A
LOVE
LIKE
YOURS

A LOVE LIKE YOURS

Robin Huber

FOREVER
YOURS

New York   Boston

Forever Yours
Hachette Book Group
1290 Avenue of the Americas, New York, NY 10104
read-forever.com
twitter.com/readforeverpub

First published as an ebook and as a print on demand: May 2019

Forever Yours is an imprint of Grand Central Publishing. The Forever Yours name and logo are trademarks of Hachette Book Group, Inc.

The publisher is not responsible for websites (or their content) that are not owned by the publisher.

The Hachette Speakers Bureau provides a wide range of authors for speaking events. To find out more, go to www.hachettespeakersbureau.com or call (866) 376-6591.

ISBNs: 978-1-5387-3285-4 (ebook), 978-1-5387-3286-1 (print on demand)

*For my sister, Karen, who gave me
my first romance novel.*

She slept with wolves without fear, for the wolves knew a lion was among them.

R. M. Drake

Prologue

Lucy, Eleven Years Old

I pick at my peanut butter and jelly sandwich, tearing off the crust and shoving it to the side of my paper plate. I keep my eyes down to avoid making eye contact with the two boys sitting across the table from me. I don't know their names, but they're my new foster brothers. Their mother is standing over my chair with a fisted hand on her hip. "You get three chances a day to eat around here. Breakfast, lunch, and dinner. You don't eat now, you'll be hungry 'til morning."

Her firm voice draws my eyes up. Her yellow hair is tied in a knot on the top of her head, and a ring of dark brown roots surrounds her stern face. I nod obediently as she takes a drag from the cigarette hanging from her lips. But I can't eat, not when my stomach is full of rocks, like it always is when I get moved to a new home. I'll be hungry later, though. Probably tonight when it's dark and everyone is asleep. I got pretty good at sneaking food at my last foster house. I sip my water and watch a trail of smoke follow her out of the room.

One of the boys gets up from the table and folds his paper plate in half. He's taller than the other one, who looks about my age. He must be older. "When was the last time you brushed this mess?" he asks, tugging my hair as he passes me.

I shrink in my chair. My hair is always tangled and it's hard to get the knots out, so I don't brush it very much. I feel the tears coming, but I grit my teeth until they go away.

The younger boy with buzzed hair and freckles reaches across the table and grabs my plate. "Thanks, I wanted seconds," he says, taking my sandwich for himself.

Another boy walks into the room and smacks it out of his hand. He's tall and thin, and his hair is the color of caramel, hanging around his face and over his eyes. "Give it back to her, Will."

Will presses his lips together and slides the plate back to me.

"You don't mess with her, you don't talk to her, you don't look at her the wrong way. Understand?"

Will swallows and nods.

"That goes for you too, Tommy," he says to Will's brother, who bobs his head. He sits down in the chair next to me and moves his hair out of his eyes, which are a mix of blue and brown, unlike any eyes I've ever seen before. "What's your name, newbie?"

"Um, Lucy," I say, looking at his strange eyes.

"You been in the system long, um-Lucy?"

"No, it's just Lucy."

He grins and nods. "Lucy . . . how long you been in?"

"Um, since I was eight. I'm eleven now, so . . ." I shrug. "Three years."

"Seven for me. Been in since I was five."

"You're twelve?" I ask, surprised that he's only a year older than me.

"Yep."

"Wow," Will says, leaning over the table. "I didn't know your kind could add or subtract. I mean, I know you can't read."

"Shut your mouth, asswipe. That's A-S-S-W-I-P-E. Do I need to write it on your forehead so you don't forget?"

Will gets up from the table and Tommy follows him out of the room.

"Just ignore Tweedledee and Tweedledum. They're morons."

I giggle quietly.

"I'm Sam, by the way. Sam Cole."

I nod and pick at my sandwich.

"You have a last name, Lucy?"

"Bennett."

"Well, Lucy Bennett, either of them mess with you again, just let me know."

"Okay." I pick up a piece of crust and tear it in two.

"You going to eat that or just pick the crust into a million pieces?"

"I'm not really hungry."

"First day's always hard. But don't worry, I've been here for a few months now. Maxine's pretty cool. She's strict, but fair. She knows her boys are assholes. She'll tear 'em up if she catches them doing anything stupid. And if they mess with you again, I'll kick both their asses."

"Okay."

"So, what's your story?"

"My story?"

"How'd you end up here?"

"Oh, um, my mom died. And my dad's in prison, so..."

"Drugs?"

I look down at my lap and nod.

"Yeah, mine are both in for drugs too, somewhere in California." He shakes his head. "I'll never touch that stuff."

"How did you end up in Atlanta?" I ask.

"My uncle. Turns out, he didn't want me any more than my parents did." He leans back in his chair. "So here I am, living the life in Brighton Park."

"I'm sure they wanted you. They probably just made some bad decisions. Everybody messes up."

He leans forward and puts his elbows on his knees. "Is that what you tell yourself? Or has your social worker said it so much that you actually believe it?"

"What?"

"Our parents didn't want us, Lucy. That's why we're here. The sooner you accept that, the better off you'll be."

"That's not true. My mom wanted me. She loved me."

"How did she die?"

"What?"

"How did she die?" he asks again, making me squirm uncomfortably in my seat. He stares at me, waiting for me to answer.

"A drug overdose," I finally say.

"And your dad...he's in prison for dealing, right?"

"Yes, but—"

"You're here because they wanted drugs...more than they wanted you."

The rocks in my stomach are the size of boulders now. I get up quickly and find the room where Maxine put my book bag, and cry into the musty pillow on the bed, hoping that no one hears me.

A few minutes later, someone knocks on the door.

"Lucy?" Sam calls, pushing it open. He's holding my sandwich in a ziplock bag.

I sit up and wipe my face as he walks into the room and sits beside me.

"I'm sorry. I was a jerk. I didn't mean it." He shrugs. "I guess after a while, you just get used to it all...to being on your own, to not having parents or knowing where you're going to live in six months. I gave up on my parents—and the idea of having a family—a long time ago. But I didn't mean to upset you. And you don't have to give up. Maybe your dad will come for you when he gets out."

"No, you're right. My dad's not going to come for me. He didn't want me to begin with. My mom was all I had."

He nods and hands me my sandwich. "Thought you might get hungry later. Just put it in your backpack so Maxine doesn't see. And don't leave crumbs, unless you have a thing for rats."

I glance around the dusty room. It's filled with stacked boxes that are overflowing with magazines and old junk.

"No." I frown. "I don't like rats." I put the sandwich in my book bag.

"Did you do those?" he asks, pointing to the colored drawings inside my bag.

"Yeah."

He pulls a few of them out and looks at each one for a few seconds. "You drew these?" he asks again.

"Yes."

"They're really good."

"Thanks."

"Do you do other stuff, like paint, or do you just draw?"

"I like to paint. I just don't get to very much. I can usually find colored pencils lying around at school, so..."

"Well, I've never seen drawings like these. They're really cool." He narrows his eyes at me and says, "Kind of badass."

"Thanks." I smile softly. "And...thanks for the sandwich."

He smiles and I see dimples in his cheeks that match the one in his chin. "You're welcome." He stands up and walks to the door, but pauses and looks at me before he leaves. "Kids like us have to stick together, Lucy."

Chapter 1

Lucy

"Are you ever going to hang this?" my future mother-in-law asks me in her polished southern accent, picking up a painting that's leaning against the cinder-block wall in the back of my art studio. "I just love the colors you used. The blue is so vibrant, like the sky on a cloudless spring morning. And the magenta is just gorgeous. So deep and rich. Like the color of love," she sings, draping her cashmere scarf around my neck.

I shake my head at her uncanny way of interpreting my paintings. But if she only knew the real meaning behind that particular one...

"What do you call it, dear?" she asks, flitting over to it again.

"Oh, um, I haven't given it a name," I say, fidgeting with the delicate gold bracelet on my wrist.

"Well, I think it should be called *True Love*," she says wistfully, throwing her arms in the air as she spins over to me. "Art inspired by life."

I choke a little, because the part of my life that inspired that painting is not the part I've spent with her son.

"Drew loves you so much, darling. What you two have is what I had with my dear Maurice." She sighs and laments, "You would have loved him."

"I'm sure I would have, Janice."

"Drew is just like him, you know. Hardworking and tough as nails. But soft as a teddy bear on the inside," she says, smiling with pride. Janice has had only three loves in her life. Her late husband, Maurice Thomas Christiansen III, her son, Andrew Thomas Christiansen, and her vintage 1986 Jaguar convertible, which was a present from Maurice the year Drew was born.

"Janice, I'm sorry, but I really need to get to work. I have a lot to do to get ready for the exhibit next month."

"Of course you do, darling." She grabs her expensive purse off my desk and smooths her short silver bob. "The best of Atlanta will be here and they'll be buzzing about the wedding."

"It's still a year away."

"Eleven months, to be exact. And you haven't even picked out your dress."

"I know, I've just had so much going on with the exhibit the last few months," I say, hoping she doesn't notice the gleam of sweat that sheens my forehead every time she brings up the lavish wedding she's been trying to plan since Drew proposed.

"Don't you worry, you just leave everything up to me." She

narrows her excited eyes. "We're going to throw the biggest party this city has ever seen."

"Oh, Janice, I don't know."

"Nonsense. You're marrying my only son." She reaches for my face and smiles softly. "You are the best thing that has ever happened to him. It's worth celebrating." She touches my cheek with the back of her hand. "*You* are worth celebrating, Lucy Bennett. My beautiful, smart, talented *future* daughter-in-law." She drops her hand to her purse and retrieves her lip gloss. "Now"—she dabs some gloss on her thin lips—"how do I look?"

I smile and sigh with inevitable defeat. "You look great, Janice. Oh, don't forget your scarf," I say, removing it from my neck.

She takes it from me and wraps it around her neck several times as she sashays through the studio. "Well, I'm off. Oh, Sebastian, darling, you look as handsome as ever," she says to my assistant, passing him on her way out.

"Thanks, Jan. You look gorgeous as always. Are those new diamonds?" he asks, touching his earlobes.

She spins around with a big grin on her face. "Do you like them? They were an early birthday present."

"Oh? From who? A new suitor?" he asks, perking up in his chair.

"Heavens no. From me." She winks and pushes her big black sunglasses on. "Lucy, you should really think about covering these windows. It's awfully bright in here and you have utterly no privacy. Everyone on the street can see right in."

I press my lips together and raise my eyebrows. "That's the idea."

She nods absently and blows two kisses as she opens the door. "Bye, darlings."

"Bye, Janice."

"Oh, my God, your mother-in-law is delectable," Sebastian says, biting the end of his pen. "I'm so jealous. Paul's mom is such a drag."

"*Future* mother-in-law. And don't encourage her."

"I'm sorry, sweetie, it's just too tempting. You have Joan Rivers for a mother."

"She's not my mother," I remind him, and slouch against the front desk. "She's just the woman who took me under her wing and introduced me to a community I never thought I could be a part of. The woman who told me to believe in my talents and convinced me that I could actually make a living off them. The woman who taught me to always wash my face before bed and to never leave the house without sunscreen." I stand up straight. "Oh, my God. She is my mother."

Sebastian gives me a satisfied smile. "I bet Drew has no idea how fabulous she is."

"I'm not sure Drew would use the word 'fabulous' to describe anything."

He rolls his eyes. "You definitely scored in the mother-in-law department, but the jury is still out on her son."

"Sebastian."

"Well, she's just so amazing and full of life, and he's just so...normal."

"What's wrong with normal?"

"Nothing. If you like that sort of thing."

"Well, I do. As a matter of fact, normal is exactly the sort of thing I like. All I want is a nice, normal existence. So, case closed."

He arches one of his dark eyebrows and bites the end of his pen. "Pity."

I love Sebastian, from the top of his perfectly styled hair down to his patent leather loafers, but sometimes I want to throw a paintbrush at his head. He's been happily married to his partner for three years, he lives in arguably the coolest apartment in Atlanta, his family adores him, and he's generally pretty happy most of the time. My life is *messier*. Or at least, it was, until recently. Now, I'm well on my way to nice and normal.

"Can you help me with this?" I ask, struggling to pick up a heavy box off the floor by the front desk.

"Yeah, I've got it," Bas says, taking it from me. "Where do you want it?"

"I think it's the paints I ordered. You can just put it in my office for now."

"You got it, boss lady."

I follow him to my office in the back of the studio.

Sebastian probably knows me better than anyone, but I haven't told him very much about my past. He doesn't know why I strive so hard for normalcy. He knows that I met Drew when I was waitressing at La Pêche, one of the restaurants Drew owns here in Atlanta. But what Sebastian doesn't know is that a few years before that, I dropped out of high school and left my foster home in Brighton Park after the love of my underprivileged life was arrested for drug possession and sent to prison. Then again, Drew doesn't know either.

"Hey, Paul got tickets for fight night at the Garden this Saturday," Bas says over his shoulder. "What do you say, take a break from all this and come to New York with us for the weekend?"

"New York? Who's fighting?"

"Cole versus Sanchez. I'm surprised you don't know. I thought you were a big Sam Cole fan."

"I am," I answer with what little air is left in my lungs, while I try to find my heart. "He's fighting Mario Sanchez?"

"Yeah, it's a title fight. It'll be on HBO and pay-per-view. I know Drew isn't a big boxing fan, but you guys should come anyway. Paul got like six tickets." He raises his perfectly manicured eyebrows and puts the box down on my desk. "Perks of working for a music producer."

"Yeah," I say softly. "I guess so."

"So what do you say?"

"I, um, I can't go to New York," I say over my pounding heart. "I've got way too much to do for the exhibit."

"That's why you have me. We've got it covered. Besides, it's still six weeks away."

"Five and a half to be exact. And Drew probably has to work anyway." I try to keep my voice even, but my heart is still pounding inside my chest and my scattered thoughts are stammering around my head.

Sebastian gives me a slanted look. "Drew always has to work. In fact, as I recall, it was the very reason for your little breakup not so long ago," he says. "I thought his work demands were no longer supposed to interfere with your ability to enjoy life. With or without him."

"That's not what this is."

He narrows his eyes. "Mmm, really? How?"

"It just isn't. I don't want to go without him."

"Oh, come on, Lucy. We can go to the Met and get some inspiration for the show. It's just what we need right now."

"I'll be a third wheel, Bas."

"Have Paul and I ever made you feel like a third wheel?"

"No," I answer honestly. I adore them both, and I love hanging out with them.

"Then, come with us."

I pick at my thumbnail. "I can't."

"Why?"

"I just can't, Sebastian," I say abruptly. "Maybe some other time."

"Fine," he says, holding his hands up. "But if you change your mind..."

I nod. "Thanks for the invitation. We'll go somewhere after the exhibit is over, okay?"

"Okay."

"Hey, you know, I was actually just going to paint this afternoon. So if you want to cut out early for the day, it's fine."

"You sure? You don't need me for anything else?"

"No, not today."

He smiles and shoves his hands in his pockets. "You know, you're sort of the best boss ever, right?"

"Don't forget it." I narrow my eyes and force a small smile. "Now go, enjoy the rest of the afternoon with Paul."

"Okay, Okay. You don't have to twist my arm." He winks. "See you tomorrow."

"Bye."

When Sebastian leaves, I fall into my desk chair, drop my face to my hands, and take a deep breath to clear my head. I quickly unplug my laptop and shove it into my desk drawer. I've Googled Sam so many times, I'm surprised the letters of his name haven't worn off my keyboard yet. It's a form of self-torture I'm far too familiar with. A game of Russian roulette where the search button is the trigger, delivering a blast to the head each time I see a new girl hanging off his arm. He has varied tastes, but his favorite flavors are model, actress, and volleyball player, in no particular order.

I get up and grab my painting clothes off the back of the door, exchanging my pleated cream pants and blue silk top for my old ratty cutoffs and paint-covered T-shirt. I'm desperate for the solace only a brush will give me as I walk barefoot to a six-foot-tall canvas in the back of the studio. I grab its wide edge and shuffle it across the cement floor, holding it upright between my knees as I drag it to a spot where I like to paint.

I scan my paint cart and begin selecting various tubes and sizing up my paintbrushes, laying them out carefully as I go. I squeeze several small mounds of paint onto my palette and pull the colors together with my palette knife, blending and mixing them until they're just right.

I begin painting with large brushstrokes, thinking of Sam.

I wonder if he ever thinks about me.

I wonder if he's okay.

I wonder if he hates me.

I keep painting, until the only thing left to wonder about is if I'll ever stop thinking about him.

* * *

Lucy, Sixteen Years Old

I hold Sam's hand tightly as he leads me down a sidewalk adjacent to a chain-link fence that surrounds the airport a few blocks from our high school. "Where are we going?" I ask warily.

"It's a surprise."

"Well, I hope it's somewhere we can study, because you have a test on King Richard tomorrow, and I have a paper to write."

He looks down at me and grins. "We can do whatever we want there."

"You know, those dimples will only get you so far in life." I narrow my eyes at him.

"They worked on you, didn't they?"

"It was more than your dimples, but yes."

He pulls me off the sidewalk and pushes me up against the fence. "More than my dimples? Hmm... Was it my eyes?" he asks playfully.

I gaze up at his beautiful eyes. They're a mix of brown and blue. The left one is more brown, but it fades to blue on one side and has a gold ring in the center. The right one is mostly blue with brown around the edges and a matching gold ring. "I love your eyes, but no, that wasn't it either."

"It must have been my body, then." He can't even say it without laughing.

I laugh with him and push against his chest, which is like pushing on a wall. "Sam." I shake my head.

"No? Well, maybe it was my brains."

"I love your brains too. You're very smart, even if you dismiss it. But no, that's not it either."

"All right," he says, gazing into my eyes. "What on earth could possibly make someone like you love someone like me?"

The corners of my mouth turn up because the answer is so obvious. I place my hand on his chest and say, "Your heart."

His eyes narrow with curiosity.

"It's strong and fierce and brave. You've always made me feel so safe . . . and loved."

He drops his forehead to mine. "I do love you, Lamb. And I'll always protect you."

The corners of my mouth turn up again. "Because you have the heart of a lion."

"Like King Richard?"

I raise my eyebrows. "You've been studying!"

He laughs softly and pushes on the chain-link fence, creating an opening where the metal wire has been cut. "After you."

"Sam, are we allowed in there?"

He doesn't respond and I know that the answer is no. But I bend down and slip through the opening in the fence anyway, scraping my jeans and catching my flannel shirt on the metal wire. Sam unhooks it and follows behind me. I take his hand again, and he leads me to a place on the wiry brown grass while I examine the damage to my shirt. It now has a hole in the back to match the one in the front that was there when I bought it from the consignment shop. I take it off and tie it around my waist over my white T-shirt, letting the bright November sun warm my bare arms.

Sam drops his book bag on the ground and pulls a tattered-looking sheet out of it. He spreads it out on the dormant grass and sits down.

"You had this whole thing planned out, didn't you?"

He smiles and pulls me down next to him. "Just wait a minute," he says, pointing to a plane in the distance that's taxiing toward the runway. We're at the opposite end, directly in its flight path.

"Sam, is this safe?"

"As long as it takes off it is." He laughs.

I grimace at the thought of the plane barreling down the runway and plowing right over us.

"Here it comes," he says excitedly.

I can hear the engines roaring as it gains speed and charges toward us. We're on the opposite side of a small hill at the end of the runway, so hopefully the pilot won't be able to see us. I can only imagine what kind of trouble we'd get in if we got caught. I glance at Sam, and he smiles at me with eager eyes. *He's worth the risk.* I inhale a deep breath as the plane races down the runway.

It's getting closer.

Closer.

Closer.

I squeeze Sam's hand as the plane lifts off the runway into the air like a feather. I cover my ears as it roars over our heads, but I can't take my eyes off it. I lean back on my hands and watch the wheels retract, tipping my chin up until I'm lying on my back watching it upside down as it disappears into the sky. "Wow." I drop my head to the side and look at Sam lying beside me. "That was so cool."

"I thought you'd like it."

I smile and roll onto his chest and drop my mouth to his. "I do."

He reaches for my hips and pulls me all the way on top of him.

I sit up and place my hands on his firm stomach. "We have to study. Well, you do. I need to write a paper."

He rests his hands on my thighs and squints up at me. "I'm too happy to study."

I lean forward and kiss him again. "I'm always happy when I'm with you. If I only studied when I wasn't, I'd flunk out of school."

He crinkles his eyes. "Good point."

I climb off him and reach for my book bag.

Sam watches me, but he doesn't sit up. He doesn't like to study. He doesn't like school, period. But he tries, for me. One of the few things I remember about my mom is that she wanted me to get an education. She told me that if I made good grades, I could get out of Brighton Park. She hated what this place did to her. She wanted a better life for me.

Sometimes I still get angry at her for leaving me like she did, but I know that she was sick. The drugs ruined her. Sam and I promised each other that we'll never do drugs. Sometimes I think she's watching over me and put him in my life, because without Sam, I'm not sure how long I'd be able to avoid it. Drugs are all around us, all the time. Kids are usually buying them from other kids at school. And they can't afford it, so they steal to get the cash. It's just a big ugly cycle. The same one that sucked the life out of my mom and put my dad in prison. So I'm going to get my education and get the hell out of this place, just like she wanted me to. And I'm taking Sam with me.

"Come on," I say to him, dragging his book bag into his lap. "I'm going to start my paper. Why don't you answer the study questions at the end of the chapter...and then we'll see where it goes." I press my lips together to cover a smile.

He shakes his head. "I think that's extortion."

"Not exactly, but I'm glad your government class is rubbing off."

He grins and pulls out his history book.

Both of us sit quietly, studying and writing, and looking up whenever a plane takes off. By the time the fourth one rumbles overhead, I shout, "This may not be the best place to study."

"I think you might be right." He closes his book and tosses it aside, tackling me to the ground with kisses.

"Sam!"

He holds my hands above my head so that I can't move, and he kisses my neck.

"You didn't hold up your end of the bargain."

"You said it yourself. It's too noisy to study."

"It is. So we should probably go somewhere else. Like a library, maybe?"

"I'll make you a deal." He rubs his nose against mine and looks into my eyes.

"You're going to try to coerce me now?" I laugh.

"Stop worrying about books and papers and studying, and just be with me, right here, right now...and *then* we'll see where it goes."

I grin and shake my head, but before I can say anything, his tongue silences my retort with long, smooth strokes that fill my head with clouds and my heart with sunshine.

Another plane roars over us again, but neither of us look up.

Chapter 2

Lucy

"Are you coming to bed?" Drew asks from the doorway of the theater room, where I'm watching Sam fight Arturo Moreno for the gold.

"Yeah"—I glance up at him from the giant TV screen—"in a little bit."

"Why are you watching an Olympic boxing match from two years ago?"

"Sam Cole is fighting this weekend and Sebastian and Paul have tickets. They invited us to go."

"Here?"

"No, it's in New York City, actually. Madison Square Garden."

"New York? Luc, I have to work this weekend. I can't go to New York."

"And that's exactly what I told Sebastian." I give him a small, accepting smile.

He drops his hands on the couch and hovers over me. "You mad?"

I shrug and look up at him. "I could go by myself."

He narrows his dark blue eyes and runs his fingers through chocolate-brown hair. "By yourself?" He walks around the couch and plops down next to me. "I don't know."

"What don't you know?" I widen my eyes playfully. "Are you afraid I can't handle myself in the big city?" I smirk. "I'm a twenty-six-year-old woman. And I grew up in Brighton Park, remember?"

"Oh, I know you can handle yourself." He pulls me into his arms. "I just don't want you to ever be in a situation where you have to."

"I won't. I'll be with Paul and Sebastian the whole time."

"Paul and Sebastian don't look at you the way other men do. They don't know the kinds of things that are going through their heads." He pulls my chin up and looks in my eyes. "You are so beautiful. I don't know what I'd do if anything ever happened to you."

I look away because the guilt seeping beneath my skin feels as if it's about to reveal itself through my eyes.

Drew sighs heavily and drops his hand. "Okay."

I look up at him, feeling a strange mix of excitement and angst. "Okay, you won't mind if I go without you?" I ask, knowing good and well that I shouldn't go, that I shouldn't *want* to go. But I do. I desperately do. As soon as Sebastian mentioned Sam, all I could think about was going. I had an opportunity to see him fight a year ago, which I passed up under stronger resolve, and I've regretted it ever since. Part of me hopes that if I see him in person, it will quiet the unrest I feel in my soul whenever I think about him.

"I'll miss you while you're gone, but no, I don't mind if you go." Drew rolls his eyes playfully. "Besides, I know you have a thing for that Sam Cole guy."

The guilt winds its long ugly fingers around my neck and slowly tightens its grip.

"Are you"—I clear my throat—"are you sure? I won't go if you really don't want me to." *Say you don't want me to.*

He smiles softly and reaches for my hand. "I know I've been working a lot, especially with the new restaurant opening in Philadelphia. It isn't lost on me that you haven't said a single word about how much I've been traveling, especially with all the wedding planning." He pulls my hand to his mouth and kisses the back of my knuckles. "Not that I could get a word in edgewise with Momma in charge." He laughs and gives me a sincere look. "You know I'm doing it for us, right? For our future?"

I bob my head.

"It won't always be like this."

"I know," I say over the doubt that fills my mind.

"Before Daddy died, he told me the most important thing a man can do is provide for his family. That's what he did for me and Momma, and that's what I'm trying to do for you and our kids. One day."

The thought of kids jerks my back up off the couch with an unexpected pinch in my chest.

"You okay?"

"Yeah." I smile and ignore the unwelcome feeling.

"Go to New York with Sebastian and Paul. Have a fun time. Just promise you'll be safe, okay?"

"I will, I promise."

"I love you...so much."

"I know. I love you too."

He tucks my hair behind my ear. "I'm going to bed. I have to get up early tomorrow." He stands up, pausing halfway to kiss the top of my head. "Don't stay up too late."

"I won't."

Drew leaves the room, and I stare at the stranger on the TV who resembles the person I used to know, except that now he's huge and has tattoos everywhere—down his left arm and across his chest. There's a fierce-looking lion roaring over his heart and the phrase *Pain Is Fleeting* scrolled in cursive beneath the curve of his collarbone.

When Sam was arrested for drug possession, I was devastated. He broke the very foundation we were built on. He betrayed everything we stood for. I wasn't just hurt, I was shattered. The Sam I knew and loved was gone, and I was alone...again. At seventeen, I lost the only thing I ever wanted—a future with Sam. And for a while, I lost myself. I began ditching school and eventually I stopped going altogether. But as the months passed, my sorrow turned to anger and then determination. I refused to turn out like my mother. I wouldn't break my promise just because Sam broke his. So the day I turned eighteen, I left the broken place that raised me and got a job in the city waiting tables at La Pêche.

The restaurant was elegant and always smelled like the most delicious food. It was so very different from anything

I had ever experienced. The people who came in looked like celebrities. They dressed beautifully, they spoke beautifully, they smiled beautifully. I was definitely getting a strong dose of how the other half lived. I didn't want to be like them— I cringed just putting on my perfectly pressed black pants and crisp button-down shirt every day—but I couldn't deny the charm of a life that seemed so easy. A life that came with houses and cars and clothes that weren't purchased at second-hand stores. A life where kids went to good schools and could paint to their hearts' content. A life without thugs and drugs and guns. A life that I found myself wanting more and more.

I was making enough money waitressing to pay for the dilapidated apartment I rented, but not enough to support my habit. Painting had become my hobby turned therapy, turned obsession. It was as necessary as breathing. It was the only way I could organize all the clutter inside my head. So, in an effort to turn my obsession into a means of extra income, I got my GED and applied for the Savannah College of Art and Design in Atlanta. With the help of several student grants, I spent the next four years immersed in classes, learning new techniques, like painting with oils—my favorite— and art history. I graduated from SCAD with a bachelor of fine arts in painting, with a minor in art history. But that didn't exactly equate to a career in painting. So I began entering my artwork in local contests around the city.

Drew saw one of my paintings when La Pêche sponsored a community arts contest, and it wasn't long before he was taking an interest in more than just my artistic ability. But I was cautious, keeping him at arm's length. I was twenty-two with very little life experience, and he was twenty-eight with the life experience of someone twice his age, having already opened three successful restaurants, one of which I still worked at. Although I didn't have a lot of dating experience, I was pretty sure you weren't supposed to date your boss. But that didn't dissuade Drew from pursuing me.

* * *

Lucy, Two Years Ago

"One date. That's all I want," Drew bargains as I wait patiently for him to hand me an invitation to his mother's gala. He's been trying to get me to go on a date with him for the last two years. He's nothing if not persistent. But he's still my boss. And more importantly, he's my friend. As persuasive as he is, I just don't see him as anything more than that.

"Drew, Janice invited me personally. I don't need the invitation to attend."

"Technically, you do. The doorman won't let you in without it."

I close my eyes and shake off the foreign thought of attending a party that requires a doorman. "I'm a guest of honor," I say, ignoring the nerves that have been racking me since Janice asked to auction off one of my paintings at her annual charity ball. "And I have your mother's number. I'll just call her directly."

He taps the sturdy card against his palm and narrows his eyes. "You have my mother's number?"

I raise an eyebrow and hold out my hand. "Yes. Now, hand over my invitation."

"All right, all right," he says, giving it to me. He smiles wide and shakes his head.

"What?"

"I just haven't figured out who likes you more. Me or Momma."

I look at the vintage calligraphy on the beautiful invitation in my hand and say, "I'm pretty sure it's my art that you both like."

"Is that really what you think?"

"I don't know." I look up at him and shrug. "I mean, I'm not really like the people who will be at this party. I'm not, you know, fancy."

"Fancy," he repeats, pulling his dark eyebrows together.

"Sophisticated," I clarify.

He brings his hand up to his face and rubs his jaw. "You're right. You aren't like the people who will be at this party. Because you, Lucy Bennett, aren't like anyone. You are"—he puts his hand on my shoulder and slowly trails it down my arm—"so bright and kind and funny. All things that have nothing to do with your art." He moves his hand over my wrist and wraps his fingers around mine. "You are the strongest—and most stubborn—woman I have ever met. And you are far more beautiful than any of the high-society women who will be at this party. You don't need a trust fund to be sophisticated, okay?"

I press my lips together and bob my head. "You think I'm stubborn?"

He smiles. "That's what you took away from everything I just said?"

I laugh softly and shake my head. "No."

He reaches for my other hand and holds it in his. "Let me take you to the party tonight, Lucy. I'd be honored," he says sincerely, and it eases the nerves buzzing around inside me. "It doesn't have to be a date, it can just be—"

"Okay," I answer.

His eyes widen slightly. "Okay?"

"Yeah," I smile softly, "I'd like that."

He nods casually and tries unsuccessfully to hide a smile. "Okay."

* * *

That night I listened to Drew tell stories of how he swam with great white sharks in South Africa and climbed Mont Blanc in France. I was as captivated as the other guests by how worldly and cultured he was. Though it only reiterated how different we were. But Drew had a way of making me feel like I belonged in that room. He held my hand and introduced me with pride, and for the first time in two years, I saw him in a different light. I saw *me* in a different light. And as much as I wanted to believe that I could never love anyone besides Sam, I found myself falling for Drew, because he was all the things that Sam *wasn't*.

But that was before Sam won the US Amateur Boxing Championship and earned a spot on the US Olympic boxing team. I never even thought I'd see Sam again, let alone see him on my TV. But there he was, screaming back into my mind and staking claim on my heart, just days after Drew proposed. I couldn't believe it. Everything I'd wondered about, everything left unanswered, everything I'd given up on was right there in front of me. Sam was okay; he was *more* than okay. And suddenly, without warning, everything that felt right about me and Drew seemed *wrong*.

Sam won the gold medal, holds four championship belts, and is now the undisputed light-heavyweight champion of the world. He has twenty-two wins, ten of which were knock-outs, and only two losses. He's well on his way to becoming the greatest boxer the world has ever seen.

"Just like he said he would," I whisper to myself as I click off the television. And then I head upstairs to Drew, the man I *should* be thinking about.

Chapter 3

Sam

"Come on, champ. Come on," Joe growls in my ear while I spar with Tristan. "Block the jab, baby, block the jab."

I hold my gloves up to protect my face while Tristan throws punches at me. It takes everything in me not to hit him back, but the scar down the middle of his chest reminds me why I can't. He's my trainer and one of the toughest guys I know, but he has a weak heart. Joe just has me practicing defense with him.

Joe has been my coach since I was fourteen. He was Tristan's coach too, until Tris didn't get up off the mat one day—he was seventeen when he had his first open-heart surgery. Joe is like a father to us. He took care of Tristan when he was sick, and he never gave up on me when I was in prison. When I got out, he helped me rebuild my life, gave me a place to live, started coaching me again. He taught me how to fight professionally. He taught me how to win. Every belt I have is because of him.

"Ahhhhhh!" I scream, shoving Tris back against the ropes.

"What the fuck, man?"

"That's enough! Get out of my face!" I shout.

"Sam, take it easy," Joe says. "Take a break."

Tristan steps toward me and holds his gloves up. "You want to go for real? Come on, champ! I'm not scared of you."

"I said take a break," Joe shouts.

I duck between the ropes and climb out of the ring.

Tristan laughs and starts throwing practice jabs in the air.

"You all right?" Joe asks.

"Yeah."

"You seem wound up today. More than usual," Joe says.

"Wouldn't have anything to do with Lucy getting married, would it?" Tristan chimes in as he moves around the ring.

"Lucy's getting married?" Joe looks up at me. "To who?"

"Atlanta restaurant owner Andrew Christiansen, according to the *Atlanta Journal*," Tristan answers. "She's moving up in the world."

Joe puts his hand on my shoulder. "Sam, I'm sorry."

"It's not Lucy that's bothering me," I lie. "It's just...Sanchez. I can't stand that motherfucker."

"Yeah, well, Saturday's your chance to show him how much," Joe says. "Sit down, cool off a minute. You want your headphones?"

I nod and Joe disappears to the locker room.

"Sanchez my ass," Tristan says, but I ignore him.

Joe returns with my headphones and puts them over my

ears for me. He turns the volume up, and the screaming rap music drowns out the sounds of the gym, and Tristan.

I drop my head to my gloves as my thoughts bounce between Sanchez and Lucy, but they ultimately stay with Lucy. Like they always do.

* * *

Sam, Eighteen Years Old

I jog across the street, weaving between the passing cars, ignoring the driver shouting out of his window at me. When I reach the uneven sidewalk, I push my hood off my head. It's March, but the sun is making me hot inside my sweatshirt, even though it's still pretty cool out.

"Hey, man, you need something today?" the dealer on the corner asks when I reach the crosswalk.

"Nah, man, I'm good. I don't do that stuff."

"You a boxer or somethin'?" he asks, eyeing the gloves hanging from my backpack.

"Something like that."

"Yeah...yeah...I seen you. You that kid down at Joe's. I seen you fight before."

I nod and keep walking.

"You need a manager or somethin'?" he calls.

"Nah, man, I'm good," I call back.

"Well, if you change your mind, you come find Big T."

I ignore him and continue toward school. When I round the corner I see a small group of guys crowded together on the sidewalk. After I hear what they're saying, I know they're talking to a girl.

"Honey, you fine. Just let me get a little piece of that...Nah, she don't want yo skinny ass. She want a real man. Don't ya, baby?"

"Leave me alone."

Lucy.

I drop my backpack and charge the three guys surrounding her, knocking them back like bowling pins. "Get away from her," I shout, standing in front of her. One of them steps toward me and stands two inches from my face. He's taller than me, but I push him back and make him fall against his friend.

He gets in my face again. "What? You gonna fight me, son? Over that?" He looks at Lucy and says, "Nah, she ain't even worth it."

"What'd you say?" The anger burns inside me like wildfire. "What the fuck did you just say?" I shout in his face.

"Sam, don't." Lucy tugs on my sweatshirt, but I can barely hear her through the rage that's roaring through me. "I'm fine."

"I said why don't you back the fuck up." He pulls his jacket open and shows me his gun.

"Cole...Cole!" Joe shouts, running up to me. He pushes me back a few feet. "Come on, save it for the ring."

"Sam, let's go," Lucy says, grabbing my hand and yanking me back farther.

"Wait...wait. You're Sam Cole?"

"Yeah, he is," Joe answers, pushing me down the sidewalk.

"Oh, I'm gonna remember this. Sam Cole. I got you, Sam Cole. I got you," he shouts down the sidewalk.

"Ignore him," Joe orders, aware of the storm brewing inside me. "Keep it in until Friday. Russo won't stand a chance."

"He wouldn't stand a chance anyway," I say confidently.

"Yeah, well, that's probably true. But you've got to start channeling your anger, Sam. Use it to be better. To be great. No more street fights."

I take a deep breath and hold Lucy's hand tighter. Just thinking of what they could have done to her makes my pulse race faster.

"You left this," Joe says, handing me my math book. "Thought you might need it."

"He does need it," Lucy says, giving me a sideways glance.

Lucy is smart. Too smart for me. She's a junior, but she's in my senior calculus class. The only reason I'll be graduating in a few months is because of her. She makes me study. I don't like to, but she can be very persuasive.

"Is that what you were doing down here, coming to drag me to school?"

She looks up at me with her innocent pale blue eyes and shrugs. "I had some extra time this morning. I thought I'd meet you at the gym so we could walk together."

"See ya this afternoon, Sam," Joe says. "Stay out of trouble."

"Bye, Joe." Lucy waves at him.

"Bye, sweetheart. Make sure he gets to class."

"I always do."

After a couple of blocks, I look down at Lucy and she smiles up at me. The sun is shining on her porcelain skin, reflecting off her shiny pink lips and blond hair that's streaked pink to match. Much to her amusement, my fingertips are still stained from the Kool-Aid packets we used to dye it. It's pulled back into a ponytail, showing off the soft skin below her ear. My eyes follow the curve of her neck down to her bright yellow bra that's peeking out beneath the collar of her jacket, and they continue down to her creamy legs. I squeeze her hand and tear my eyes away from her. "You shouldn't be wearing that skirt."

"Well, I thought it was going to be warmer today, but now I'm wishing I hadn't. Why? You don't like it?"

I pull her into the doorway of an abandoned building and turn her around so that her back is pressed against the brick exterior. I place my hands on the wall by her shoulders and lean in close. "I like it. But so do the wolves." I bring one hand to her face. "You're so beautiful, Lamb. You don't even know it." I slide my hand down her neck, tracing her collarbone with my thumb, and push her jacket off her shoulder. "And so pure." I kiss the spot below her ear. "You have no idea what they'd do to you."

She raises her hand and drags her finger down the middle of my chest. "That's why I have you. You've always protected me. And I've never felt afraid."

"What if I wasn't there?"

"You always are." She smiles and presses her lips to mine.

"Yeah." I move my mouth to her ear. "I always will be." My greatest fear is that one day, I won't. I close my eyes and kiss her hard, pressing myself against her so that I can be as close to her as possible. I drop my hands to her thighs and run them up her smooth skin until they're under her skirt. I groan against her mouth and she moans into mine, sending a fire blazing through me that only she can put out.

I pick her up and she wraps her legs around me. "We can't," she says, running her fingers through my hair, kissing me. "We have to go to class."

I ignore her.

"Sam."

I kiss her harder and she kisses me back.

"Not here," she says, looking at me with a conflicted grin on her face. She lost the battle with herself.

I smile wide and put her down. "Come on." I pull her around the side of the building.

"Where are we going?"

"There." I point to a ladder that leads to the roof. "Come on."

"You want me to climb up that?" she asks, watching me yank on the bottom of the ladder to test its stability.

"Yeah, it's safe. You can go first. I'll follow, in case you slip."

She gives me a slanted look. "Wouldn't have anything to do with the skirt, would it?"

I grin. "Of course not."

She begins to climb the ladder, and I follow behind her. About halfway up, the wind blows her skirt up, and I groan quietly.

"Knock it off," she says.

"Not possible."

She pauses and looks down at me, pursing her lips.

"Don't stop, you're almost there." I wink and give her a gentle push over the top. I climb over after her.

"Holy crap, it's cold up here," she says, rubbing her arms.

I drop my backpack and pull her into my arms, and hold her against me until she warms up. When the wind stops blowing, it feels ten degrees warmer in the sun. "Better?"

"Yeah. It's actually really beautiful up here. So quiet. Kind of makes you forget all the crap down there."

I look out at the low brick buildings that make up Brighton Park. The sky is so clear, I can see all the way to downtown Atlanta where the tall buildings stagger across a small section of the horizon. "We're going to get out of here one day, Luc."

"Promise?"

"Yeah. I promise."

She sighs. "How?"

"You're going to get a scholarship after you graduate next year and you're going to go to college."

She props her chin on my chest. "No, I'm not."

"Lucy, yes you—"

"No," she says firmly, "not without you."

I made the grades to graduate, but I won't be getting any scholarships.

"Joe thinks I have a real shot at boxing. Maybe that's my ticket out. If it is, I'll work night and day to be the greatest boxer this world's ever seen."

She smiles wide. "Like Muhammad Ali?"

"Float like a butterfly, sting like a bee."

"And we'll live in a big house?"

"The biggest."

"And we'll eat pancakes every morning?"

"With bacon."

"And I'll be able to paint whenever I want?"

"Whenever you want."

"And we'll have a family? A *real* family?"

I tuck a windblown piece of her hair behind her ear and nod. "Yeah, we'll have a family."

"I love you, Sam. Even if none of that ever happens, I'll still love you. You're my family."

I take her face in my hands. "I love you too." I kiss her softly until we melt into each other, numb to the cool air that's wrapping around us. I pick her up again and she wraps her legs around me like before, kissing me slower this time.

She pulls my sweatshirt off and drops it on the concrete rooftop beneath us, and pushes my sweatpants down on my hips. She reaches under my shirt and runs her hands over my chest and stomach, making my muscles tighten where she touches me.

I sit down on my sweatshirt with her in my lap and lift her shirt above her bra, but I notice goose bumps on her skin, so I lower it back down and hold her close to me, kissing her slowly until I feel the heat between us.

Her tongue moves over mine, and I feel it everywhere.

I push her jacket off her shoulders so that it's still covering her arms and kiss her neck, but she shrugs the rest of the way out of it. "I'm not cold anymore," she whispers, taking her shirt off.

I run my hands up her thighs and tug on her panties. I

might spontaneously combust if she doesn't take them off soon.

"Do you have a condom?" she breathes.

Fuck. No, I don't. I look at her, desperately hoping that she has one.

"I have one," she says, smirking, reaching for her backpack. "I want a family with you, but not yet." She tears it open and puts it on me, and I welcome her warm hands.

She pulls her panties off and climbs over me again, and I hold her hips while she sinks down on me until she's flush against me, surrounding me and making me forget everything else. There's only me and Lucy in the entire world.

She reaches for my face and kisses me slowly while she moves up and down, sending electricity coursing through my body.

I grip her warm thighs and she moans against my mouth, igniting the fire that's scorching through me. I wrap my arms around her and lift her up and down on me, again and again, listening to every breath, every moan, every whisper she makes.

"Sam." She tightens around me and her body trembles under my hands, making me lose control.

I hold her tight and let go, groaning against her neck as I come. "Luc," I grit through my teeth.

I reach for her face and kiss her softly, but the wind blows and raises goose bumps on her arms again. I grab her T-shirt and jacket, and she slides both back on.

"What would you have done if I hadn't shown up earlier?" I ask, watching her pull her panties back on.

"Sam."

"Just humor me."

"I would have done what you taught me. Throat, knee, groin. And then I would've shown 'em my right hook." She smiles.

"Show me," I say, getting to my feet.

"Sam."

"Show me. Make a fist."

She curls her small fingers into her palm and wraps her thumb around her knuckles tight.

I push against her fist with my hand. "Good. Keep it strong." I hold my palms up. "Now show me. Let me see that right hook."

She pulls her right arm back and hits my left hand, but I barely move.

"Harder."

She does it again, a little stronger.

"Harder."

She does it again and my hand actually moves back an inch.

"Good."

She shakes her hand.

"You can't be afraid to hit, Luc. They won't be afraid to hit you."

"I just don't like hitting you."

I smirk. "I think I can take it."

"I don't care if you can. I don't like it."

I reach for her wrist and spin her around, locking her in my arms with her back to my chest. I hold her tight. "Now what do you do?"

She squirms in my arms but barely moves. I'm using only a fraction of my strength.

"Come on, Luc, what do you do?"

She squats down fast, spins out of my hold, and brings her knee up to my crotch. "Lower my center of gravity."

"Good."

"Am I done now?"

I nod and hug her. "I don't know what I'd do if something happened to you."

She hugs me tight. "I know the feeling."

"Hey, I got something for you."

"You did?" She smiles up at me.

I pull a small black box out of my backpack and hand it to her.

"What's this?" she asks suspiciously.

"Just open it."

She opens the box carefully and touches the small gold bracelet inside. "Sam." She gives me a shocked look. "Is it real?"

"Yeah, it's real."

She looks at it again. "How did you buy it?"

"Joe's been paying me a little to clean up the gym after hours."

"He has? Since when?"

"I've been doing it for a few months now."

She gives me wary look. "Really? Why didn't you tell me?"

"Because I wanted to surprise you. Here, put it on." I take it out of the box and fasten it around her wrist. "Do you like it?"

She bobs her head and looks up at me, but I can't tell what she's thinking.

"If you don't, I can—"

"No, Sam." She smiles softly. "It's beautiful. Really. I love it."

"You do?" I ask, unable to hide the smile on my face.

She nods and touches it. "Yeah." She wraps her arms around my neck and whispers, "I'll never take it off."

"Good," I breathe against her cheek.

"Thank you for giving it to me." She places a soft kiss on my lips.

"I got you something else too."

"Something else?"

I reach into my backpack and pull out three small bottles of paint and a new package of paintbrushes. "I got them at the drugstore. They only had red, blue, and yellow."

"Sam, that's perfect. Thank you." She sits down and pulls her drawing pad out of her backpack.

I sit down beside her and watch her wipe off a section of the concrete and squirt a small amount of each color onto it.

She tears open the package of brushes and grabs the biggest one first, dipping it into the blue. She brushes it over the top half of the paper until it's the color of the sky. Then she takes another brush and paints the bottom half red, blending it up into the blue. She mixes the two colors together, adding some yellow, and paints very carefully across the middle of the paper where the blue and red meet.

I watch her for several minutes while she works, biting her lip and concentrating.

When she's done, she holds the paper out in front of us, and I see the same cityscape that's in the distance.

"Wow, that's incredible."

"You like it?"

"Yes." I take the pad from her and hold it in my lap, noticing every brushstroke, every detail, every color she created. "You're so talented."

"I used red here because that's us," she says, pointing to the bottom half of the page. "You and me, up here above all the crap down there. It's love."

I wrap my arm around her neck and kiss her cheek.

"And the blue"—she points to the top half of the page—"that's everything that's waiting for us. Our future. Big and bright."

Chapter 4

Lucy

I gaze out of the window over the wing of the airplane, watching the familiar mass of buildings and skyscrapers that make up the New York City skyline come into view as we approach JFK. Since opening my own studio, I've fallen in love with the Chelsea neighborhood, home to more art galleries than all of Georgia, and home to some of my favorite artists. To be among them and sell my paintings in New York would be the pinnacle of my career. Atlanta's art district is still waiting to be discovered, but I'm aiming to change that with my exhibit next month. If all goes well, it will get me one step closer selling my artwork in New York.

"We're beginning our descent into New York, folks," the pilot says over the speaker. "The current temperature is fifty-three degrees. Please stay seated with your seat belt fastened until after we've landed."

I give Sebastian a worried look. "Fifty-three degrees? I hope I brought warm enough clothes."

"It's early," Paul says. "It'll warm up by the afternoon. It usually does in October."

"And if it doesn't, just buy something new." Sebastian winks at me. "I'm sure Drew wouldn't mind seeing you in a new dress when you go home."

I know that he's teasing, but just thinking about Drew ties my stomach into knots. Surely if Drew knew about my history with Sam, he wouldn't have wanted me to come. I've never been able to bring myself to talk about it with him. I wanted to once, but the more I thought about what Sam and I had, the more precious it became. I couldn't bear to pretend that it was anything less than a once-in-a-lifetime kind of love. And I couldn't bear to hurt Drew with the truth—that I'll never be able to love him the way that I loved Sam. So I keep Sam tucked away safely in a corner of my heart that will always belong to him, and I live with the secret pain, taking the blows every time I read an article, watch an interview, or see a picture of him on the internet.

"You okay?" Sebastian asks me. "You look nauseous. Do you need the baggy?" He grabs the paper bag from the seat back in front of him and holds it out for me.

"No," I say, batting it away. "I'm fine."

I peek out of the window as the plane angles down and the horizon disappears.

We're in the clouds.

Below the clouds.

And racing toward the runway.

I close my eyes as we bump along the tarmac until the plane eventually comes to a stop. I open them when we begin to taxi toward the terminal. I've flown only a few times in my life, and only since I met Drew. I don't mind the flying part, but I could do without taking off or landing.

Sebastian hands me my carry-on bag from the overhead compartment, and I follow him and Paul off the plane. Before we even make it inside the airport, Sebastian starts rattling off to-do items from the itinerary he made us.

"Okay, I got us early check-in at the hotel, so we can drop our bags, and then we have lunch reservations at Balthazar. It's too far to walk from Midtown, so we'll take the subway to SoHo. After that, I thought we'd do a little shopping, and then head back to the hotel to get showered and dressed. We'll take the subway to Grand Central Station and have cocktails at the Oyster Bar before the fight, and from there we can take a taxi to the Garden."

"Take a breath, Bas," Paul says, reaching for his hand as we file through the mass of people moving around the airport.

I laugh. "What about the Met?"

"Tomorrow," Sebastian says with wide, smiling eyes. He loves it as much as I do. "And if we have time, we can look for a new gallery to check out in Chelsea."

"Before we embark on the Sebastian Tour of Manhattan, we should probably get our bags," Paul says, tugging him in the direction of baggage claim.

I walk behind them, admiring their affection for each other. Paul laces his fingers with Sebastian's in the most casual yet caring way, and I can't help but envy them. I fantasize about Sam and I walking through the airport together, our fingers intertwined as he leads me to a car that's waiting to take us home. I imagine our house and kids...and pancakes. My heart glugs heavily in my chest and my feet drag as if bricks are tied to them. I admonish myself for fantasizing about a life I already have with Drew. Sans kids, at least for now. I know Drew wants them, but I can't imagine taking care of someone else when I can barely manage my own emotional well-being. Still, I often think of what my and Sam's kids would look like. A little boy with caramel hair and eyes like his. A little girl with light hair and eyes like mine.

"Come on, slowpoke," Sebastian says, pulling me from my thoughts. I've fallen several paces behind them.

"Sorry." I blink a few times to push down the sorrow. I feel it whenever I let go of that dream.

* * *

"To good friends." Paul raises his martini glass, and Sebastian and I do the same.

"And to sexy husbands," Sebastian adds, raising an eyebrow at Paul.

"And good assistants," I add, winking at him.

"And good bosses." He winks back.

"And to that beautiful hunk of a man who's going to be up on the stage tonight," Paul says exuberantly.

"It's a ring, not a stage," Sebastian corrects, lowering his glass.

"Oh, put your glass back up," Paul says to him. "You

know I'm only here to see Sam Cole, half-naked and sweaty."

I laugh awkwardly. "Cheers," I say, ending our much too long, and now somewhat uncomfortable, toast. We all clink our glasses together and sip our martinis.

"Well, some of us actually came to watch the fight," Sebastian says. "Right, Lucy?"

"Oh, uh, mm-hmm," I say, taking another sip of my drink. My eyes dart around the dimly lit bar that's tucked away inside Grand Central Station like an old hidden tavern. The arched ceilings are covered in century-old chevron-shaped tiles that glow amber in the ambient light.

"You know, our seats are close enough to see the sweat beading on their faces," Paul says, and butterflies immediately flock to my stomach.

I want to see Sam tonight, but I don't want him to see *me*. A million thoughts race through my head. *He won't see me, he'll be focused on the fight... What if he does see me and loses focus on the fight?... Would he even recognize me if he saw me?... What if he sees me and doesn't recognize me?... What if he recognizes me and he doesn't care?* My heart pounds inside my chest. "I can't believe our seats are that close," I say, just louder than a whisper.

"What?" Paul asks, leaning in to hear me better.

"I can't believe our seats are that close," I say again, louder.

"Maybe we'll be on TV," Sebastian says excitedly.

"Oh, God, I hope not."

"Honey, in that dress, you'll definitely be on TV," Paul says, smirking at me.

My face feels hot and my hands automatically move to the taut material covering my thighs. I swallow hard and look down at the navy-blue cocktail dress. I tug at the material that's barely hiding my cleavage. "You told me to wear this," I say, shoving Sebastian's arm.

"Yeah, because you look hot!"

"I'm too dressed up."

"We're all dressed up," Paul points out. "You're supposed to be."

"Luc, why are you freaking out? You look gorgeous." Sebastian tussles the ends of my long hair. "Your hair is super shiny and your skin looks like porcelain. You have nothing to worry about."

I bob my head. *Right. Nothing to worry about.* Except that I'm secretly stalking the estranged love of my life during a title fight against his biggest rival, in which he may or may not see me, at which point he may or may not care. *I think I might throw up.*

"Can you just give me a minute?" I ask, getting up from the small cocktail table we're sitting around.

"Yeah, but hurry, we need to leave in about ten minutes," Paul says.

"Okay, I'm just going to the restroom. I'll be right back." I balance carefully on my stilettos to the bathroom, where I lock myself inside a stall and take slow, deep breaths. *It's going to be fine. It's going to be fine,* I repeat over and over in my head. The thought of not seeing Sam tonight, as anxiety-inducing as it may be, would be much worse for me in the end. I'd regret it forever. Not to mention that if I back out now, I might never fully regain Paul's faith in my sanity, even if Sebastian eventually comes around. I'm just going to have to suck it up and get my dress-clad, stiletto-wearing butt ringside.

* * *

Lucy, Seventeen Years Old

"Are you ready?" I ask Sam, who is sitting in a folding chair across from me in the chaotic locker room at Joe's. His hands are wrapped in tape and Joe, who has been trying to manage the disarray and mayhem that accompanies an amateur boxing match, is sliding Sam's gloves on.

Sam nods, but he doesn't answer me, because of his mouth guard.

"He's ready," Joe says, wiping the sweat from his forehead. He's been supervising the ebb and flow of anxious boxers and coaches all afternoon. Sam is one of four boys from the gym who have a match tonight, and all of them, along with their coaches, opponents, opponents' coaches, and officiators, are squeezed into the relatively small space. I fan myself with a folded promotional flyer that Joe had printed up. It's usually freezing in here, but there are so many moving bodies creating heat, I'm actually sweating.

"Craig. My man," Joe says, shaking the hand of an official. He's one of the many volunteers who helps Joe get these matches set up. It's a lot of work, but there's usually a cash prize for the winners of each weight class, and the event helps generate revenue for the gym. Joe runs a nonprofit facility. He grew up in Brighton Park and, after some success as a professional boxer, decided to open the gym to give underprivileged kids a place to come after school. After he saw Sam get into a fight four years ago, he convinced him to join and has been coaching him ever since.

Sam stands up. It's almost time for his match.

I hug him and he holds me to his chest for a moment. "Be careful," I say to him, and an eager smile lights up his eyes. As confident as I am that Sam will win tonight—because he always wins—I hate knowing he could get hurt. The last time he fought Anthony Russo, he was left with a fractured rib and covered in bruises. Russo looked even worse.

Sam says that pain is fleeting. I wouldn't know. I've never been hit before. I leave the fighting to him. Just watching it is painful enough.

"Lucy, you should go grab your seat," Joe says, tightening the strings on Sam's gloves.

"Go get 'em, Rocky," I say, winking at Sam, before I'm absorbed by the crowd of people flowing from the gym floor into the locker room. Once I squeeze past them, I find my seat in the front row next to the ring. It's marked by a sign with my name on it. Joe always reserves a seat for me up front.

Sam and Anthony climb into the ring and take their corners and, after a quick introduction by the referee, begin the dance I've come to know as boxing. The footwork, the balance, the cardio, the strength, the technique required for a boxer to gain victory over his opponent...it's a little theatrical, but what can I say, I'm a fan of the arts. To me, boxing is just a very violent ballet. Much less chaotic than the street fights I've witnessed. Even the cheers and jeers from the crowd are synchronized to the movements of the match.

Sam takes a jab to the jaw, and I cringe, but it doesn't seem to shake him. He throws a left hook, followed by an uppercut that leaves Russo stumbling backward into the ropes.

The gym erupts even louder than before.

By the middle of the third round, Anthony and Sam both look exhausted. But everyone is still screaming and cheering them on. I'm too anxious to cheer. I'm just trying not to chew my nails down to the quick.

Sam takes an uppercut to the ribs. And another.

Dammit. This seems to be Russo's favorite move. It's how he broke Sam's rib before. *Come on, Sam! Move!*

Sam steps back and throws a jab, followed by a left hook, a right hook, and another jab that knocks Russo to his knees.

Yes!

The referee stands between them and pushes Sam into his corner. He holds his hand up and counts to eight while Russo gets to his feet, gauging whether he can keep fighting. I don't think I could watch if they just pummeled each other until one of them couldn't get up, like they do in professional boxing. The ref calls the fight and the crowd roars with excitement. By the sound of it, there were a lot of bets on Sam. The ref takes Sam's hand and raises it up in the air, and a smile stretches across my face when Sam winks at me, followed by a wave of relief that I always feel when a fight is over.

* * *

My heart might literally beat through my chest. If it weren't for the booming thuds reverberating through the arena speakers, I'd swear you could actually hear it. Everyone is on their feet, cheering and clapping as the music grows louder and the lights dim over the crowd.

"These are seriously the best seats you've ever gotten us for an event," Sebastian says to Paul. "Aren't they fantastic?" he shouts to me over the music as we shimmy along the row to our seats, which are directly behind the rail that separates the ring from the stands.

"Um, yeah, they're great," I say, keeping my eyes down to be sure my stilettos meet the floor and not someone's toe, and also because I'm terrified to look up at the ring, which I can see in my peripheral vision and know is only a few yards away from where we're sitting.

"I love your dress," a woman in our row says, touching my arm as I pass her. I thank her and smile graciously, but I feel nothing of the sort. Dresses that get compliments get attention, and that's the last thing I want right now.

When we reach our seats, I sit down, hoping to disappear behind the rail and the arena staff on the other side of it, but Sebastian grabs my elbow and pulls me back to my feet. "You can't sit down! This is amazing!" he shouts, rocking his head back and forth to the blaring music with a huge smile on his face.

I force a smile and try to move a little to the music, but my nerves have pushed me to the brink of paralysis. I curl my fingers into my palms and try to rub the sweat off them as I take in the well-lit ring before me.

It's so close. *Too* close.

Whether Sam sees me or not, I'll see *him*. I mean, *really* see him. Not through the filter of a screen, or even through a sea of people I assumed would be between us. But up close, in person. We'll be breathing the same air. I swallow hard and take slow, deep breaths. *It's been years. You were a child when you were together*, I think, trying to convince myself that what we had was nothing more than puppy love. *It's what everyone experiences . . . and then moves on from. It's perfectly normal to feel like this*, I tell myself, wanting so badly to believe it. But nothing about me and Sam was normal. Nothing about either of our lives was normal. Being orphaned by our drug-addicted parents as children wasn't normal. Having lived in twelve different homes, collectively, by the time we were in high school wasn't normal. Relying solely on each other until we were practically adults wasn't normal. The way that we loved each other wasn't normal. A shallow ache throbs inside my chest. We didn't just love each other; we lived and breathed each other. He was my universe. And I was his.

At the time, the universe seemed a lot smaller.

Blue and white spotlights bounce around the arena as the giant scoreboard monitors over the ring flash images of Mario Sanchez. There's a steady roar of applause from the crowd as the announcer highlights his career achievements. And then the showcase moves to Sam, and the roar of applause turns into rumbling thunder as the crowd cheers and screams and stomps their feet.

I gaze up at Sam in high definition, and I'm overwhelmed with emotion. Being surrounded by nineteen thousand people who are screaming for your childhood love is definitely not normal. I beam with pride, as if I somehow had anything to do with his accomplishments. Just knowing what he came from and how hard he's had to work to get here fills me with awe. *He's just a kid from Brighton Park.* An orphan who came from nothing. And now he has all this. It's everything he ever wanted.

Everyone's attention turns to the far corner of the arena where an entourage of people and flashing lights begin moving toward the center of the floor.

My heart stutters and my breath catches. I can't really see much through the crowd, but I feel light-headed. I look up and see Sanchez on the monitors over the ring and exhale the breath I didn't realize I was holding. I close my eyes and open them again.

Sanchez climbs between the ropes and holds his gloves up in the air, bouncing from foot to foot, encouraging the excited crowd. I can literally see every detail of his face, the white birthmark on his olive-colored torso, the blue-and-white stripes on his shoelaces. Before I have time to think about seeing Sam that close, the cheers from the crowd turn into thunder again, and everyone's attention shifts to the opposite corner of the arena. This time, I know that Sam is making his way toward the ring.

My heart races and heat flashes across my skin. My breath catches again. I can't move. I can't breathe. I can't blink.

"Hey, look up," Sebastian says, pointing to the monitors that must be showing close-ups of Sam. But I can't.

My eyes are frozen on the moving bodies inching closer and closer to the ring.

"Hey," Sebastian says again, but his voice fades into white noise. I can barely hear him.

I blink once, slowly, and everything is quiet. I no longer hear the thundering cheers or the blaring music. I don't notice the flashing lights. I only see *him*.

Sam is walking toward the ring, toward me.

My heart pounds in my ears as the arena air swirls through my lungs and past my lips. I watch him climb between the ropes and stand in the center of the ring like a warrior, mighty and strong. I can see every line in his torso and every muscle that's wrapped around his body like armor. I can see the details of his tattoos and read the ones that are spelled out.

He raises his gloves and, to my utter shock, I see the word *Lamb* scrolled in cursive on his rib cage, small enough that his arm covers it when he puts it back down.

My eyes flash to his face and fill with tears. I stare at him, trying to memorize the way his eyes crinkle when he smiles at the crowd, the way he licks his lips and nods with the cheers, the way the small muscles flex in his jaw when he talks to the referee. His confidence is a stark contrast to the anxiety I'm feeling.

The noise rushes back into my ears like a tsunami, nearly knocking me over. I stumble, but catch myself on Sebastian's arm.

"You okay?" he shouts.

"Yeah, sorry, it's just the heels. They're hard to balance in."

"This is crazy. They are so close."

"I know."

"Sam Cole is hot! Holy crap. He's way too pretty to be a boxer. No one should be allowed to hit that face."

A feeling that I haven't felt since I was seventeen suddenly washes over me. It's the feeling I used to get when I watched Sam fight at Joe's, knowing that he would be hit, knowing that he could be hurt. It's different watching him fight through the filter of TV. On TV, it's not real; he's not real. But here, now. This is real. He's real. He's *so* very real.

We take our seats as the fight begins, and the dance commences, leading the roar of the crowd.

Sam Cole takes the first hit of the night, the commentator announces, and air hisses through my teeth.

"Keep those hands up, Sam, keep 'em up." We're close enough to hear Joe shouting at Sam, and it takes me back in time. He looks exactly the same, except that his hair has a little more gray in it now.

Sanchez hits Sam again.

Cole takes another hit to the head.

"Throw the jab, Sam, throw the jab," Joe shouts.

Sam returns two body slaps to Sanchez's ribs and then throws an uppercut that knocks him into the ropes.

Okay, okay.

Sebastian puts his hand on my bouncing knee. "Don't worry, Luc. Sam's got this."

I give him a tight-lipped smile and nod.

The second round starts, and Sam takes the first hit again.

Jesus. I don't know how I'm going to watch this whole fight.

Sam throws a jab at Sanchez's face, and another, leaving him with a bloody nose.

"Holy shit, did you see that?" Paul shouts, leaning over Sebastian. "Forget seeing them sweat, I just saw blood fly out of Sanchez's face!"

"Yeah, it was totally gross," Sebastian says.

I wrinkle my nose. "It *was* pretty gross."

By the tenth round, Sanchez isn't the only one who's bleeding. Sam took a punch to the eye in the seventh round that split his eyebrow. But it hasn't slowed him down. He throws a right hook, followed by an uppercut that knocks Sanchez to the mat.

The referee counts, *One . . . two . . . three . . . four . . .*

The arena is going crazy.

By *five*, Sanchez is back on his feet. He throws a jab at Sam, but misses. He's tired. So is Sam. They lean against each other, hugging, until the referee pulls them apart. Then they explode like two volcanoes, taking turns throwing jabs and uppercuts at each other like they were both saving their last ounce of energy until right now.

The crowd erupts and everyone is on their feet.

Paul's on his feet. Sebastian's on his feet. I'm on my feet, screaming for Sam.

He's beating the hell out of Sanchez, and Sanchez is beating the hell right back out of him.

Tears burn in my eyes. *I can't take this anymore.* I just want it to be over.

Sam takes one last hit to the head, and once again everything around me falls silent. I watch Sam fall to the mat in slow motion, his glazed eyes finding mine before they close, and the only sound I hear is my own voice screaming, "Sam!"

Chapter 5

Sam

I open and close my unfocused eyes a few times, ignoring the sweat and blood stinging them.

Lucy?

"Get up, Sam. Get up!" Joe shouts from beside the ring.

Four . . . five . . . six . . .

"Get up!"

I pull my knees under me and grab the rope.

Eight . . .

I'm on my feet.

The referee grabs my gloves. "Come here, you good?"

I nod and take my stance in front of Sanchez.

Sanchez throws a punch at my face, but misses.

"Ahhhhhhh!!!!!" I scream, feeling a roar inside me, louder than I've ever felt before. I throw everything that I've got at him. A left hook, a right hook, another right hook, and an uppercut that sends him flying backward.

He lands on his back.

One...two...three...four...five...six...seven...eight...nine...ten!

The crowd erupts and my team climbs into the ring.

"You did it, baby!" Joe screams.

Sam Cole has done it once again. He has successfully defended his title as the undisputed light-heavyweight champion of the world!

I feel hands on my back and arms. People are congratulating me from every direction.

I spit out my bloody mouth guard and wrap my heavy arm around Joe's neck. "Lucy," I shout in his ear. "I saw Lucy."

Joe gives me a confused look.

"She's here. Have someone find her before she leaves."

"Yeah." He nods. "Okay."

"I mean it."

"Yeah, yeah...okay. Hey, Miles," he says, turning to my manager.

I'm consumed by the people crowding in around me and blinded by the flashing lights. I hold my belt up for the pictures, faking a smile for the camera.

Lucy was here. She came. I can't keep up with the thoughts racing through my pounding head. *Was she alone?* My eyes could barely focus. All I saw was her creamy skin and blond hair, her pale blue eyes. When she shouted my name, I knew it was her. Her voice would stand out from a hundred thousand other voices. *Why did she come? Did she want me to see her? Has she come before?*

My team leads me through the crowd to my dressing room,

where I'm greeted by the physician. I take the seat across from him and wait impatiently for Miles to return while the doctor examines me.

Miles walks in and reports, "I couldn't find her, Sam. If she was here, she's long gone."

"Well, fucking ask around. I'm telling you, she was here. She was ringside, for God's sake. Find out who she was with."

"I'll find out what I can." He crosses his arms and stands over the doctor. "How's he look, doc?"

"Gonna need a couple of stitches over that eye, and an ice bath wouldn't hurt."

"Stitches? Can't you just put some glue on it?" I ask.

"Yeah, I can put glue it, but it'll leave a scar."

"It's fine."

* * *

My phone buzzes, waking me from a deep sleep.

Fuck. Everything hurts.

I sit up slowly and swing my legs over the side of the bed. I reach for a bottle of ibuprofen on the nightstand, ignoring the ache in my shoulder, and shake a couple into my hand. I swallow them down and answer my phone. "Yeah."

"No signs of her being at the fight last night," Miles says on the other end of the line. "We checked all the ringside tickets."

"That doesn't make sense. She was there."

"You got hit hard. Maybe you just thought you saw her."

"She was there, Miles. Get the recording."

"Recording's already been sent. A copy to the office and a copy to your place. It should be there when you get home."

I rub my stiff neck. "Yeah, okay."

"Flight for Atlanta leaves at one. I'll come by your room around eleven."

"All right."

"You need anything?"

"No, I'm okay."

"Order room service. Get some food in your system."

"Yeah, okay."

"Bye, champ."

I get up and walk over to the mirror, holding my aching ribs. My eye looks like shit. It's swollen and blue under the glob of hard glue that's holding my eyebrow together. I lift my arm over my head and stretch my aching muscles. *Fucking Sanchez.* He used my ribs as a punching bag.

I run my fingers over the word *Lamb* that's camouflaged by bruises.

I don't think I can wait until I get home to see the recording. I have to find the fight; I have to see if Lucy was really there. It has to be on the internet somewhere. I sit back down on the bed, grab my phone, and search for the fight. I scroll through several video clips until I find one that's close enough to see the people sitting next to the ring. I watch it for about thirty seconds before I see her, and my heart stops. I pause it. *She was there.*

I take slow, deep breaths because just knowing that she was really there, that I didn't imagine it, does all sorts of fucked-up things to my head. I squeeze my eyes shut and grip the phone. *Why were you there, Lucy? What the hell are trying to do to me?* I open my eyes and look at the screen again. I want to press play, but I know what seeing her is going to do me, and I'm not sure if I'm ready for it. I throw my phone across the bed and fall back against the pillows, grimacing at the ache in my chest, which now accompanies the pain in my ribs. But after a few seconds, I grab it again, and press play.

When the camera focuses on Lucy, I pause the video and stare at her for a long minute, until my pulse stops thumping in my neck.

She looks exactly the same, but different. Her hair is long and straight, and still the same shade of blond. And her face hasn't changed at all, except that maybe she's gotten prettier. She's wearing makeup, but it's not caked on like it is on the women I usually meet. I can still see the beauty mark under her eye and the one by her mouth. I can see her clear blue eyes. She looks worried. I unpause the video and watch her pull her hand to her mouth. She looks down and shakes her head. The camera cuts to the ring and zooms in on me. I just took a hit from Sanchez. I rewind the video and watch her again. She's sitting on the edge of her chair, leaning forward with one hand on the rail in front of her. I take the hit and she grips the rail tighter and pulls her other hand to her mouth. Her face screws up at the same time, and she shakes her head.

She was worried about me.

I watch it again.

And again.

I let the video keep playing this time, but it stays on me and Sanchez for the next several minutes. Finally, when the camera pans out again, I see Lucy standing up, cheering. I just knocked Sanchez on his back. She has the biggest smile on her face. I pause it and stare at her for a long time.

God, it hurts just to look at her.

I put my phone facedown on the nightstand and fall back on the bed. I fold my hands over my chest, close my eyes, and inhale a deep breath to try to clear my head. But the only thing I can think about is Lucy. I squeeze my eyes shut tight and pull my palms to my temples, pressing against my thoughts, trying to clear my mind. I listen to my breathing. I focus on my pulse. I try to think about anything except for Lucy. But it doesn't work.

* * *

Sam, Fourteen Years Old

Something wakes me from a light sleep. I turn my head to listen for it again, but the only sound I hear is the whistling of a train in the distance, cutting through the cold, quiet night. *It was probably just the heat kicking on.* My mind is so messed up right now, I doubt it would take much to wake me. I'm getting placed in a new home tomorrow. It will be my fifth foster home, my fifth so-called family, and my fifth time starting over. It's also the first time I wished like hell I could stay where I'm at.

I got into a fight today. My fourth fight this year. So my social worker is putting me with a family that has better "core values" and can help put me on the "right path." It's not like

I'm some kind of hothead that just goes around beating people up. I was defending Lucy. And I would do it again. She
tends to stand out from the crowd, especially at our school.
The guys give her a hard time because they think she's pretty.
And the girls give her a hard time because they know the
guys think she's pretty. She *is* pretty. She's different-looking.
She's a year younger than me, but I'm constantly fending off
the older boys who live on our street.

Tomorrow it will be *her* street. I'll be three blocks away,
and she'll still be living under the same roof as Will and
Tommy. *I swear to God, if they even look at her.*

A noise pulls me from my thoughts, and this time, I know
it's coming from Lucy's room.

She whines and cries. *No.*

A burst of heat flashes across my skin, and my pulse races
as I jump from my bed, ignoring the noisy springs that creak
inside my mattress. I step into the hallway to assess the danger, but everything is quiet, besides Maxine's snoring, which
is loud enough to hear through her closed door. Will and
Tommy's door is closed too.

Lucy whimpers again.

"Lucy?" I whisper, pushing her door open. I find her curled
up in her bed, gripping the sheets. "Lucy," I whisper again,
touching her arm.

She startles awake and looks up at me with wide eyes.

"Hey, it's okay. You were just having a nightmare."

She blinks at me a few times, and the gray moonlight coming through her window fills her pale, watery eyes.

"Luc, what's the matter?"

She rolls over and pulls the sheet up to her chin. "Nothing, go back to your room," she says with a wobbly voice.

I tug on her arm through the sheet. "Not until you tell me what's wrong. Was it the dream? Are you okay?"

She buries her face in her pillow and cries.

I'm not really sure what to do, so I sit beside her and wait for her to finish.

After a few seconds, she looks up at me and sniffs. "I'm crying because it wasn't just a dream, you're really leaving me...just like everyone else."

My face screws up at the tight feeling in my chest. "Lu—" I swallow hard. "Lucy." I wrap my fingers around her shoulder. Her skin is hot under my hand, and it sends a strange sensation through my body that makes me uncomfortable and excited at the same time. "I'm not. I'm not leaving you."

"Yes you are."

"I'm just leaving this house. Not you. We'll still see each other at school."

"For now. But what about next year when you go to high school? I'll never see you."

"That's not true. You'll see me all the time. I'll leave early every day and walk you to school, just like I do now."

She sits up and looks at me with sad eyes, and it makes me want to kick the shit out of myself for getting into that stupid fight today. *I'm such an idiot.* "I'm sorry," I say, wishing a thousand times that I could go back and walk away from it, like she told me to.

She nods and a tear rolls down her cheek. "I know." She

wraps her arms around my neck and hugs me tight. "You're my best friend, Sam."

I push down the feelings she's stirring up inside me and hold her while she cries.

She sniffs again and asks, "Will you stay with me tonight, just for a little while?"

"Yeah." I swallow hard and banish the uninvited thoughts that invade my mind when we lie down. She rolls onto her side and reaches for my arm, draping it over her shoulder, and I intentionally move my hips back a few inches away from hers. I pull her against my chest and hold her tight.

This isn't the first time she's asked me to stay with her in the middle of the night. She has nightmares about her mom overdosing sometimes. She was there when it happened, and she remembers things about it that no kid should know. But tonight feels different. *She* feels different.

I close my eyes and breathe in the smell of her hair and skin, knowing that this is the last time I'll be able to comfort her in the middle of the night. My chest feels heavy when I think about tomorrow. Lucy is the closest thing that I have to family. She needs me...to protect her, to keep her safe. I knew it from the second I laid eyes on her. She was so innocent, like a little lamb or something. She didn't belong in this place. She still doesn't. But I need her too. I don't remember being happy before her. But she makes me happy. She makes me curious. She makes me want to do good things. I don't know if love is really a thing, but if it is, it must be what I feel for her, because I've never felt like this about anyone before.

"I love you," I whisper, wanting her to know. But I don't

think she hears me. She must be asleep. I close my eyes, feeling pleased with myself. I've never said that to anyone before, but I like how it feels to say it to Lucy.

"I love you too," she whispers, and a strange feeling—a mix of joy and awe—settles over me.

No one's ever said that to me.

* * *

"Sam! Sam!" Someone pounds on the door and calls my name again. "Sam!"

I grab my phone. *Shit.* It's 11:25. I jump up and answer the door.

Miles marches into my hotel room. "I guess you don't want to go home today."

"I fell asleep."

"Well, you might as well go back to bed, because you're not making a one o'clock flight out of JFK now."

"Just get the next flight, then." I reach up and rub my stiff neck. I'm still just as sore as I was earlier this morning.

"Damn," he says, eyeing the bruises on my ribs. "Did you take something for that?"

"Yeah. I'm fine. Just let me get a shower before we go." I head to the bathroom and strip down.

"You get some food?"

"No, not yet."

He grabs the room service menu and stands outside the shower. "What do you want? An omelet? Eggs Benedict? Pancakes? All of the above?"

"Not pancakes."

"I forgot, you don't like pancakes."

"I never said I don't like them."

"Then have a cheat day. You won last night."

"Just order me the fucking omelet, Miles."

"Well, you could've said that to begin with. I'm ordering you some coffee too. You're grouchy." He shuts the bathroom door. "Guess I would be too, if I looked like a punching bag," I hear him say from the other side of the door.

I close my eyes and stand under the hot water, thinking about Lucy.

I spent every day in prison worrying about her. I wrote letters, but everything I sent to her foster home came back returned. I tried email, but her school account was deactivated. Gaining access to her file was like trying to pry open a locked vault. Family Services wouldn't tell me anything. The only person who would give me any information at all was her last foster mom, Ms. Jenkins. She told me that Lucy dropped out of school and took off on her eighteenth birthday, but she didn't know where she'd gone. The Lucy I knew would have never done that. Then again, the Lucy I knew would have never given up on me. When they put me in Central State Prison and she didn't come, I knew it was over.

I turn off the shower and grab a towel.

"Breakfast is here," Miles says through the door. "Oh, and I think I got some information for you."

I swing the door open. "What information?"

"The ringside seats. Not everyone who paid was there. Antwon Cruz, a record producer out of Atlanta, was a no-show. But it was a packed house, there were no empty seats. So I called his office. Apparently, he sent someone from his staff instead. A guy named Paul Ford." I listen quietly, waiting for his point. "I just Googled him. His partner, Sebastian, is Lucy's assistant. She runs an art studio in Atlanta. I found an article about an exhibit she's hosting next month. He was mentioned in it."

I let out a slow breath and lean against the door frame.

"They must have come together."

"She runs an art studio?" I drop my head and say quietly to myself, "Makes sense."

"Sam, are you listening? You were right, she was there last night. Or at least, it's possible that she was."

I glance up at him. "Yeah, no, I heard you."

He hands me a folded-up piece of paper. "It's the address to her art studio."

I take it from him and frown.

"If you don't go talk to this girl, I'm going to go do it for you."

I roll my eyes.

"I'm serious. These girls, they mess with your head, Sam. Maybe not the chicks you drag up and down red carpets and bang in the back of the limo afterward. But this one"—he points to my head—"she's in there deep. I can see it. So, please, for my sake...go talk to her, once and for all. Say goodbye, get closure, or do whatever you need to do so that you can forget about this girl and get on with your life. I need you focused on what's important. Your career. Your next match. Okay? You hear me?"

I crease my eyebrows. "Yeah. I hear you."

Chapter 6

I sip my coffee and gaze at the beautiful painting before me. "This one's my favorite," I say, admiring the smooth flesh tones of the partially nude woman lying on her back amid her discarded clothes and tousled hair, carefully balancing a vibrant, feathery-winged bird on her delicately splayed fingers. She looks so carefree, like she has no worries in the world.

I envy her.

"Woman with a Parrot," Sebastian reads the painting's label aloud. "Looks more like a parakeet. You could paint a better parrot."

"Are you comparing me to Gustave Courbet, one of the most important artists of the nineteenth century?"

"I'm not comparing. I'm saying you're better than him."

I laugh a short but loud laugh that echoes off the walls of the quiet museum. I quickly cover my mouth. "Gustave

Courbet led the realism movement in France. He's arguably one of the best realistic painters of all time."

"Well, I think you're better."

"Sweet, sweet Sebastian," I say, pressing my lips together over an amused smile. "You've got so much to learn."

"Look, I may not have studied art in college, but *that* looks like a parakeet."

"He's right," Paul says, teaming up with Sebastian. "It does look like a parakeet. I think you could paint a better parrot."

I laugh quietly this time. "I love you guys, but you're both crazy."

Sebastian gives me a sideways glance. "Speaking of crazy, maybe now you can tell us what happened last night."

Paul gives Sebastian a disapproving look, but Sebastian ignores him and raises his eyebrows at me expectantly. Clearly I've let the employee-employer line blur a bit too much. You'd think he was my older brother or something by the scornful look on his face.

"Nothing happened. I just"—I shake my head, unsure how to explain why I bolted from the arena before the fight was even over—"I just wanted to get out of there." I *had* to get out of there. When Sam hit the mat, he looked at me. His eyes met mine and, if only for a second, he *saw* me. And I saw him. I saw him sitting at the kitchen table when he was twelve, pushing his hair out of his unusual eyes. I saw him in my bed protecting me in the dark, whispering *I love you* for the first time. I saw him lying on the grass beside me watching the planes fly over us. I felt his long fingers laced with mine. I felt his heart beating against my chest. And I felt *my* heart break into a thousand pieces, like a pane of glass shattering inside me. It hurt as much as losing him the first time. But once again, I had to let him go. And that's exactly what I did when I walked out of there. I ran, actually, which wasn't easy in my heels, but I was too busy wiping tears from my eyes to worry about my ridiculous choice in footwear, until one of my heels got caught in a sidewalk seam and broke off somewhere between West Thirty-Fourth and West Thirty-Sixth Streets. I was a barefoot bawling mess by the time I got to the hotel.

Suffice it to say it wasn't the best night for me. Except that it *was*. Seeing Sam in that ring, hearing everyone cheering for him and calling him *champ*. It was incredible. I've never felt so happy for someone in all my life. I'm immeasurably proud of him. It might have been one of the best and worst nights of my entire life.

Sebastian stands between me and *Woman with a Parrot* and places his hands on my shoulders. "Okay, you know I love you. But you are acting a little bit crazy."

I roll my eyes and shift my weight from one foot to the other.

"Are you pregnant?" he asks very seriously.

I let out a sharp puff of air. "No." *Can you imagine the look on Janice's face if I told her I was having a shotgun wedding?* I suppress a giggle.

"Are you sure? Because when my sister was pregnant, she acted crazy too. With a capital 'C.'" He widens his suspicious eyes.

"Sebastian. I. Am. Not. Pregnant."

"Well then, what is going on with you?"

"Nothing. I just have a lot on my mind right now."

"You walked out of the Garden during the last two minutes of a title fight, featuring your favorite boxer, who won, by the way, because of the exhibit?" He shakes his head. "No, I'm not buying it."

"Bas, drop it." Paul winks at me.

"Yeah, knock it off. I have a lot on my mind, I'm not pregnant, and I don't really want to keep talking about this. I left a boxing match early. I didn't rob a bank. You can put my crazy card right back where you found it."

"Fine. But if you take off like that again, without telling anyone where you're going, I'm pulling it back out, and I'll be forced to show it to Drew."

Drew would have a heart attack if he knew I walked nine blocks alone in the dark, barefoot no less. I'll definitely be leaving that detail out when I tell him about the trip. I cringe at the thought of telling him anything about it. At this point, I just want to pretend that it didn't happen. *I shouldn't have come.* All it's done is left a new hole in my heart that I'll have to pretend isn't there.

"I'm sorry that I took off last night, I just didn't feel good."

"Crazy and nauseous. Hmm...Sounds like you're pregnant."

I hit Sebastian with my purse. "I am *not* pregnant. Now, let's go so that we don't miss our flight."

* * *

"You're back," Drew says, greeting me as I walk through the front door.

"Hey," I say, surprised to see him. He was supposed to leave for Philadelphia this morning. "What are you doing here?"

He wraps his arms around me and pulls me up into a big bear hug. "I rearranged my meetings tomorrow so that I can leave in the morning instead."

"Oh," I say with a wobbly voice. I was expecting to come home to an empty house and wallow in my sorrow and guilt alone.

"You okay?"

"Yeah," I lie.

He kisses the top of my head and murmurs, "I missed you."

I nod and wrap my arms around him. "I missed you too."

"I didn't like being here without you."

"I thought you had to work all weekend."

"I did. But when I wasn't working, I was here alone. I've gotten used to you being here." He smiles at me. "I'm so glad you decided to move in before the wedding."

I rest my chin on his chest and force a weak smile. "Me too."

"Did you have a good time?"

"Mm-hmm." I press my cheek to his chest, unable to look in his eyes when I answer.

"How was the fight?"

"Loud."

He laughs and squeezes me in his arms. "Didn't Sam Cole win?"

I swallow the hard lump in my throat and nod against his chest. "Yep."

"I thought you'd be more excited."

I shake my head and look up at him. "I'm just happy to be home. And to see you," I say honestly. In his arms I feel quiet and calm, a welcome reprieve from the last twenty-four hours. "I'm glad you stayed."

He unwraps my arms from around him and drags my bags over to the stairs. "Leave these here," he says, taking my hand.

"What are you doing?" I laugh. "I need to unpack and take a shower."

"Just a little surprise."

It smells like he's been cooking. *I hope he made dinner.* I'm starving. Our flight was delayed and all I've eaten today was the airline cookies they passed out on the plane. It's well past dinnertime now.

He pulls me into the kitchen, and my mouth pops open when I see flowers and candles flickering on the kitchen island, which he's set for two. "It's been a while since we've gone on a date, so I thought we could have one here tonight."

My eyes mist over because he's so incredibly sweet and thoughtful and I don't deserve him. "Drew."

"I had Sebastian text me when you landed, so everything's warm." He pulls a stool out for me to sit down at the island and busies himself in front of the stove. He returns moments later with a bottle of wine and two small plates of what looks like something amazing. "Lobster macaroni with gruyère and cheddar."

"Oh, my God, thank you. I'm starving." I quickly get a forkful and shove it into my mouth, moaning over the bite. "It's *so* good."

He smiles and pours us both a glass of wine. "Don't fill up. There's more."

I widen my eyes and smile, a genuine smile, maybe the first one I've had all day. "This was a good surprise. Thank you."

He leans in and kisses me. "You're welcome."

After the lobster mac, Drew presents me with a gorgeous fillet that is melt-in-your-mouth delicious. Then for dessert, fried cinnamon ice cream. It is the perfect meal and the perfect way to end a very crappy day.

Drew smiles at me and I smile at him, but he doesn't say anything.

"What?"

I see a familiar look in his eyes, and I know exactly what. I'm frozen under his lustful stare, unsure how to tell him that I'm too raw from seeing Sam to be with him right now. I just need a day or two for everything to go back to normal, back to the way it was before I lost my mind and decided to go to New York. I anxiously bite my lip, which he takes as an invitation.

He presses his mouth to mine and kisses me, softly at first, and then deeply, taking my face in his hands. But instead of tasting him, I just taste *dinner*. I take a deep breath of his cologne and try to focus on how good he smells and how good he looks. I consider all the reasons he should be turning me on right now—besides the fact that he *loves* me...he's handsome, he's tall, he dresses well, he can cook—but I can focus only on why he isn't.

He drops his mouth to my neck and unbuttons my shirt, dragging his lips across my collarbone down to my bra. I close my eyes and force a soft moan, trying so hard to feel some-thing, but all I feel is uneasy.

"Lucy, I want you so bad," he says, unclasping my bra, and even his voice feels wrong.

"I want you too," I say automatically, but when he drops his mouth to my breast, it makes me shiver for all the wrong reasons. I roll my shoulder away from him and slip out of his arms. "Take me to bed," I whisper, trying to sound seductive, hoping that by the time we get upstairs, I'll be able to shake whatever is wrong with me.

He scoops me up and, even though I feel pathetic in his arms, I let him carry me up the stairs to our room. He drops me onto the bed and climbs over me. His mouth goes right to my boob again, and it feels just as weird as it did before.

Something's wrong. I close my eyes and try to will it to feel good, but I can't. It doesn't.

He sits up and pulls his shirt off, and I welcome the space between us, as fleeting as it may be. He somehow manages to get my jeans and panties off in the same few seconds it takes him to get naked. He's moving with the speed of a train, unable to see the signs blurring past him, telling him that something's wrong, that I'm not into this at all.

"Wait." I sit up and put my hand on his chest, and he freezes.

"What is it? What's wrong?"

I stare at him for a second, trying to think of a way to tell him about Sam. He deserves to know the truth. But I can't do it. "I don't feel good. I think maybe from the flight."

"Oh. Okay," he says, trying to mask his disappointment.

"Is it your head or your stomach?" He puts his hand on my forehead. "You don't think it's the food, do you?"

"No, the food was delicious. It's just a headache, probably from the flight. I'm sorry."

He nods thoughtfully and rubs my thigh. "You don't have to apologize. I know you and planes don't mix well. I should have thought to ask."

I shrug. "Do you think maybe you could get me some Tylenol?"

"Sure." He gets up and puts his pants back on.

I reach for my robe on the end of the bed and slip it on. "Hey." I grab his hand before he leaves. "Rain check?"

"Just say the word." He winks and leaves to get me some Tylenol, which I could actually really use now.

Chapter 7

Lucy

"Good morning, sunshine," Sebastian says, handing me a cup of coffee. "It's a latte macchiato. Two percent milk. You're welcome."

"Thank you." I take it from him and smile.

He gauges me and says, "You look very sunny today. I take it you liked Drew's surprise last night?"

Before I can answer, a man walks into the studio, carrying a large vase of white roses. There must be at least three dozen of them. "Delivery for Lucy Bennett," he says, eyeing the paper in his hand.

"You can put them there," Sebastian says, pointing to the corner of the front desk. When the delivery guy leaves, he plucks the card from the vase and reads it out loud, "Ready for that rain check." He raises an eyebrow. "I love you. Drew."

I sip my coffee and smell the roses, ignoring Sebastian's stare.

He puts the card down next to me. "Rain check?"

"What?" I look up at him. "I was tired from the trip."

"Ahh." He turns the vase until the roses are positioned to his liking. "You were tired."

"Yes." I laugh awkwardly. "Is that so hard to believe?"

"No. I just wish you'd tell me what's really going on with you."

"Sebastian, there's nothing going on."

"Lucy, your fiancé, the man that you love, rearranged his travel schedule to surprise you with an incredible dinner, and you asked him for a rain check."

"So what? I loved the dinner. I just didn't feel like having sex, okay?"

He holds his palms up and nods. "Okay."

I exhale an exasperated breath and sip my coffee under his watchful stare.

"Just... you know that you can talk to me about anything, right?"

I nod and smile softly. "I know." *But not about this.*

He gives me a sincere look and raises his dark eyebrows.

"There's nothing to talk about, Bas. I just want to enjoy my coffee and roses, okay?"

He squares his broad shoulders, inhales a deep breath, and exhales with a smile. "Okay. Well, I think today's going to be a great day. The sun is shining, the sky is blue, there's a nip of fall in the air... and one of us got laid last night."

"Sebastian."

"What? I'm allowed to bask in the glow. You should try it sometime."

"Sebastian, you're like the sun. You never stop glowing."

"I'll take that as a compliment."

"It was meant as one."

He wraps his arm around my neck. "Come on, we still have about a mile of red tape to get through for the exhibit."

"What's on the agenda today?" I ask as we walk to the back of the studio.

"The schedule, the waivers, the price list, the theme. Want me to go on?"

I had no idea what an undertaking the exhibit would be. If it weren't for Sebastian, I might have thrown in the towel already. "Let's get started."

* * *

Sebastian stands up and pulls me up off the cement floor, where we've been sitting for the last three hours, scheming and planning and organizing for the event. "I don't think I can brainstorm anymore. My cloud has run dry."

I stretch my arms over my head. "I know, mine too."

"How about I go get us some lunch? Sustenance will help. Fill our stomachs, nourish our brains."

"Okay." I look around at the mess we've made. We're standing in the middle of a storm of scattered papers, open notebooks, our laptops, my iPad, and about twenty prints of potential artwork we're considering for the exhibit. "I'll clean up while you're out and peruse the internet for a conference table, so we can actually work like grown-ups." I laugh.

"Why would you do that? This is what I love about this job. We can sit on the floor, make a huge mess and be creative, and no one can say anything about it. I cannot be creative around a conference table."

I laugh again. "Well, maybe just some floor pillows, then."

"That's more like it. I'll see if I can find some while I'm out."

"Don't take too long or we'll be eating dinner here too."

"I won't."

Sebastian leaves and I begin organizing the chaos on the floor. Unlike the front of the studio, which is wall-to-wall white and adorned with my paintings, the back is all cinder block and exposed pipes and air-conditioning ducts. I like the industrial feel, and there's plenty of windows for light, so I've never bothered finishing it. I just added a big area rug, an old leather couch, and a couple of chairs, which we never actually sit in. It's a nice contrast to the clean, vibrant storefront. The two spaces contradict each other like the halves of my brain.

I get up and take my laptop to the desk in the front of the studio. I need a change of scenery. And I need to catch up on the emails I've been ignoring all morning. I sit down and look at the open space, wondering how I got here. I still feel like I need to pinch myself to be sure I'm not dreaming. Just a few years ago, I was struggling to make ends meet. Now I own my own gallery. Well, I'm running it anyway. It's technically still in Drew's name, but he's gifting it to me for our wedding. Which is why this exhibit *has* to be a success. I want to earn back every cent he put into it, and the only way to do that is by selling my paintings. Over time, I should be able to pay him back. It's the only way I can accept it.

I begin reading through my emails. I reply to a few and flag the ones I want to come back to later. After a few minutes, I look up from my task, and I'm startled to see someone standing outside on the sidewalk, staring at me through the glass.

The studio seems to turn upside down, and I have to grip the desk, because it feels as if I might fall out of my seat and land on the ceiling. My eyes lock with the most beautiful set of eyes I've ever seen, eyes that have seen places inside me that no one else knows exist. My lips part, desperate for a breath that will bring the sweet relief of oxygen to my lungs.

Sam gazes at me and I gaze at him for what feels like an eternity, one I never want reprieve from, and then he mouths the word *hi*.

Hi, I mouth back, and it brings a flood of emotions screaming to the surface, feelings that I've repressed, ignored, and denied for so long. I hold my breath as he reaches for the door and pulls it open, stepping through my protective bubble, which pops and vanishes into thin air.

My heart is racing so fast I think I might pass out.

He walks into the studio and all I can do is watch him, terrified. I'm terrified of why he's here. I'm terrified of what to say. I'm terrified of what he's going to say. But mostly, I'm terrified of the way that he's making me feel right now.

I get up and carefully walk around the desk. I'm also terrified of falling on my face, because I seem to have lost all feeling in my knees.

He stands just a few feet away from me, and we stare at each other for another silent eternity. He's bigger up close. *Has he gotten taller?* He's definitely more muscular, but I've seen him without a shirt on enough to know that. I try not to look at the tattoos that are peeking out of his rolled-up sleeve. I know them by heart, but seeing them in person makes me feel like a stalker for having memorized them. I keep my eyes on his handsome face. His eye looks terrible—the cut over his eyebrow is glued shut, and it's bruised around the side—but he's still the most beautiful man I've ever seen. His caramel hair is cut short, and his chiseled jaw is covered in light stubble that surrounds his full lips. I would give anything to see his dimples, but his face is too intense right now.

I swallow hard and try to force something out of my mouth. "How did you—"

"The fight," he says before I can finish, and my heart quickly runs and hides somewhere inside my chest. "I saw you there." He waits for me to say something, but I can't form any words. I just want to hear him speak again. I want to hear the warm familiarity of his voice. "What were you doing there, Luc?"

I feel a piece of my heart splinter off when he calls me that, like no time has passed at all, like he's still the only person I've ever let in. I drop my eyes to the floor, to the walls, to my paintings that seem so irrelevant now, to anywhere but his face. I can't look in his eyes and lie, but I can't tell him the truth either.

He boldly places his hand under my chin, and I suck in a breath. "Hey," he says, lifting my face so that I'm forced to look at him. I can barely keep my eyes open because the sensation traveling from his fingertips is surging through me with the force of a hurricane.

I pull my chin away and take a step back to put some space between us again.

"Sorry," he says, pulling his eyebrows together, like it's just occurred to him that he crossed an invisible line, a fracture in the earth at our feet separating our lives.

"It's okay," I whisper, unable to speak any louder.

He stares at me again and more silence passes between us. "I just, I want to know why you came. Are you...okay?"

Okay? No, I'm not okay. I love you and I don't even know you anymore. And I'm engaged! A few of the tears I'm working so very hard to contain make it to my eyes, but I blink them back, hoping he doesn't notice. "I'm, um..." I close my eyes and shake my head. If I say anything else, even just a single word, the dam is going to break. I open my eyes, force a weak smile, and nod over the lump in my throat. But he's watching me with so much intensity, like he's desperate for me to say something, anything to answer the question in his eyes.

"I mean, you came to the fight, but you didn't try see me afterward or anything, so..." He pauses and stares at me again.

I swallow hard and look into his familiar eyes, and I'm wrapped in a blanket of warmth that shields me from the elements and protects me from the hurt and the pain and the anxiety of the moment. He feels like *home*. I'm compelled to answer him honestly, to tell him that I'm *not* okay, that I still think about him all the time, that I was wrong, that I miss him, that I'm sorry, that I'm proud of him, but the studio door swings open and Sebastian walks in with our lunch, balancing several square pillows against his chest that are stacked high, covering his face.

"A little help," he says, but before I can blink, he stumbles and the pillows scatter across the floor. He looks at me and he looks at Sam, then he looks at me and he looks at Sam. I've never seen him so shocked before. His eyes fix on Sam and his mouth pops open. "Sam Cole."

Sam presses his lips together and nods.

"You're Sam Cole."

Sam nods again and Sebastian gives me a confused look. "Why is Sam Cole here?"

"Sebastian, can you give us a minute, please?" There's no way to evade his questioning, but I can at least postpone it for now.

He bobs his head and raises the bag in his hand. "Got lunch," he says, still sounding perplexed. Perhaps he's putting some version of the puzzle together in his head. He makes his way to the back of the studio, and Sam and I are alone again.

"Your assistant?"

I crease my eyebrows and nod.

"I had my team call around after the fight. You came with him and his partner."

"His husband," I say, though it's irrelevant.

"Why did you come to the fight, Lucy? Why did you come and sit right beside the ring? Did you think I wouldn't see you?"

"Who's your team?" I ask, skirting his question.

"Joe, Tris, my manager, a few other people in my circle. Will you please answer my question?"

"Tristan Kelley. He's your trainer now, right?"

"Yes."

I exhale a quiet breath. "You did it." I shake my head slowly. "You really did it." I can't help but smile and gaze up at him with the same awe I felt during the fight when everyone was cheering for him.

I can tell that he's frustrated because I haven't answered his question, but the corners of his mouth turn up defiantly, just enough to show me his dimples, and my heart comes out of hiding. "I told you I would."

My smile quickly vanishes and I'm filled with guilt. I press my lips together tightly, trying to hold in another wave of emotion, but it's too big to contain now. The tears leak slowly onto my cheeks.

"Are you happy?" he asks.

Say yes, you're happy with Drew. I look into his eyes, contemplating my answer, but the truth is I don't know anymore. I shrug and answer, "It's not that simple."

He looks at me with his beautiful, strange eyes, the blue mixing with the brown like paints running together. "It *is* that simple."

I shake my head and wipe my cheeks. "You have no idea what all I went through after you left, what I had to overcome without you, or what I've struggled with every day since you showed up on my TV."

He drops his chin and says quietly, "I'm not the one who left."

"You went to prison for drugs, Sam. What was I supposed to do?"

"You were supposed to believe me." He reaches for my wrist, just as boldly as when he reached for me before, and runs his thumb over the gold bracelet dangling from it.

I swallow hard and say softly, "It was all I had left of you."

"I bought this for you with the money I earned mopping floors at the gym. I never sold drugs," he says quietly, and a cry bubbles out of me because I want so badly to believe him. I've gone over it in my head so many times over the years. I want to believe anything but the truth. That Sam chose drugs over me.

"I'm getting married," I say, overcome with frustration, because I never would have met Drew if Sam hadn't been arrested. "You weren't supposed to leave."

"Neither were you." The pain in his voice makes me cry harder.

"I'm sorry," I whisper. My heart aches, knowing that I can't go back and change the past, doubting that I would now even if I could. I love *Drew*. He's my reality now.

"It's too late for sorry, Lamb."

I want to cry even harder when he calls me that. I inhale a shaky breath and wipe my eyes. "Please don't call me that."

"Why?"

"Because that's not who I am anymore. We have different

lives. We're different people now," I say resolutely, double knotting Drew to my heart.

He stares at me for a few silent seconds and then shakes his head. "No we're not. You're still the little girl sitting across the table from me, picking at her sandwich. The girl who called me to her room night after night because she couldn't shake the memories of seeing her mom dying on the floor in front of her. The girl I walked to school for six years and protected from the wolves that stalked our neighborhood. The girl I called *Lamb* because she was so pure, she was unlike anyone I'd ever met before. The girl who was, and still is, the most beautiful thing I've ever laid my eyes on."

I look away, as if I can somehow hide from his words, from our history, from the memories.

"And I'm still the boy who fell in love with that girl. The boy who promised to always protect her. The boy who lived and breathed for her happiness." He creases his eyebrows and runs his hands through his hair. "I came here to tell you goodbye, Lucy. To tell you that you were wrong. To finally let you go."

My heart weeps in a dark corner inside my chest.

"But you see, the problem with that is, I don't know how."

My heart stammers.

"So just tell me that you're happy, tell me that your fiancé is the love of your life, so I can let you go." He watches me intently, waiting for me to respond, but I can't bring myself to answer him.

Admitting the truth, that Drew *isn't* the love of my life, would mean acknowledging it, and the implications of that scare the hell out of me. But if I lie, I could lose Sam for good. My heart cries from the corner it's been painted into. If I answer honestly, life as I know it will change irrevocably. But part of me deep down knows that it already has. It changed the second I looked up and saw Sam standing outside on the sidewalk. When he mouthed the word *hi*, my fate was sealed.

He stares into the deepest part of my soul, seeking the truth, but I close my eyes before he can read me. When I open them again, he reaches for a pen and a piece of paper on the desk and scribbles something down.

"When you're ready," he says, gazing at me. But before I can respond, he turns toward the door and leaves me just as breathless as when he walked in.

I watch him jog across the street and get into a very expensive-looking car.

"Bye, Sam."

I reach for the piece of paper and read his familiar handwriting. An address? Here in Atlanta. *His* address? I look up as he's pulling away from the curb and fall against the desk.

"Oh. My. God." Sebastian rushes over to me, holding a tissue in his hand. He sniffs and wipes his eyes, and promptly pulls me into a hug. "Sweetie, why didn't you tell me?"

"I couldn't. I've never told anyone. Drew doesn't even know," I say, looking at him desperately.

He takes my hand and drags me to the back of the studio, and we fall onto the old leather couch together. He hands me a box of tissues and demands that I tell him everything, so I do.

"Lucy, I don't even know what to say," Bas responds after I've finished.

"There's nothing to say."

"Actually, I think you've got tons to say, to Sam." He exhales loudly. "I cannot believe that Sam Cole was your boyfriend. Or childhood soulmate, or whatever he was. It's insane. Paul is going to flip."

"Bas, can you just keep it to yourself for now?"

He sighs. "Fine. But what are you going to tell Drew?"

I cringe at the thought of telling Drew anything about Sam. I can't. Especially not that he came to see me today. "I don't know. Nothing, for now."

"Well, whatever happens, I'm here for you." He smiles and puts his hand on mine. "You don't have to figure it out alone."

My eyes well with tears. "You're kind of the best assistant a girl could ask for. And by assistant, I mean friend."

He makes a fist and gently knocks it against my chin. "Aw, kid, you know I'd do anything for you."

I wipe my eyes and nod. "Thanks, Bas."

Chapter 8

Lucy

It's been two weeks since Sam showed up at my studio and effectively ruined my life. Since then, I've been silently struggling with how to tell Drew about him, but with each passing day it's grown harder and harder. How do I tell Drew that I've been keeping a secret from him for years, a secret that popped up at my studio out of the blue and made me question every decision I've made since I was eighteen? I could risk losing everything that's good in my life. Which is why I decided not to.

I glance in the rearview mirror, checking my makeup for the third time in twenty minutes. That's how long it's been since I pulled out of the driveway I share with Drew, drove down our tree-lined street, and left our gated suburban neighborhood. Drew is seven hundred miles away in Philadelphia and, as much as I wanted him to stay and give me a reason to not go see Sam, as soon as he left I knew that I had to. I have to tell Sam that I'm happy with Drew, that I'm going to marry him, and that he can't come see me again. Then I'm going to go home, wait for Drew to return, and tell him about the boy I used to love.

I inhale a shaky breath and run my thumb back and forth over the seam in my black skinny jeans. I settled on these, a white T-shirt, and my white Chuck Taylors, opting for comfort over style, something I think I'm going to need today.

I follow the directions on my GPS through the city, squinting through my Ray-Bans as I chase the afternoon sun through the tall buildings that make up downtown Atlanta. All too soon I'm pulling into an unfamiliar parking garage below a shiny high-rise apartment building that matches the address Sam left for me. I'm stopped by a security guard who steps out of his booth as I approach the gate.

I lower my window and smile at him. "Hi, I'm here to see Sam Cole. He lives here," I explain, gesturing to the high-rise building.

The smirk on his face tells me he knows.

Sam is famous, I remind myself, *the whole building probably knows.* The thought makes me uneasy. What if word gets out that a mystery blonde in a silver Volvo is visiting Sam Cole at his home? *Maybe I should have told Drew first.*

"Name?"

"Lucy Bennett."

"ID, please?"

I reach for my wallet and pull out my driver's license.

The guard takes it from me and returns to his booth.

Am I supposed to be on some kind of list? Sam doesn't even know that I'm coming today.

After a few seconds, the gate raises up and I feel a strange mix of relief and reluctance.

The security guard smiles and gives me back my ID. "You can park in spot 322 on level three. Mr. Cole reserves it for his guests."

"Okay. Thank you." I shove my license back inside my wallet, take a deep breath, and pull forward.

I wind through the garage until I'm on the third level. *322...322...* I see it. And I pass it.

Not once.

Not twice.

But three times.

As I approach the spot a fourth time, I wonder if the guard is watching me on a security camera, thinking I'm some kind of half-wit. I park out of pride, but sit in my car for another ten minutes, until I finally get the nerve to open my door. When I do, I see an expensive-looking car parked beside me in spot 323 that I'm pretty sure is the same car Sam was driving the day he came by the studio.

I grab my purse and black leather jacket off the seat and take the stairs to the first level of the garage, hoping to buy myself some time to figure out what I'm going to say.

Less than a minute later, I'm standing at the entrance of the apartment building looking through the giant glass doors. I take another deep breath, reach for the shiny handle, and pull the heavy glass door open.

I walk inside where, once again, I'm greeted by a security guard who promptly addresses me. "May I help you?"

"Hi. Yes, I'm here to see Sam Cole. He lives in"—I eye the paper in my hand—"unit 2500."

He gauges me with the same scrutiny as the parking garage guard. "Your name, please?"

"Lucy Bennett."

He looks at his iPad and scrolls over the screen a few times. "Yes, ma'am," he says, smiling at me. "I'll just need to see your ID."

I can't help but wonder if this level of security is afforded to all the residents in this building, or just Sam. I hand over my ID and, after the guard reviews it, he hands it back and says, "I'll let him know that you're here."

Oh. I nod nervously. *There's no turning back now.*

"You'll want to take the elevator to the twenty-fifth floor."

I wait for him to give me further instructions, but he just smiles and says, "That's it."

"O-oh, okay." I smile shyly. "Thank you."

Has he got the whole floor?

When I reach the bank of elevators, I press the call button and eye my blurry reflection in the shiny stainless steel doors. I look like an abstract painting, with the black and white colors of my outfit blending together. *There couldn't be a truer depiction of my life right now.* The *ping* of the arriving elevator startles me, and I consider turning around and getting back in my car, but the security guard in the lobby is still watching me, probably wondering if I need help. I smile at him and wave, then I take a deep breath, step inside the awaiting elevator, and look for the button for the twenty-fifth floor.

23–24–PH. *The twenty-fifth floor is the penthouse?*

I take another deep breath and press the button. *Expensive cars and penthouse apartments.* I shake my head at the foreign thought.

The doors close and I'm whisked to the twenty-fifth floor before my stomach has a chance to catch up. When they open again, I step out of the elevator and take a second to steady myself. But the feeling doesn't last long. Sam opens his apartment door—the only door in the small foyer surrounding the elevator—and the floor falls away again.

The corner of his mouth turns up just enough to gift me with a dimple that sends my heartbeat sprinting. "Hi," he says over a crooked smile, and my heart pounds even harder.

"Hi," I say softly, letting him pull the heavy blanket of emotion off me, until I feel like I'm floating.

He's wearing gray joggers that look like they're tailored to the lower half of his body and a white V-neck T-shirt that hugs his tattooed chest. His hair is messy and he's barefoot. "I, um, I hope it's not a bad time. You didn't leave a number, so I couldn't call..."

He crinkles his eyes, and I wonder if it's on purpose. "It's not a bad time." He holds the door open for me. "Come in."

I smile shyly and slip past him, taking in the soft scent of sandalwood and laundry detergent that clings to his shirt.

Holy crap. His apartment his *huge.*

I glance at the open space that is encased in floor-to-ceiling windows, the only thing I have time to notice before he draws my attention back to him. It feels intrusive to be standing in his apartment, as if seeing his personal space is going to expose a life I don't want to acknowledge he's had all this time. Just the thought of him standing in my living room and seeing proof of the life I've lived without him fills me with anxiety. I'm suddenly plagued with dread, for fear of what I might see when I look around, or who I might see. *Why didn't I think of this before? Why didn't he just ask to meet him for coffee somewhere?*

"Do you want a drink or something?" he asks, eyeing me carefully.

I've never been good at hiding my emotions. "Water would be great."

I take my jacket off and follow him to the kitchen, keeping my eyes on him the whole time. I'm pretty sure it's an impressive kitchen, by the gleam of the marble counters and the shine of the stainless steel refrigerator door that swings open, but I can't say for sure because I'm staring at a small freckle on the back of his neck.

He turns around and the freckle is replaced by the V of his T-shirt and the tattoo peeking out of it. "You okay?" he asks, pulling my attention up to his face.

"Your eye. It looks so much better," I say, examining it in the bright light. The bruising is gone and there's just a thin line where the glue was holding his eyebrow together two weeks ago.

"Yeah, I guess I was still kind of mess from the fight when I stopped by."

I shudder at the thought of him taking that hit from Sanchez.

"I'm sorry about that."

A puff of air passes between my lips. "You're apologizing for having a black eye?"

He hands me a bottle of water but doesn't let go of it when I take it from him. "No, I'm apologizing for coming to see you. I wasn't thinking."

I gaze up at him and begin to feel the oxygen slowly seep from my blood, leaving me with a woozy head and a heavy heart. He's exactly *right*. He shouldn't have come to see me. So why does it hurt so much to hear him say it?

"I didn't mean to upset you." He takes a step closer, forcing me to step back until I'm bumping into the counter behind me.

I blink up at him, wrestling with my emotions, but I can't think with him standing so close. "It's, um, it's okay."

He lets go of the bottle and leans against the counter beside me.

I quickly open it and take a sip. Unwilling to look at him, I'm forced to take in my surroundings, but much to my surprise, there isn't anything in the kitchen that appears harmful to my emotional health. Just a large wooden bowl filled with bananas, a coffee maker, a stack of papers, and a laptop.

"You're a minimalist," I say over the rim of the plastic bottle.

"I'm not here very much."

"You travel a lot."

He shrugs. "It's part of the job. I leave again in the morning."

"Where are you headed?"

"Las Vegas."

"Ahh." I raise my eyebrows. "Big party to attend?" I cringe at the thought of him partying in Vegas with God only knows who.

"No. I got Vegas out of my system a couple of years ago." He smirks and I feel my face twist up as I recall reading a story about him partying all night in Vegas. "It's for a charity fight."

"Oh. You can fight again that soon?" His eye looks better, but it's not completely healed.

"Doc said two weeks. It's been two." He watches me take another sip of my water. "I thought maybe you lost my address. Or threw it away."

"Sounds like you've had a change of heart about coming to see me. Maybe I should have," I say, feeling insecure about my decision to come see him now, especially if he doesn't care one way or the other who I marry.

"I don't regret coming to see you, Lucy. I just regret upsetting you."

I take another sip from my half-empty bottle.

"I'm glad you came today," he says.

I nod, unsure what to say. But the silence doesn't last long.

"So are you going to tell me why you came to the fight now?" he asks, just like he did at the studio, his eyes still desperate for the answer.

I gaze into the familiar mix of blue and brown, and answer honestly. "Because I wanted to see you."

His shoulders soften and slope a little. "Why?" he pushes,

and my stomach tightens, because I think he has as many questions as I do, but he has no hesitation to ask them.

I give a weak shrug.

"You know, there was a time when you would tell me anything."

"I guess the longer you keep something in, the harder it is to get out."

"You don't have keep it in. You can tell me."

I laugh quietly, because what he doesn't realize is that *he* is what I've been keeping in all this time.

"What is it?"

I drop my chin. "It's everything. It's all of it. The articles, the pictures, the videos, the interviews, the girls."

"Me?"

"Yes, you. *You* are what I've been keeping in all this time. The more famous you've become, the harder I've had to hold on to the secret."

He pulls his eyebrows together and drops his chin. "Secret. That's what I am." He walks out of the kitchen, forcing me to follow him into the living room, which is filled with contemporary-looking furniture that surrounds a large stone fireplace. But once again, my eyes stay fixed on the back of his neck, so I don't see much else. Surely there are pictures and memorabilia in here, ready to stab at my heart.

He turns around when he reaches the couch. "Are you embarrassed of me?"

"Embarrassed? No. Why would you—"

"It's okay, I get it. Your life is different now." He drops his eyes over me. "Sophisticated. I'm just a fuckup from Brighton

Park who got lucky with a pair of gloves." He sits down on the long gray sectional couch, rests his elbows on his knees, and laces his fingers together.

"Sam." I sit beside him. "You are not a fuckup from Brighton Park. And I'm a little offended that you think I would ever be embarrassed of you."

"Then why would you keep me a secret? I mean, no one knows about us? Not even your—"

"No." I can't bear to hear him say *fiancé*. "But not because of the reason you think."

"Everyone close to me knows about you, Lucy, so I don't really know what to think."

"They do?"

"Yes." He sits back and looks at me. "My life was on pause for three years while I was in prison. And I spent the majority of that time worrying about you and wondering about you and praying that I'd get to see you again. It's why I started fighting again. Because I knew I could win. I knew I had to. So you could see who I really am, who I've always been. Who I could have been for you, if you'd only believed me."

I swallow the giant lump in my throat and try to tame the wild thoughts that are running rampant through my mind.

"So yeah, they know who Lucy Bennett is. The girl I spent my whole life fighting for, and fight for still, even if it is in vain."

"Sam." I close my eyes and warm tears roll down my cheeks.

"I'm just having a hard time understanding why that same girl would keep me a secret."

I drop my head into my hands and mumble, "Because you hurt too much."

"What?"

I sit up and wipe my eyes. "Because you hurt too much. I was in a dark place for a long time, Sam. Drew eventually pulled me out of it, but I couldn't bear to talk about you with him or anyone else." I close my eyes and recall the pain I felt when he went to prison. "When you pled guilty, it was like the earth crumbled beneath me and everything I believed, everything I knew to be true, disintegrated."

"I pled guilty because my lawyer told me to. He said it would lessen my sentence, and it did. I told you that."

"But when you did that you were guilty." I shake my head. "I really believed that. And I felt so betrayed. For a really long time. Because you were the only person I trusted."

"I didn't betray you, Lucy. You have to believe that. I would have never done that to you."

I shrug, because it doesn't change anything. "It doesn't matter. You were gone. And so were we. Then one day, I turned on the TV and there you were, bulldozing your way back into my life and demolishing the walls I'd built around my heart. You were real. And I knew that what we had was real. But it didn't change anything. It only made it harder."

He holds his folded hands to his mouth and inhales a deep breath. "Then please, just tell me that you're happy."

I clench my teeth together and prepare to say the words, but my tongue won't cooperate. I can't lie to him. "Does it really matter?" I finally ask.

"Yes." He drops his hands away. "It matters."

"Why?"

"Because I need to know that it was worth it, that I didn't spend three years in prison waiting for you to change your mind and call me, or visit me just once, for no reason."

My eyes well with more tears, but I hold them back this time. "I have a bad track record with people leaving me," I say numbly. "The only memory I have of my father is a scar he left on my mother's chin and the drugs he left in her veins that eventually killed her. And the last memory I have of my mother is a paramedic pulling a needle out of her lifeless arm."

"Luc—"

"She loved me too, Sam." I close my eyes and reach for the bracelet on my wrist. "I'd never been given a gift like this before. I didn't know how much it cost. When the police questioned me, I began to question everything too. And the more I did, the angrier I became. I was losing the person I loved and trusted more than anyone to drugs *again*. And I was alone again." I exhale an uneven breath. "I was so hurt."

He stares at me quietly for a second. "Do you remember the last day we were together?"

I swallow down my emotion and nod. "Yes."

"I mean *together* together. On the roof of that old building?"

I nod softly. "Yes."

"You were over on Brentwood Avenue, where you had no business being—"

"I was going to meet you at Joe's," I recall, like it was yesterday.

"You shouldn't have been there." He creases his eyebrows. "You remember the guys who were messing with you?"

"Yeah, I remember."

"Aaron Lewis, Tyler Jones, and Alex Brown."

"How do you know their names?"

"Aaron Lewis has three arrests for possession. Tyler Jones has one arrest for possession with intent to sell. Alex Brown has two arrests for possession with intent to sell and is currently serving out a fifteen-year sentence."

Anxiety pricks across my skin and my mind races with questions, but none of them make any sense. "What are you saying?"

"The tall one, Aaron. He said he would get back at me. Do you remember that?"

"The one with the gun?"

"Yes."

"Wait...you think?" I pull my hand to my mouth and gasp. "Oh, my God." I exhale, putting the jagged pieces of the truth together.

* * *

Lucy, Seventeen Years Old

"That's twenty, forty, sixty. Good job tonight, kid," Joe says, stacking three twenty-dollar bills in Sam's hand.

Sam shoves the money into the pocket of his sweatpants and reaches for my hand. Even with the gloves, his hands always take a beating during a match. His red knuckles are rubbed raw.

"Sam, your hands." I lift them to my mouth and kiss his knuckles. "You need ice."

"It doesn't hurt."

"You still need ice," Joe says, plopping a soft ice pack in his lap.

Sam jumps and makes a groaning sound that makes me laugh. He picks up the ice pack and holds it to his hand as I inspect his face.

"I don't see any bruises this time," I say, running my hand over his eyebrow and his cheekbone. I walk around him and examine his back and shoulders. "Nothing back here." I run my hand down his spine. "Except for some goose bumps," I say softly, and kiss his shoulder. I lift his arm and gasp when I see a deep-blue-and-purple bruise covering his ribs.

"What?" He looks down where my hand is tracing the edge of the bruised area. "Oh."

I call for Joe, who left the room.

"Lucy, it's nothing. I'm fine."

"Joe," I call again, ignoring him.

Joe walks back into the room and sees the dark spot on Sam's side. "Jesus."

"Do you think his ribs are broken?"

"Nothing's broken," Sam says, putting his arm down. "Doc already cleared me."

"He didn't mention anything to me," Joe says. "But the bruises might not have been showing when he examined you. You sure he checked?"

"He checked," Sam says.

"Just keep an eye on it, okay? Take some Tylenol tonight," Joe orders.

"I will." Sam stands up and pulls his T-shirt on over his head, grimacing through the pain he says he doesn't feel.

"Here." I take his hoodie from him. "Let me help."

He shrugs into it and slings his book bag over his shoulder. "Come on, it's late. You need to get home or Momma Jenkins is going to have your ass." My current foster mom isn't very lenient with my curfew, but she likes Sam, which is the only reason she lets me come to these matches.

"Hold up, I'll walk out with you," Joe says, turning off the lights in the locker room. He follows us through the gym and locks the door behind us when we step outside.

"It's freezing," I say, hugging myself, and I'm immediately enveloped in Sam's arms. I snuggle against his sweatshirt.

"Come on, I'll give you a ride home," Joe says, and we walk a short distance to where his car is parked in front of the gym.

Sam opens the passenger door for me, but as I'm getting in, I'm startled by a car that roars up onto the curb in front of us—a shiny black sedan with flashing blue and red lights on the dashboard.

The police? My heart begins to race and my skin pricks as I consider the imminent danger that must be nearby. I stand up quickly and cling to Sam. His hands tighten around my arms and he pulls me against him, but my mind is flooded with potential threats. A break-in, a robbery, a drug deal gone bad.

The armed police officers approach us.

"What's going on, officers?" Joe asks, but they ignore him.

"Sir, you need to step back," one of the officers says, placing his hand over his gun.

Joe takes a step back and holds his hands up.

"Sam Cole." The other officer steps toward us, and Sam holds me tighter. "You need to let go of the girl."

Frightened and confused, I shout at the officer, "What? No!"

"You need to step aside," the officer says to me, but I grip Sam's sweatshirt tighter.

"What's going on? What's happening?" I feel someone's hands wrap around my arms from behind. "Let go of me," I say frantically, clinging to Sam.

Sam struggles to hold me close, but the officers pull us apart. "Let go of her!" Sam shouts, reaching for me.

The officer pushes Sam's face down against the hood of Joe's car.

"I didn't do anything!" he says, but I can barely hear him through the fear that's consuming me.

"I don't understand what's happening," I cry. "Why do they want Sam?" I ask Joe.

"Easy, easy," Joe says. "There must be a misunderstanding."

"We're going to need to search your bag, son," the other officer says to Sam, ignoring Joe.

"You have some kind of warrant or something?" Joe asks.

The officer pulls a folded piece of paper out of his shirt pocket and shows it to Joe, and then Sam.

"Go ahead, I'm not hiding anything," Sam grits through his teeth.

The officer opens Sam's book bag and begins rummaging

through it, placing his belongings on the hood of the car—his gym shorts, a notebook, a bag of pretzels, a few pens, and a small plastic baggie that's tied in a knot and stretched around a ball of white powder.

Oh, my God.

"That's not mine, someone put that there," Sam says, but the officer ignores him and reaches for his handcuffs, locking them around Sam's wrists.

I think I'm going to be sick.

"You have the right to remain silent. Anything you say can and will be used against you in a court of law. You have the right to an attorney..." The officer's voice, the night sky, and the dimly lit buildings around us blur together into a fog that begins to consume me.

Is the sidewalk moving? I turn to Joe and he catches me when I stumble toward him.

The officer puts his hand on Sam's head and places him in the back seat of his car.

"Sam?" I cry, feeling my heart crumble into pieces.

"It's okay, Lucy. Everything's going to be okay," he says before he disappears behind the tinted glass.

Joe drops his head and paces a few times, then he pulls out his phone and dials a number. He has a quick conversation with the person on the other end of the line and hangs up. "Come on," he says, opening his car door for me.

"Who was that?"

"My lawyer."

I swallow the hard lump in my throat and get in the passenger seat. "Where are we going?" I ask numbly. "To the jail?"

"No, I'm taking you home," he says, pulling away from the curb.

I shake my head slowly, feeling as though I'm slipping out of my body. "He's my home. Sam is my home."

* * *

"Anyone could have put the drugs in my bag that night," Sam says, getting up from the couch. "The gym was open, everyone was crowded around the ring, no one was watching who was in the back."

My heart throbs inside my chest when I realize that he's right. Anyone could have done it. I swallow the giant lump in my throat and get up from the couch. I walk over to the window and stare at the horizon, unable to face him and admit that I was wrong.

I should have believed him.

An overwhelming wave of grief washes over me, flashing pictures of the life we could have had together, and I'm stricken with guilt, because *I'm* the one who threw it away. Not Sam.

How could I be so quick to think he would betray me? He did everything for me. Even when I gave up on him. I squeeze my eyes shut, as if I can somehow hide from the truth. *I'm the one who left.*

"That's what happened, Lucy. Even if you don't believe it."

"I do, Sam." I turn around and look at him with tear-filled eyes. "I believe you."

He inhales a deep breath and closes his eyes. "That's all I've ever wanted to hear."

I bite my trembling lip and think of what could have been, but then I realize it erases Drew...and everything else that's good in my life. "I'm sorry."

He shoves his hands in his pockets and nods. "Yeah, me too."

I swallow down my sorrow and walk back over to the couch. "Have you told anyone else? Your lawyer, maybe? There must be some way to charge those guys."

He shakes his head and shrugs. "What's done is done. I've spent enough time trying to figure out what happened back then. I'm done living in the past." He closes the space between us and looks into my eyes. "I want to focus on what's in front of me, right now."

My eyes are everywhere, except for him. If I don't get out of this emotional rabbit hole now, I may never find my way out. I look around, expecting to see his pictures and personal things, but all I see are a bunch of empty shelves, a few staged vases, and a couple of empty bookends. I turn around and take in the space, which looks a bit like a hotel. A very expensive hotel, but a hotel nonetheless. Definitely not a home. "Do you live here?" I ask, glancing around.

He raises an eyebrow. "Last I checked."

"Sorry, I just meant, there's no stuff. Where's all your stuff?"

"My stuff?"

"Well, yeah."

He drops his head and laughs quietly. "I told you, I'm not here very much."

"How long have you lived here?"

"About a year." He walks over to the wall of windows and slides one of the glass panels to the side. "It's a bit much, but it's got a great view."

I follow him outside onto the balcony, which wraps around the corner of the building. "It's freezing up here." I wish I hadn't taken my jacket off. I wrap my arms around myself and peer over the edge of the balcony. "Wow." He's right, the view is spectacular.

He leans against the ledge and looks out at the city. "It sure is a different view up close, isn't it?"

"Yeah. Which way is Brighton Park?"

He pushes away from the ledge and leads me around the corner. "Right there." He points to a place in the distance with certainty.

I gaze out at the skyline and wonder how many times he's looked this way. An airplane angles up into the sky from the same point on the horizon, and I know with equal certainty it's the place where we found each other, where we grew up together, where we loved and eventually lost each other.

"Hard to believe it's only a few miles away, isn't it?"

"It's a long way from all of this," I say, gesturing to his penthouse apartment.

He nods but doesn't say anything.

"You should be really proud of yourself, Sam."

"It's got a great gym. That's really the only reason I've stayed here as long as I have."

"Oh, yeah, I think I passed it downstairs."

He grins and I see the shadow of his dimples before he tries to hide them. "Not that gym." He leads me back inside, and

I follow him through the living room, watching his bare feet meet the dark wood floor as he takes me down a short hallway with a door at the end of it. He pushes it open and gestures for me to go inside. "This gym."

I walk in and I'm standing in the middle of Joe's, boxing ring and all, except that this gym is state of the art and situated twenty-five stories above the ground. "Wow." I breathe in the distinct smell of the rubber floor mats, a sort of industrial smell that I'll always associate with Joe's, and with Sam. I look over my shoulder and smile at him. "Okay, this is pretty great."

He walks past me and grabs one of the ropes around the ring. "It kind of is," he says, unable to mask his pride.

I smile and walk over to him, and wrap my hands around the bottom rope.

Sam grins and climbs up into the ring, shaking the rope in my hands, and my heart flutters when I see his bare feet against the worn mat. He leans down and reaches for my hand, which I reluctantly offer up. He pulls me up into the ring effortlessly, making me giggle as I find my footing.

"Well, this is a first," I say, trying to wrap my brain around the fact that I'm standing in the middle of a boxing ring with Sam, in his gym, inside his high-rise apartment.

He bounces from foot to foot. "You remember the moves I taught you?" he asks playfully, his eyes alight.

"What?" I laugh softly. "Get out of here."

"Come on," he says, still bouncing on his feet.

I hold the rope behind me and shake my head.

"Come on, humor me."

I fight a smile and finally say, "Throat, knee, groin."

"And?"

"And what?"

"Show me your right hook."

"Sam."

"Come over here and show me. I want to see if you still got it."

I let go of the rope and walk across the mat to him.

"Make a fist," he says, holding his palms up in front of him, making it difficult for me to concentrate on anything other than the flexing muscles in his arms and the tattoos covering them. "Luc," he says, grasping my attention.

I make a fist with my right hand, just like he taught me when we were kids, and he pushes against it. "Good. Keep it tight. Make it strong." He holds his palms up again. "Now show me."

I pull my arm back and hit his left hand as hard as I can, but he doesn't move. Not at all. "Ow!" I shake my hand.

He stifles a laugh. "Come on, you can hit harder than that."

Determined, I pull my fist back again and hit his left hand with all my strength, but once again, he's like a stone statue. "Seriously?"

"Okay, we clearly need to get you in here working out." He laughs openly now.

"I work out," I protest unconvincingly, which is met with a dubious look. "Painting can be very strenuous." I raise my eyebrows and laugh.

He narrows his eyes and then reaches for my wrists and

spins me around abruptly, locking me in his arms with my back to his chest.

My breath leaves me in a rush, and my heart takes off in a wild sprint. I know exactly what he's doing, because he's done it a hundred times before, but if he weren't holding me up right now, I'd be a puddle at his feet.

"Now what do you do?" he asks softly against my ear, the warmth of his breath falling onto my heated cheek.

I look down at the mat and see his bare feet planted firmly on either side my Chuck Taylors, his strong legs encasing mine, which I pray he can't feel shaking.

"What do you do?" he murmurs again.

I breathe in and out, trying to find my voice, but I only manage to whisper, "I, uh, I..."

"What are you going to do, Lamb?" he pleads softly, and I lose all feeling from my knees to my toes.

My heart pounds inside my chest and my eyes prick with tears when I grasp the question he's *really* asking. I swallow hard and squirm in his arms, but I barely move, he's holding me so tight.

"Come on, Luc, what do you do?" he grumbles, and I feel overcome with frustration.

I struggle in his arms, praying he doesn't let go and see me crying, but after a few seconds, his arms soften and I realize that he's holding me, not restraining me.

"It's okay, I'm sorry," he whispers against my ear. "I'm sorry."

Afraid to turn around and face him, I stand with my back to his chest, feeling him breathe in and out against me, letting him hold me up in his strong arms, unsure if I can use my legs. I stare at the shelves in the back of the gym that hold his awards, his gold medal and his championship belts, trying to absorb the magnitude of everything he's accomplished. "Lower my center of gravity," I finally say, and Sam loosens his hold on me. I squat down and slowly spin out of his arms and face him. "Lower my center of gravity," I say again softly.

He smiles gently. "You remembered."

I press my lips together and look into his eyes. "I never forgot." I climb down out of the ring and take a deep breath to clear my head. I dodge a large punching bag that's hanging from the ceiling as I make my way to the back of the gym, where I take my time reading the inscriptions on each of his awards.

Sam walks up behind me, but he doesn't say anything. He just watches me read them, one by one.

I touch the felt-lined case displaying his gold medal. "This is . . ." I can't find the words to express how truly unbelievable it is. "It's incredible."

He manages a soft smile, but it's clouded in sadness, a reflection of the joy and pain I feel when I see all that he's accomplished and who he's become without me. "I did it for you," he says, burying my heart under a heap of guilt and confusion.

"Sam."

"It's true." He shoves his hands into his pockets.

"Sam . . . I can't." I close my eyes. "I just . . . can't—"

"Are you hungry?" he asks abruptly.

"What?" I blink a few times.

"I'm hungry. Are you hungry?" he asks again.

I shrug and nod mechanically.

"Let's go see what's in the fridge." He leads me out of the gym and out of the fog I drifted into.

Chapter 9

Lucy

I stand behind Sam, watching him pull an arsenal of food out of his fridge and pile it onto the kitchen counter. I guess I shouldn't be surprised that he requires so much food, but I'm surprised that he knows how to cook it.

"You cook?" I ask.

He pauses and looks at me and then eyes the greens in his hand. "Oh, um, I, uh...no," he finally says, laughing.

I smile and take the leafy bunch from him. "Do you even know what this is?"

"No."

"It's Swiss chard. It's kind of like kale. You can cook it down or put it in a smoothie. Why do you have all this food if you don't cook?"

He rubs the back of his neck. "I have a chef. He comes over and cooks for me."

"Ahhh..."

"I was hoping to find some leftovers, but I guess I ate them all."

I push my lips together over a smile and ask, "Want me to make something?"

"Are you sure?" he asks, raising his eyebrows. "We can just order something."

I look at the various ingredients heaped on the counter and begin sorting them. "Let's see..." I reach for the limes, some cilantro, and an onion. "Do you have any honey?"

He opens one of the cabinets and pulls out a little golden bear. "Is this okay?"

"Yeah, that's perfect." I peer into the fridge and find two thawed chicken breasts. "How long have these been in here?"

"Just today. Jean-Luc stocked the kitchen this morning so that he can cook while I'm gone."

"Jean-Luc," I say, unable to hide the amusement on my face. *So fancy.*

"What?"

"Nothing." I shake my head and take inventory of the refrigerator shelves. "Okay, how about some sriracha?"

He reaches over my shoulder and the scent of sandalwood fills my nose. "Right here," he says, handing it to me.

"Thanks." I set the ingredients on the white marble counter beside the sunken sink and turn toward Sam's grocery mound by the fridge. I start loading it all back inside, and Sam steps beside me to help. "Can you see if you have any quinoa?" I ask, needing to put some space between us.

"Sure."

"It kind of looks like rice."

"Okay."

I finish loading the fridge and close the shiny stainless steel doors. "Salt and pepper?" I call across the kitchen, wondering where he disappeared to.

"In the cabinet," he answers from somewhere nearby.

Which one? I begin opening the cabinet doors until I find one that's filled with spices. I grab some kosher salt and a pepper mill. Still no sign of Sam.

"Sam?"

"Yeah?"

I follow the sound of his voice.

"Where did you go?" I ask, rounding the corner. I find him standing in the middle of a small room that appears to be the pantry, scanning the shelves dutifully. There's enough dry ingredients in here to feed him for a year. I stand beside him and scan the stocked shelves until I see the quinoa. "There." I stand on my tiptoes to grab it, but barely brush it with my fingertips.

Sam reaches over me, gently pressing me against the shelves as he stretches for it, and I breathe in his warm scent as his body blankets mine.

He lowers the box between us. "Here."

I blink up at him. I'm desperately trying to absorb the oxygen in the small room, but there doesn't appear to be any left. "Thanks."

"So what exactly are you planning on making with this?" he asks, trying to hide a small smile, which calls his dimples front and center.

I take a step back. "You'll just have to wait and see."

"I'm good at waiting."

I chew the corner of my mouth and spin around. "Where are your pots and pans?" I ask as I walk back into the kitchen.

He opens a deep drawer below the gas range and pulls out a very large stockpot. "Will this work?"

I laugh and shake my head. "That's a little too big." I find a saucepan and a sauté pan and set them on the metal grates. "These will do. Where are your knives?"

He points to a drawer beside me. "In there."

I open it and find a chef's knife, a santoku knife, and a couple of wooden spoons. "I'll need a couple of cutting boards too."

He finds two plastic cutting boards and places them on the counter beside me. "Can I help?" he asks, watching me take the paper off the chicken breasts.

"Sure." I set the onion on the cutting board in front of him. "Can you chop this up?"

"Absolutely," he says confidently, reaching for the chef's knife.

"Not that one." I hand him the santoku knife. "This one is for chopping vegetables."

He eyes the knife curiously and takes it from me.

I point to the little divots on the side of the blade and explain, "Those help break the suction when you cut into the onion so that the pieces don't stick to the blade."

"Oh, okay," he says, creasing his eyebrows.

I begin slicing the chicken breasts into cubes, watching him fight with the onion skin out of the corner of my eye. He picks at one end, pulling a few slivers of the papery skin off, and then starts on the other end.

"Try cutting it in half first. It should come off easier that way," I encourage, but he gives me a dubious look. I smile and say, "Trust me."

He cuts the onion in half and manages to get the skin off one side by the time I've completed my task.

I wash my hands and reach for his knife. "Here, let me show you." I cut the end off the side that still has the skin on it and add, "If you cut one of the ends off after you cut it in half, the skin should peel right off."

He watches me intently.

"Then you just make long slices along the top," I explain as I begin cutting. "And because there are layers in the onion, you just have to cut across to get little dices." I look up at him. "Want to try?"

"Okay." He takes the knife from me and begins slicing.

"Good." I place my hand over his and guide the knife a little closer to the edge. "Like this, so the pieces aren't too big."

He pauses and looks at me, and his skin flames under my palm.

I pull my hand away. "Keep going." I look down at the small pieces of chicken on my cutting board, struggling to remember what I need to do next. "Olive oil," I eventually say. "I need olive oil."

Sam looks over his shoulder. "Try the cabinet next to the stove."

I walk across the kitchen, taking a deep breath of Sam-free air to clear my head, and find the olive oil. I drizzle it into the sauté pan and turn the burner on. It clicks and flames under the pan. I go check Sam's progress while I wait for it to get hot. "Good job," I say, eyeing the pile of diced onion.

"Are you sure?"

"Yeah, that's perfect. You want to drop it in the pan over there?"

He carries the cutting board over to the stove while I season the chicken with salt and pepper. "You want me to put it all in?" he asks.

"Yep, just scrape it right into the pan." When it hits the hot oil, it sizzles and fills the kitchen with its savory aroma. "Grab a spoon and stir it around a few times until the onions begin to sweat."

He turns around and looks at me. "Until they what?"

"Sweat."

"That can't be the technical term for cooking onions."

I laugh and walk over to him, and take over with the spoon. "Look, see how the juices are coming out? Onion sweat." He shakes his head and grins at me, and I give him back the spoon. "You just keep sweating your onions and I'll get the chicken."

"Does it sweat too?"

"No." I drop the pieces in. "Chicken doesn't sweat. Only onions sweat."

"I don't know, that looks like chicken sweat to me," he teases.

I scrunch my nose. "Chicken sweat is gross. There's no chicken sweat."

He holds his hands up. "Okay, okay, you're the expert."

I press my lips together over a small smile and he shoves the spoon in the pan again. "No, not yet. Let it sear for a few minutes. Get a bowl and a whisk and we can make the sauce while it cooks." I go grab the limes and slice them in half.

"Now what?" Sam asks, placing a bowl on the counter beside me.

"Add the sriracha and honey and squeeze in some juice from the limes."

He follows my directions and begins whisking the ingredients together while I tend to the chicken and get the quinoa going. He stands beside me, holding the bowl, still whisking obediently.

"Okay, now pour it over the chicken," I instruct, and when he does, it fills the air with sweet, savory spice.

"That smells amazing," he says, smiling, and I can't help but smile back. It really does.

By the time the quinoa is done, the sauce has thickened and coated the chicken. I fill a couple of bowls with the fluffy quinoa. "Okay, scoop the chicken into the bowls, and don't be shy with the sauce."

I grab the cilantro, give it a quick rinse, and tear a few leaves over the top of each bowl.

"And that, Mr. Sam Cole, light-heavyweight champion of the world, is how you make sriracha chicken and quinoa." I smile and hold the pretty bowls up between us.

He smiles and nods. "Should we go sit?"

I nod once and follow him to the long rectangular kitchen table. He sits at the end of it, and I take the chair next to him. I'm actually really hungry. I was too anxious to eat earlier today, and by the look of the sky outside, it's starting to get late. The sun is glowing orange in the reflection of the mirrored building across the street.

Sam takes a bite and so do I. "Oh, wow," he says over his mouthful.

"You like it?"

He nods and gets another forkful. "With you around, I might have to fire Jean-Luc."

My heart flutters inside my tight chest. *Is he planning on me being around?* I force a smile over my bite, which suddenly feels too big to swallow.

"How did you learn to cook like this?" he asks, and I see the realization fall over his face before I have to answer.

I press my lips together into a flat line and shrug. "I had a good teacher."

He pulls his eyebrows together and drops his chin, and pushes his food around with his fork a few times.

"Eat," I say, stabbing a piece of chicken with my fork. I pop it in my mouth and give him big eyes, and after a few seconds he does the same.

We eat in semicomfortable silence, until we've finished our bowls, then we take our dishes to the kitchen sink. Sam rinses them and loads them into the dishwasher, and we clean up the rest of the kitchen together.

I watch him dry the last pan after I wash it and something about seeing him standing barefoot in his sweats, holding a dish towel, drying a pan we cooked a meal together in, fills me with sadness. *This is how it was supposed to be.*

He puts the pan away and we both look around the spotless kitchen.

Sam reaches inside the fridge. "Do you—" "I should—" We both speak at the same time.

"Do you want a beer?" he asks.

Do not say yes.

"Sure," I say, against my better judgment.

He opens a bottle and hands it to me, and I follow him into the living room where we take our previous places on the couch.

The sun is pouring into the room now, painting the pale gray walls amber. Sam watches me sip my beer, and I feel my fair skin flush under his stare. He must notice, because the corner of his mouth turns up. "Do you love him?"

I lower my beer and answer honestly. "I wouldn't marry someone I didn't love."

He sips his beer.

"He's a good man, Sam."

He takes another sip of his beer and rests his arm on the back of the couch. "You never told me why you came to the fight in New York—why you wanted to see me."

A long silent second passes between us as I contemplate an answer to the question he asked me earlier. "I don't know. My head has been kind of a mess lately, and I just thought that seeing you might help, or help me realize that I'm insane, which I must be."

"I was really happy when I saw you that night." He smiles softly, and I fight the urge to touch the dimple in his cheek.

"You were?"

He narrows his eyes. "Happy is probably an understatement. But I was also really confused."

I ignore the way my heart is twirling around inside my chest. "You said that you had your team try to find me after the fight."

"Yes," he says tentatively.

"Have you done that before?"

"Lucy, I'd be lying if I told you I didn't have the resources to find you. The truth is, I didn't want to come looking for you if you didn't want to be found."

I crease my eyebrows and consider that.

"But when I saw you"—he studies me with his knowing eyes—"I wondered if maybe you wanted to be found."

I pick at my thumbnail and shake my foot, which is dangling off the couch. "I'm happy, Sam," I finally say, but I can't look up at him.

He sips his beer and watches me carefully. "I think if you were happy, you wouldn't be here right now."

I mask my disquiet with a smile. "Well, I am." I've already hurt Sam so much. How do I tell him that I came here only to say goodbye?

He leans in and whispers, "I know what happy looks like on you."

I pull in a weak breath that does little to ease the wooziness in my head. "Are you happy?" I ask, diverting the question to him.

"Depends."

"On what?"

"The day. The match. The party. The girl," he says, throwing a dagger at my heart.

I look down at my lap and accept the deserved stab. "Yes, you are quite popular with the ladies." I peek up at him, but he's looking down at his beer bottle now. "Is there anyone special?"

"No. The girls I go out with are...they're not..."

"I know. You've got a reputation to uphold. It can't be easy being boxing's most eligible bachelor," I say, quoting a headline I saw once.

His eyes flash to mine. "They're not *you*."

My heart flutters wildly inside my chest like it's grown wings.

"It's hard to meet people that don't want to take advantage of someone in my position," he adds. "Everybody wants something."

I pick at the seam that runs along the inside of my jeans, feeling sad for him. "That must get pretty lonely."

He holds my stare and laughs softly, but I don't get the joke. I crease my eyebrows and wait for the punch line.

"I slept in a cement room without windows for three years...waiting for you to come visit me. *That* was lonely."

I look down at my lap and part my lips, hoping to ease the pain in my stomach with a quiet breath. I worked so hard to block out thoughts of him living in prison, I never really came to terms with it. The reality of it now is overwhelming. "I'm so sorry, Sam. I can't imagine what it must have been like for you."

"It wasn't all bad. I got my GED. I even got an associate's degree."

A smile spreads across my face. "You did?"

"I know it's not a four-year degree, but..."

"That's wonderful," I say, smiling so big now it hurts.

He smiles too and I see the pride in his eyes. "I knew you'd want me to."

I press my lips together and hold my breath until another wave of emotion passes. "I'm really proud of you, Sam."

"I've waited a long time to hear you say that."

I stare at him, feeling completely lost in an emotional black hole.

"So tell me about your studio," he says, shifting my thoughts. "It seems pretty great."

"It is," I say, blinking at him. "I, um, I'm still getting used to the idea of it being mine, but it's a dream come true. It's starting to get some notice now, and I'm hosting an art exhibit later this month that will hopefully open a lot of doors for me."

"Is the exhibit for your paintings?"

"Some. And other pieces that were submitted to me from artists around the city. If it's a success, I might have a chance to participate in a show in New York next year."

"New York?"

I smile and nod. "That's my real dream. There's this gallery in Chelsea that's hosting an exhibit for emerging contemporary realist painters next year. If I can get their attention with my show, I might be able to earn an invitation."

"Well, they'd be lucky to have you." He smiles and sips his beer.

I tuck my hair behind my ear and glance up at the windows. Twinkling lights have come on around the city, and the

indigo sky is almost dark now. "I should probably get going."
I stand up and Sam follows my cue.

"I'll get your jacket," he says, taking my beer to the
kitchen. He returns a few seconds later with my jacket and
purse. "You know, I didn't really have a chance to look around
when I was there, but maybe you could show me your studio
sometime. If that's okay. I'd really like to see your paintings."

A strange feeling exudes from my chest and tingles down
to my fingertips at the thought of seeing him again. *Say no.*
"Okay." Drew flashes through my mind, and I remember my
original plan to tell Sam that he can't come see me again. But
the thought of this being our last goodbye is almost unbear-
able. I can't do it. Not yet.

"Why don't you put my number in your phone and you
can call when it's a good time," Sam suggests.

"Okay." I pull my phone out of my purse and tentatively
add *Sam* to my contacts. "What's your number?" I ask, ignoring the warning signs my mind is holding up. *Proceed with
caution... Dangerous territory.*

He recites his number and I enter it carefully.

"I'm really glad you came by today, Luc."

"Me too," I say, giving him a friendly hug goodbye. But
when he winds his hands around my back and pulls me close,
I don't want him to let go.

"I missed you," he whispers, and I could die right here in
his arms. If he's a stranger, he sure as hell doesn't feel like one.
He feels like family, like *my* family that I've missed so very
much.

I close my eyes and breathe him in, nodding silently

against his warm chest, savoring how it feels under my cheek. "I missed you too."

My phone buzzes in my hand like a warning shot sounding, and I let go of him and look at the screen. I hit ignore on the call from Drew and feel the blood drain from my face.

"Everything okay?"

"Yeah," I say, dropping Drew into my purse, which suddenly feels like a ton of bricks.

Sam walks me to the elevator and presses the call button, and the doors open not a moment too soon. But my heart pounds when I step inside the empty elevator.

"Have a safe trip tomorrow," I say casually over the pulsing in my ears.

He stands across from me, looking into my eyes, and it feels as if there's a rubber band wrapped around us, pulling us back together. He takes a step toward me, but the elevator doors close, snapping the rubber band as I'm whisked away from him.

I close my eyes and clutch my stomach, but I don't think this feeling is going to go away anytime soon. I look at my blurry reflection in the shiny steel doors, grateful that I can't see my face. I don't think I could bear to look at myself right now.

Chapter 10

Sam

I pull my hand away from the elevator door and grab my shirt. I try to rub away the ache in my chest, but it's no use. "Fuck!" I slam my fist against my door and push it open. *I'm so incredibly screwed.* I close the door behind me and lean against it, and look around my empty apartment. I've never felt more alone than I do right now. I close my eyes and slide down the door until I'm sitting on the floor. I pull my knees up and fold my arms over them. *She loves him.*

After a few minutes of feeling sorry for myself, I get up and pace around my apartment. *She isn't happy.* I could see it in her eyes when I asked. I fall onto the couch and lean against the cushion where she was sitting, and breathe in the soft scent of her perfume. I can't believe how beautiful she is. She was always pretty, but now ... I couldn't take my eyes off her.

I fucking hate Andrew Christiansen. Does he know how lucky he is? Does he know how amazing Lucy is? Does he know all that she went through? Maybe it was wrong to spend the afternoon with her, but I don't care. He has the only thing that ever made me happy. I'm not looking to do him any favors.

I walk into my bedroom and lie on the bed. The truth is, I envy him. I grab the remote off my nightstand and lower the screens over the windows. I close my eyes and lie in the dark, listening to the sound of the ceiling fan, hoping sleep will put me out of my misery, but after a few minutes I open my eyes and resort to the only thing that has ever helped fill the hole Lucy left in my heart. I grab my phone and scroll through my contacts until I reach the M's.

"Molly. Let's go out."

* * *

"Sam, get up," Miles calls from the living room, waking me from a deep sleep. "Come on, champ, we've got to go," he says again, walking into my bedroom. I try to ignore him, but he slaps me on the ass. "Let's go."

"Jesus, Miles!" Molly shouts, covering herself with the sheet.

"Remind me again why you have a key to my apartment?" I ask him.

"Because if it weren't for me barging in all the time, your sorry ass would miss every event you commit to."

"That *you* commit to, not me," I grumble, and sit up.

"Good point. If it weren't for me, your sorry ass wouldn't have a career." He grabs my arm and pulls me up. "Let's go."

"I'll see you later, Sam," Molly says, gathering her clothes off the floor.

"Thanks for last night," I say to her.

She shoves her hand into my hair and gives me a sincere look. "You know I'm here if you need me, right?"

"Yeah, Molls, I know."

She gives me a soft smile. "Goodbye, Miles," she calls over her shoulder as she leaves.

"Goodbye, Molly," he says, rolling his eyes.

I stretch and head for the shower.

"You're still banging that chick?" Miles asks, following me into the bathroom.

"She's not some chick, she's my friend."

"I thought *I* was your friend."

"You are my friend. But I'm not going to sleep with you. So stop begging." I strip down and turn the shower on.

"Don't worry, I'm not in the market for an STD."

"Hey." I step out of the shower. "I don't have unprotected sex, and I get tested every six weeks. I'm clean."

"Calm down. I was kidding." He shakes his head and walks out of the bathroom. "I'll be in the kitchen. I'm going to make some coffee."

I stand under the hot water not thinking, until Lucy comes creeping back into my mind like a weed. It was all I could do to block her out while I was with Molly, but now all I can think about is seeing her again.

When I'm through with my shower, I turn off the water and grab my toothbrush.

"You got something to tell me?" Miles asks, walking

back into the bathroom, holding something sparkly in his hand.

"What is that?" I ask with a mouthful of toothpaste.

He holds up a diamond ring, and I know instantly that it's Lucy's. I spit out the toothpaste. "Where did you find that?"

"It was on the kitchen counter."

"It's Lucy's."

"Lucy who?" His eyes widen. "Lucy, Lucy?"

"The one and only."

"How the fuck did you end up with her ring?" He drops his hand and gives me a hard look. "Tell me you didn't." He closes his eyes and starts pacing around the bathroom. "I said I needed you focused on getting closure, Sam! Not on the girl who wrote you off the second you had a pair of handcuffs slapped on your wrists."

"You don't know what you're talking about. It wasn't like that," I say, feeling a shift in my stance on everything I believed for nearly a decade.

"Oh, I think I know." He stops pacing. "But maybe you need a reminder. The only people who gave a shit about you back then are the ones who stuck with you when you were incarcerated. Joe, Tris...they never gave up on you the whole time you were in that shit hole. You didn't have to prove anything to them. They knew you weren't guilty. They knew you were great. They knew you could be the champ. The only thing she ever saw was a criminal."

I shake my head and let out a controlled breath. "You're wrong."

"Where was she when you were locked in that cell, huh? In

some fancy house in some stuck-up suburban neighborhood. She wasn't thinking about you. She was too busy banging her way into high society."

I lunge across the bathroom and pin him against the wall with my forearm, pressing it against his neck. "You don't know what you're talking about," I growl at him.

"Get off me," he grits through his teeth, and I struggle to contain the fire raging through me. "Get the fuck off me!"

I let go of him and step back.

"Are you crazy?"

I grab the counter and take a deep breath.

"You want to risk everything you've worked for, go ahead. But don't say I didn't warn you." He slaps Lucy's ring down on the counter.

"I didn't sleep with her." I turn around and he runs his hand through dark hair.

"So what, she just came over and took her engagement ring off so you could chat?"

"She must have taken it off when we were cooking."

He pulls his eyebrows together. "You were cooking to-gether?"

I cross my arms over my chest and shrug.

"I told you to go tell her goodbye. Not ask her on a date."

"I tried. But...it's complicated." I shake my head. "And it wasn't a date. We just talked."

"Listen to me, Sam. I'm not just telling you this as your manager, I'm telling you this as your friend. You are treading on very dangerous ground here. Just promise me you'll think before you do anything stupid."

"You don't have to worry, Miles."

He lets out a heavy sigh. "Yeah, I've heard that before."

"I'm sorry about that," I say, nodding to the wall behind him.

"What, you mean the wall? That you shoved me into?"

"Yeah."

"Don't worry about it. Stupid idiot."

I grin. "Still haven't figured out why you like me so much."

"Well, I'd lie and say it was about the money, but the truth is you're like a brother to me. And somebody's got to look out for your ass."

"Ah, Miles, I love you too."

"Shut up."

* * *

"That was a hell of a fight," Joe says encouragingly, buttoning up my shirt.

I hold my casted hand out so he can roll up my sleeve. "It was pathetic."

"Ahh, it doesn't count. It was for charity."

"It's still a draw. The first one of my career."

"You weren't exactly in your head tonight, were you?"

"No."

"You know better than to throw a punch like that. You're lucky you didn't break every bone in your hand."

"Just the one."

"Yeah, well, it's a small hairline fracture. It should heal pretty fast."

"Is the cast really necessary?"

"No. But it's the only way to keep you off the bag. You've got a big fight coming up. Your hand needs to heal as much as possible before then, so you can be ready for it."

"I'll be ready."

He pats my cheek. "I know you will, champ. Take the next few days to work out whatever's eatin' ya, okay?"

"Yeah, okay."

Miles walks in and eyes my cast. "Jesus Christ." He holds his hands out and looks me up and down. "You got any other injuries I need to know about?" He takes my unbruised face in his hands and inspects it. "I don't believe it. The only injury you got, you did to yourself."

"I'm my own worst enemy."

"You said it." He grins and wraps his arm around my neck. "You look good. You ready?"

"Yeah." I follow him to a media room for a panel interview and take my seat beside him.

Everyone begins asking me questions at once, but Miles picks the reporter he wants me to respond to, and the room gets quiet.

I lean in to the microphone and ask, "Can you repeat the question?"

One by one, they take turns asking me the same question a different way, all of them wanting to know about my hand and what my plan for recovery is. But the last reporter surprises me when she says, "You said you were distracted tonight. I don't mean to get personal, but I can't help but wonder if a girl isn't responsible for your loss of focus in the ring?" She smiles and the room joins her in quiet laughter. The status of my love life regularly comes up in interviews, but for the first time, it's actually relevant.

Miles puts his hand over my mic, leans in to his, and says, "Okay, we're not here to talk about his love life."

"So you're still single?" she presses.

"Come on," Miles says, irritated.

I lean in to my mic, look directly into the camera in front of me, and say, "For now."

Chapter 11

Lucy

My phone vibrates on my bathroom counter, but my hands are covered in face wash, so I don't answer the call. It's been forty-eight hours since I left Sam's apartment, and in that time, with plenty of space between us to think clearly, I've decided that I have to let him go. As painful as that decision is, my life is here with Drew. And it's a good life. A comfortable life. A nice, *normal* life. The kind of life that I used to dream of as a kid. Drew loves me and he doesn't deserve to be the third point in a love triangle that he doesn't even know about. Not to mention that his mother took me under her wing, made me feel like family, *and* singlehandedly launched my budding art career with her clout in the community. I owe her so much.

I rinse my face and hands under the warm water, and my phone buzzes again. I grab a hand towel, pat my face dry, and look at the screen. *Sebastian.* I put him on speaker so I can continue with my nighttime routine. "Hey," I answer, dotting my eyes with anti-wrinkle cream that Janice gave me. She says I'll thank her in my forties if I use it in my twenties.

"Sam broke his hand."

I stop dotting. "What?"

"He broke his hand during the Vegas charity fight."

The fight wasn't televised live here, so I haven't watched it yet. "Wait. What? How do you know? How could he break his hand?" *Isn't that what gloves are for?*

"Turn on ESPN."

I run into my bedroom and turn on the TV. I know all the sports networks by heart, so I find the channel quickly. Sam is sitting for a panel interview surrounded by cameras and reporters. The news scroll at the bottom of the screen reads: *Sam Cole breaks his hand during a Las Vegas charity fight.*

I pull my hand to my mouth. "Oh, my God."

"I know."

"I'll call you back." I hang up the phone and stare at the screen, watching Sam intently.

He nods and answers the reporters' questions. His hand is in a hard cast that wraps around his outer three fingers and covers his wrist.

What happened? I listen to his manager explain how he fractured his fifth metacarpal throwing a bad punch, a surprisingly common injury in inexperienced boxers. *But Sam isn't inexperienced.*

He assures the media that it's a simple fracture that should heal quickly. Joe chimes in and tells the crowd that gloves are intended to protect the face, but good wrapping and proper technique are what protect the hands. When asked if his hand was wrapped properly before the fight, Sam leans in to his microphone and says, "Everyone on my team makes sure I'm ready before each fight. Tonight was no different. If there's anyone to blame for this stupid mistake"—he holds up his casted hand—"it's me. I was the only one who came unprepared tonight. I was distracted and I lost focus out there. That's on me."

Distracted? I chew the corner of my mouth, but when that doesn't provide the relief I need, I pull my thumbnail to my teeth. I chew it nervously throughout the remainder of the interview, until Sam answers the final question.

He smirks at the bubbly brunette reporter who asks him if he's single, and then he looks directly into the camera, into my bedroom, into my soul, and says, "For now."

I swallow hard and stare at the TV, even as the network switches to a different story. I rewind it and watch it again.

For now.

. . .

For now.

. . .

For now.

My phone rings and I know it's Sebastian. I hold the phone up to my ear.

"Oh. My. God."

I don't say anything.

"Lucy!"

"What?"

"Did you see the interview?"

"I saw it."

"And?"

"And what, Bas?" I ask, irritated.

He's quiet for a second. "Oh, okay, we're doing the denial thing. In that case, I didn't see a thing. Not a single thing. Especially not Sam looking directly into the camera suggesting he doesn't plan on staying single for long. Or when he said he was too distracted to focus on the match, in which he broke his hand and received the first draw of his career. And I certainly didn't contemplate what on earth could have been so distracting to a world champion boxer that he could forget how to throw a proper punch."

"Are you trying to make me feel like shit? Because it's working."

"I'm trying to make you realize that the boy is still crazy about you."

"So what if he is? It doesn't matter."

"It matters if you feel the same way."

Drew walks into the bedroom with his bag slung over his shoulder. "I have to go. Drew just got home."

"Did you find your ring yet?"

"I have to go, Sebastian," I say again, ignoring his inappropriately timed question. I hang up the phone and turn off the TV. "I didn't hear you come in." I smile at Drew, trying to ignore the way my heart is pounding inside my chest.

"What was Sebastian making you feel like shit about?"

"Oh, my ring," I say impulsively, feeling the need point it out before he notices that it's missing. "I took it off at the studio to paint and can't remember where I put it. Sebastian was just giving me crap about it on your behalf." As soon as the lie slips off my tongue, I regret it. *Just tell him the truth. You took it off at Sam's apartment while you were cooking and didn't realize it was missing until the next morning because you were too busy crying yourself to sleep over the fact that you've decided to let him go.*

Drew pulls me up off the bed by my left hand and looks at my naked ring finger, but I pull it away before he notices that it's shaking. I swallow hard and prepare myself to tell him about Sam, but it's about as easy as jumping off a cliff. "Drew, I, um..." I swallow hard and blink up at him. "I—"

"Sebastian doesn't know me very well." He smiles and pulls me close. "If you took your ring off at the studio, it's there somewhere." He kisses the top of my head. "You'll find it."

The breath I was holding rushes out, but he doesn't seem to notice.

"I need a shower." He pulls his shirt off and drops it at my feet. "Want to join me?"

I give a weak smile and shake my head. "I already showered."

He winks and walks into the bathroom. "I'm still waiting for that rain check," he says before he closes the door.

I know.

I climb into bed, close my eyes, and hide under the covers, hoping to fall asleep before he returns.

* * *

"That one," Sebastian says, pointing to one of three paintings I'm considering for the last spot in the exhibit. "It's dark and depressing, just like you," he says, staring at the canvas, smirking.

I narrow my eyes and glare at him, but he ignores me.

"Fine. That one," I say, stalking off to my office to sulk. It's been a week since Sam's interview, so I know he must be back in Atlanta, but I still haven't found the courage to call him. Much to Sebastian's dismay, the angst is making me miserable, but every time I reach for my phone, I'm paralyzed with anxiety. I don't know what I'm more afraid of: looking into Sam's beautiful eyes and saying goodbye, or knowing that I might not be able to. But I can't wait much longer. I have to get my ring back. Drew left for Philadelphia again this morning, so there's no excuse to delay any longer.

The day is almost over now, I justify to myself. *Tomorrow is better.*

"Darling," Janice calls from the front of the studio.

I walk out of my office and find her hanging off Sebastian's arm, clutching a large white garment bag. "I have a surprise for you," she sings, and snuggles in close to Sebastian. "I brought you the most beautiful wedding gown to try on," she squeals.

Sebastian smiles at me with big animated eyes but does nothing to dissuade her. Before I can say anything, she's dragging me to my office.

"Oh, Janice, I don't know if right now is the best time."

"Darling, there's never going to be a best time. That's the price you pay for being Atlanta's most talented up-and-coming artist. You're in high demand. It's a sign of success. Don't be discouraged. But you're going to have to learn to be flexible or this wedding is never going to happen."

I swallow down my reluctance and try to be gracious.

"Sebastian, wait out front," she instructs. "You can be the judge."

"Okay," he says, spinning around with a smirk.

I stand still for the next several minutes while Janice cinches me into the ivory lace dress. When she's finished, she pulls her hands to her mouth and gasps. "This is it. This is the one."

Do I get a say? I look in the mirror to see what all the fuss is about, and a sharp pinch shoots across my chest when I see my reflection. The dress is beautiful. It's simple and elegant. It's exactly my style. But something about wearing it feels wrong.

"Let's go see what it looks like in the light. Come on, you can show Sebastian," she says, gathering the train in her hands.

I lift the bottom of the dress and walk out to the front of the studio with Janice trailing me.

"Oh, Lucy." Bas pulls his bottom lip between his teeth and breathes deeply. "It's really beautiful."

Janice spreads the delicate train out on the floor, beaming as she admires the dress from every angle. She turns me from side to side and spins me around to look at the back of the dress in the light. "Oh, hello," she says, looking over my shoulder, and I cringe because I know someone just walked in, probably thinking they're in the wrong place.

I turn around to see who she's speaking to, and the earth stops spinning. Sebastian and Janice disappear and all I see is Sam. He looks at me as if no one else is in the room and says, "Hi."

"Hi," I breathe, drinking him in. His hair is combed back and he's freshly shaven. He's wearing a snug navy-blue V-neck sweater with the sleeves pushed up, slate-gray pants, and brown leather utility boots. His casted hand is hanging by his side and his other hand is dangling from his pocket.

"I'm Janice Christiansen," Janice says proudly, reaching out to shake his hand.

"Hi, I'm Sam," he says warily.

She looks at me and then smiles at Sam curiously. "Are you a friend of Lucy's?"

Sebastian coughs.

"Um, yes," he says, glancing at me, "a very old friend."

"We grew up together," I add. I don't want her getting the wrong idea. Or the right one.

"Really?" she breathes. "I've never met anyone from Lucy's past before." She puts her hand on my back and coos, "I just thought she dropped straight down from heaven, like a little angel."

Sam lowers his eyes to the dress and follows the delicate ivory lace all the way up to my face. "I can see why you would think that."

I close my eyes and shake my head. "I'm sorry, let me go change. I was just trying this on." I fumble over my words and gather the material up in my hands.

"Wait a minute, you're the boxer." Realization flashes

across Janice's face, and I freeze. She grabs Sam's hand and drags him across the studio.

"Janice, what are you doing?" I ask anxiously, following on their heels.

Sebastian gives me big eyes and shrugs.

She pulls Sam to the back of the studio and stops in front of the canvas I've been working on for the past month. Before I can stop her, she pulls the drop cloth off the painting. "It's you"—she smiles at him—"right?"

I feel Sebastian's hand wrap around mine and squeeze tight. Sam takes a step back and stares at the six-foot canvas. He reaches for the back of his neck, and I watch his shoulders rise up and down slowly.

"It's him, isn't it?" Janice asks me with a smile still plastered on her face.

"I, um..." I swallow hard and let go of Sebastian's hand. I pick up the drop cloth and drape it back over the canvas. "I'm not finished with it. It isn't finished," I explain, feeling wildly self-conscious under Sam's eyes, which I can't even look at.

"Oh..." Janice puts her hand over her mouth. "Did I ruin the surprise?"

I shake my head with disbelief. "How did you even know about it?" I ask, feeling utterly exposed.

"Oh, you know me," she says, flippantly. "I'm just so nosy, I couldn't help myself. Were you saving it for the exhibit?"

"Yes," Sebastian interjects. "She was."

Sebastian! I shoot daggers at him with my eyes.

"Oh, good." She claps her hands together. "It's perfect. Has Drew seen it?"

An audible gasp escapes me.

She doesn't wait for an answer. She grabs Sam's arm and declares, "I have the best idea."

Oh, no.

"We should get together and have dinner on Saturday...all of us."

What? Absolutely not!

"My place is a mess, my kitchen is under a total remodel, but I'm sure Drew wouldn't mind cooking for us when he gets back in town." She looks at me with excited eyes. "Right, Lucy?"

Is this really happening?

"Sebastian, you should bring Peter."

Who's Peter?

"I think you mean Paul," he corrects.

"Oh, yes, of course, bring Paul. It will be a great time."

No, it will not be a great time!

Sebastian looks as shocked as I feel, but when I look at Sam, he has a mischievous grin on his face. "That sounds great. I'd love to," he says, to Janice's delight, and I look at him like he's grown a second head.

"Wonderful. It's set, then. Lucy will give you all the details." She spins around. "I have to get going, but it was lovely to meet you, Sam. Lucy, I'm leaving everything in your capable hands." She leaves the room, taking all the air with her.

Sebastian gives me sympathetic eyes, but I'm still irritated at him for offering up my painting for the exhibit.

"Sebastian, right?" Sam asks, reaching out to shake his hand.

Sebastian nods and shakes Sam's hand. "Yes, that's right." He looks at me and then casually tucks his hands into the pockets of his slim-fit chinos. "I need to get going."

I look at him with panicked eyes, but he backs away heedlessly.

"It was good to see you again," he says to Sam. He gives me an eager look. "I'll lock up on my way out."

I bob my head reluctantly, feeling the edges of anxiety prick down my arms and legs, especially when I realize that Janice trapped me in this dress. But when I look at Sam, all the worry and sorrow I've felt over the last week begins to evaporate.

"Hi," he says, looking into my eyes, sending my heart sprinting.

"Hi," I say, gazing up at him. I try to shake off the remnants of Janice's overbearing presence. "Sorry about Janice. She's a little over the top."

He holds my stare for a long second. "You didn't call."

I look into his eyes but don't know how to tell him that I didn't call because I'm not ready to say goodbye to him yet.

"I guess I'm not as good at waiting as I thought." He glances down and my dress. "Looks like you've been busy."

I shake my head and huff. "This was Janice." I look down at the dress awkwardly and notice his casted hand. I reach for it and carefully lift it up. "Your hand."

"It's fine."

"Does it hurt?"

He shakes his head and pushes his lips into a small pout. "Pain is fleeting."

My eyes flash to his.

"It's missing from the painting."

I lower his hand and try to hide my embarrassment. "I know... tattoos aren't exactly the easiest thing to paint."

He looks at me curiously.

"It's like trying to copy someone else's artwork. Besides, I can only get so much detail from a picture." I point to the tattoos covering his forearm. "You were a blank slate when I knew you."

The corner of his mouth twitches. "You still know me."

"You know what I mean." I glance at his arm again. "Did that hurt?"

"My tattoos?"

I nod.

"You don't have any?"

"No."

"Good."

I give him a reproachful look. "That's a bit of a double standard, isn't it?"

He smiles softly. "It would be a travesty to mar something so beautiful."

My breath leaves me in a rush, and his words burn across my skin like wildfire.

"And yes, they hurt."

I swallow hard. "You said pain is fleeting."

"It is. But sometimes it reminds us that we're still alive."

I nod, trying to slow the thoughts that are racing through my mind.

"Do you want to see them?"

Excitement and apprehension fight for their place in line.

"Maybe then you can finish the painting."

I close my eyes and sigh. "I wasn't exactly planning on anyone seeing it."

He looks at me with sincerity in his eyes that calms my racing heart. "Can I see it again?"

I chew the corner of my mouth. "Okay." I turn around, take a deep breath, and pull the drop cloth off the canvas, letting it fall to the floor.

Sam stands beside me and stares at the painting for several silent seconds. "It's really incredible."

I glance up at him hesitantly. "You think so?"

He looks at me with awe in his eyes. "I'll never get over how talented you are."

I smile and touch the canvas, lightly tracing my fingers over his gloves. "I had a pretty remarkable subject."

"Are you really going to use it in your exhibit? Or was Sebastian just trying to rile you up?"

I blink a few times, surprised by his intuition.

"That's never been very hard to do." He masks a smile. "He must know you pretty well."

I close my eyes briefly, thinking about Sebastian's brazen declaration. "He does. And...I don't know. Maybe. If I can finish it in time."

The corners of his mouth turn up. "I can help you with that."

I laugh softly. "You want me to finish it now?"

He shrugs. "Unless there's somewhere else you need to be."

"No." I shake my head. "Nowhere else." And if there was,

I'd cancel. I'd fake an illness or a flat tire. I'd say I was robbed at gunpoint if I had to, just to spend another minute with him. The thought is more than troubling. How am I going to say goodbye to Sam when I can barely stand the thought of him leaving? "Just...let me change out of this."

I hurry to my office and close the door behind me, grateful for a minute alone to calm my racing heart and clear my clouded head. But I soon realize that I can't reach the buttons on the back of the dress. *Janice!* I reluctantly open the door and call for help. "Sam?"

He walks into my office with an inquisitive look.

"I can't reach the buttons," I say, turning around and squeezing my eyes shut.

"Oh, okay," he says, walking up behind me, standing so close I can feel the heat coming off him. He reaches for the top button and unhooks the silk loop from around it. "Good thing they didn't wrap up my whole hand," he says, and I laugh awkwardly. He's quiet as his fingers move down my back, but I feel his warm breath against the exposed skin between my shoulder blades each time he unloops another button.

"Sorry." I force my eyes open and try not to sound breathy. "This dress is ridiculous."

He leans in so that his mouth is right next to my ear and whispers, "It's beautiful."

I breathe in and out slowly, trying to find my heart. "I think I've got it from here."

He takes a step back, and I welcome the space between us.

"I'll be right out," I say, closing the door behind him when he leaves. I lean against it and wait for the feeling to return to my legs, then I step out of the dress and carefully place it back in the white garment bag, trading it for my painting clothes on the back of the door. I pull on my old tattered cutoffs and look at the ratty T-shirt in my hands. *I can't wear this.* I glance around my office and see a plastic dry-cleaning bag draped over one of the chairs. *Thank you, Sebastian.* I tear into it and find a plain white poplin shirt, the most expendable item of the bunch, and quickly slip into it. I button up the front, roll up the sleeves, and head back into the studio.

Sam raises an eyebrow when I pass him.

"I just need to get my paints," I say, walking across the cool cement floor on my bare feet. I return a few seconds later, dragging my paint cart behind me.

Sam smiles and crosses his arms over his broad chest, watching me intently as I prepare everything. I grab a small paint-covered remote from my cart and point it at the ceiling. "Lighting," I explain, adjusting the lights until they're just right.

He uncrosses his arms and reaches for the hem of his sweater with his good hand, pulling it up over his chiseled abs and chest, and I watch with anticipation like the unveiling of a masterpiece.

"I think I might need some help," he says, struggling to get it over his head with one hand.

"Oh." I step toward him and assess the situation. "Other arm first." I laugh, tugging his sweater back down. I raise his arms above his head, and he holds them there while I work the sweater up over his stomach and chest. I stand on my tiptoes to get it over his head and shoulders, breathing in the familiar scent of sandalwood and laundry detergent that lingers on his warm skin. He tries to take over, but his sleeve gets caught on his cast. "Here," I say, carefully pulling it down his forearm and gently tugging it over his cast.

His eyes meet mine, and I could dive right into them and swim around for days. "Thanks," he says, low and husky. He lowers his hand to his side and stands before me like a perfectly sculpted statue, wearing slacks and boots.

I drop his sweater on the floor. "Sorry," I say, realizing what I did. I lean down to pick it up, but Sam catches my wrist.

"Leave it." He pulls me back up and inadvertently closer to him, making me stumble backward. But he puts his hand behind my back to catch me. "Careful." I feel the warmth of his skin under my hands and his breath on my forehead, but I don't look up, because I know that if I see even a glimpse of the yearning I feel right now in his eyes, I might not be able to pull away from him.

His hand falls away, and I'm both relieved and disappointed at once.

I raise my eyes slightly, but only as far as his chest, which I study carefully. I drop my head to the side and examine every detail and explore every line of the tattoos that cover him. I bring my hands up between us and touch the words scrolled beneath his collarbone. *Pain Is Fleeting.* I trace the letters, following the loops and memorizing the curves of the font with my finger. Sam lets out a heavy breath, and goose bumps flash across his skin.

"Sorry. It gets cold in here sometimes."

"I'm not cold," he says hoarsely.

My eyes flash to his, but I quickly avert them when I see the way that he's looking at me. I pause and quietly explain, "It helps me feel how I should paint it." I concentrate on my task, tracing the beautiful lion that covers his heart, memorizing its ferocious eyes and teeth with my fingers. I follow its mane over his shoulder, turning him slightly to see how it connects to the tattoos that cover his arm. "Okay," I say, when I'm ready to start.

"You forgot one." He holds his hand above his shoulder, showing me the small tattoo that's scrolled across his rib cage.

I inhale a deep breath of the thick air surrounding us and press my fingers to it lightly. I trace the cursive letters carefully. *L-a-m-b.*

"That one hurt the most," he whispers, piercing my heart and stealing the breath from my lungs. He finishes me with a devastating look that stokes a fire burning deep inside me.

I pull in a slow breath, but the oxygen only fans the flames higher. I swallow hard and reach for my paint cart with shaking hands. "Don't move," I say, just louder than a whisper. I reach for a tube of raw umber and squeeze a little onto my palette, then I add some ultramarine green and mix them together until I get a dark shade that's almost black. I dip my paintbrush into the little mound of paint, wiping it on my palette several times until my hand is steady enough to begin. I position my brush over the canvas, but I freeze when I feel Sam standing behind me.

"Lamb," he whispers in my ear, pleading.

I breathe in and out, desperately trying to extinguish the

fire, but it sears through my veins with abandon. When his lips brush my ear, I stop breathing and close my eyes.

"I know you feel it." His warm breath falls on my cheek.

"I—" I gasp. "I can't—"

He reaches for my face and turns me around, and I drop the paintbrush. "Open your eyes."

If I look at him, I'll lose my grip on the small shred of willpower I'm holding on to, so I keep them closed.

He rubs his thumb over my cheek, coaxing me, and I feel it down to my bones. "Look at me," he urges, closing the space between us until I'm flush against his heated body. His chest rises and falls against mine with tortured breaths. "Please," he begs longingly, "I *need* you, Lamb."

I open my heavy eyes to a fiery storm of blue and brown. "Sam," I whisper, knowing that I'm on the precipice of a monumental decision. The kind that alters the universe and changes the lives of everyone in it.

"Please," he begs again, dropping his mouth to mine, pushing me closer to the edge. "I can't go another second without you," he whispers against my lips.

A tidal wave of emotion washes over me, flashing images of the life I'm supposed to have with Drew. My nice, normal, *safe* life with Drew. But choosing that life will erase Sam forever. My panicked thoughts thrash around my head, rocking me to my fiery core. *I can't lose Sam again.*

I close my eyes.

Take a breath.

And jump.

"Yes." I nod fervently against his lips. "Yes," I say again, until I'm silenced by their sweet relief. He presses his mouth firmly against mine and holds me as I fall into an inferno I have no way out of. I shove my hands into his hair and kiss him with every fiber of my being, pouring my heart and soul back into him. He groans into my mouth, claiming my tongue with his, and I'm cloaked in a warm, familiar, velvety blanket that I never want to let go of. I close my fists in his hair and moan into his mouth.

He breathes heavily against my cheek and drops his hand to my waist, finding his way under my shirt. He presses his hand to my back and pulls me against him, but it isn't close enough. I reach for the buttons on my shirt and Sam takes over, yanking the two sides apart. He pushes it off my shoulders and drops his mouth to my neck. *Oh, God.*

Drew wanders back into my mind like a boat drifting out of the fog.

Oh, *God*. I can't do this. "Stop," I say urgently against his lips. "We can't do this. I can't do this." I cry, because I want him so badly I can barely breathe.

He squeezes his eyes shut and lets out a tortured breath. "Why?" he asks, just as pained, rubbing his thumb across my cheek.

"You know why."

He gazes into my eyes, into my soul, and says the words I've wanted to hear since the moment he ripped back through my heart. "I want you, Lucy. I want you *back*." His proclamation reverberates through my head, and my heart doubles in size. "I know we've made mistakes," he says urgently, "but we can leave it all behind us and start over. Together. It can be like it was always supposed to be."

"Start over?" My throat suddenly feels tight. "I've worked so hard to get here."

"I'm not asking you to give up your career," he says with a small, apprehensive smile.

"Just my life," I whisper.

He lets out a frustrated breath and drops his hand. "Your boyfriend would suffice."

I pull the two sides of my shirt together and step out of the hazy cloud of desire. I walk over to the couch and sit down. "He's not my boyfriend. He's my fiancé. And we live together."

"I'm aware."

I give him an impossible look and explain, "Everything I have is tied up in him, Sam. Everything. My career. My *studio*." A sick feeling is suddenly plaguing me.

"Lucy, if you're worried about money, it's not an issue."

I let out a distraught breath. "How could I do this to him? How could I do this to Janice? After everything they've done for me."

"Is that what this is? You think you owe them something?"

I get up and stand in front of him. "I do owe them something. I owe them everything! They became my family when I thought I had no one left. They helped me make my dream come true—my career took off because of them. The exhibit I'm hosting next week is only happening because of them." I close my eyes and let out a remorseful breath, because I doubt the exhibit will still happen now. *Sebastian is going to be so upset.*

"Do you even love him, Lucy?" he asks skeptically.

"I told you, I wouldn't marry someone I don't love."

"That's not an answer. Do you...love him?" His eyes burn into me, imploring for the truth.

I swallow hard and chew the corner of my mouth, afraid to make any sudden moves. I'm aware that I'm standing on a very thin sheet of ice that's filled with cracks, just like the ones I put in Sam's heart. One wrong move and I could lose him forever.

"Yes," I answer honestly, "I love him. But...not the way that I loved you. I could never love anyone else that way."

"The way you *loved* me." The corners of his mouth turn down, and he drops his chin. "Maybe that's the problem." He reaches into his pocket and pulls out something shiny. "You see, I *still* love you." He hands me my engagement ring, and my heart shrinks inside my chest. "I never stopped."

"Sam." I reach for him, but he walks over to the painting and picks his sweater up off the floor. He slips it on over his head, but it gets caught on his cast.

I approach him carefully and reach for his sleeve. "Let me help," I say softly.

"He doesn't make you happy."

"You don't know him."

He reaches for my hand and says firmly, "I know *you*."

"Sam."

"I can make you happy, Lucy. You know that I can."

I swallow down a quiet sob. "I know you can, but it's not that easy."

"Yes it is."

"No, it's not," I cry.

He reaches for my face and cups my neck. "I want you, Lucy." He drags his hand to my chest and places it over my heart. "I *want you*," he groans. "But if you tell me that you don't want me back, that you don't love me anymore, I'll walk away and I'll let you go." His face screws up and he closes his eyes. "If that's what you really want, I'll leave right now and I'll say goodbye to you for good."

"No." I shake my head and blink back tears. "I can't tell you that. Because I still love you too."

He exhales an uneven breath and wraps me in his strong arms. "Then come back to me," he pleads against my ear. "Come back to me, baby. Please."

A small cry bubbles out of me. "I want to. More than anything. But I don't know how."

He unwraps his arms from around me and looks into my eyes. "Yes you do."

I stare into his beautiful eyes and nod, but the thought of giving up the safety of my life with Drew and ending my career before it's even started is overwhelming. "I...I just need some time, okay? I need to figure everything out." I blink up at him, begging for his understanding. "Please."

He tucks my hair behind my ear and nods. "Okay. But don't take too long. Because I don't know how much longer I can live without you."

I ignore the storm of emotions brewing inside me. "I won't."

Chapter 12

Lucy

Pick up. Pick up. Pick up.

When the unanswered call goes to Drew's voicemail, I huff loudly and hang up the phone. I immediately try to call him back, desperate to talk to him before the guilt eats me alive, but once again it goes to voicemail. "Always too busy with work," I grumble quietly to myself, shaping my guilt over kissing Sam into something that resembles anger and unfairly pointing out Drew's shortcomings. I pace around my studio, unsure what to do with myself since Sam left ten minutes ago. *Call Sebastian.*

"Hey," he answers on the first ring.

"Sebastian, I need you. Can you come back to the studio?"

"Yeah. Is everything okay?"

"No. I don't know. Maybe."

"What's going on? Are you okay?"

"I can't tell you over the phone. Can you just come back, please?"

"Lucy Marie Bennett, if you think I'm going twenty minutes without knowing if you're okay or not, you have another thing coming."

"I'm fine, Sebastian. I just kissed Sam," I say quietly.

Just? I think, and drop my face to my hand.

Sebastian gasps. "I'll be right there."

I hang up and fall onto the worn leather couch, breathing deeply in hopes that it will bring some small shred of comfort to kissing Sam and altering the course of both our lives—and Drew's. But it doesn't. I close my eyes and rub my tight chest. Drew is going to be devastated. And Janice is never going to speak to me again. I look around my beloved studio. I'm going to lose it. Which means no exhibit. And no invite to the show in New York next year. My heart sinks inside my chest.

After a few minutes of feeling sorry for myself, I get up and walk over to the unfinished painting of Sam. I stand in front of it, gauging the additions that I need to make. Then I close my eyes and try to remember the way each word was scrolled across his skin. After several lingering seconds, I reach for my paints and mix them on a new palette. I grab a clean brush and begin painting the word *Pain*, but I stop after I make the loop for the *P*.

Pain Is Fleeting.

I really hope so, especially for Drew's sake.

I look at Sam's eyes in the painting, which are a perfect reflection of the eyes that bore into my soul when we kissed. I reach out and touch his full lips, which felt so right against mine. I trace his broad chest and shoulders and follow the curves of his muscular arms. I've always felt safe with Drew, but when Sam held me, it felt like he could protect me from the entire world. *He probably could.*

I begin painting again, thinking of the way that he called me *Lamb* and the way that he said he needed me. The way that he kissed me. My conflicted heart beats inside my chest like a bass drum, and I have to work hard to keep my hand steady. I love Drew, but Sam is woven through my soul like a piece of steel thread that can never be broken. After all these years, it hasn't weathered; it hasn't wavered. It's just as strong today as it was when I was seventeen. Strong enough to cut right through my nice, *normal* life with Drew.

* * *

"Lucy?" Sebastian calls from the front of the studio.

"Back here."

He finds me in front of the large stainless steel sink in the back of the studio scrubbing my hands and paintbrushes.

"Hey," he says cautiously, "were you painting?"

"Yeah." I dry my hands on a paper towel and toss it in the garbage, but as soon as I look at him, my face flushes with shame, and tears fill my eyes.

"Oh, Lucy." He steps toward me and pulls me into a hug. "It's okay."

"How? How is any of this okay?" I cry into his thick sweater. "What am I going to do?"

He gently pushes my shoulders back and dabs the middle of his sweater with his sleeve. "Well, first, let's find you something else to wear." He flips the bottom of my shirt up and runs his thumb over the broken thread where a button used to be. He raises an eyebrow. "Must have been one hell of a kiss."

I spin around to go find another shirt in my office, and Sebastian follows me.

"Are you sure that's all it was?"

I turn around and lean against my desk. "Yes." I tuck my hair behind my ear and nod. "But it could have been more," I admit. "If I didn't make myself stop, if I didn't *force* myself to stop—"

"But you did stop."

"Yeah." I shrug, but it doesn't make things any better. I didn't *just* kiss Sam, I gave myself back to him. What could hurt Drew more than that? I close my eyes and confess, "I didn't want to stop. I wanted Sam, more than I've ever wanted anything before."

He puts his hand on my shoulder and says delicately, "It's okay."

"No, it's not okay. I'm engaged and I kissed someone who isn't my fiancé."

"Yes, well, I can see how that might put a damper on the wedding plans." He narrows his eyes, but I don't laugh.

"I can't marry him." I exhale and blink back tears. "I can't marry Drew." Saying that out loud practically sends me into hyperventilation. "Oh, my God, Sebastian. What have I done?"

"Okay, just slow down." Sebastian lifts his hands and inhales a slow, deep breath, then he lowers his hands as he exhales. "You just need to breathe." He puts his hands on my shoulders and says calmly, "It's going to be fine. You kissed

Sam. You didn't sleep with him. I'm sure if you explain your
history with Sam to Drew, he'll forgive you and you can still
get married. In years to come, this will be nothing more than
a little bump in the road."

"I meant, how could I have promised my heart to Drew
when it still belonged to Sam?"

"Oh." He drops his hands.

"And I knew it did, Sebastian. I knew it. But I fought it—
that feeling in my gut that told me Drew wasn't the one, that
told me *not* to say yes when he asked me to marry him, that
led me to break up with him shortly after he proposed."

"Wait, I thought you broke up because he was working too
much."

I shake my head sheepishly. "That was just an excuse. I
needed space. Because even though there were a hundred reasons for me to marry Drew, there was one reason not to."

"Sam."

My shoulders slump and I fall into my desk chair. "I spent
those two weeks that we were broken up going over every
possibility of ever being with Sam again and subsequently
striking them all out. The odds were stacked so high against
us that I eventually gave up."

"And you decided to marry Drew."

My eyes fill with tears. "I love Drew."

Sebastian sits in the other wooden swivel chair in my office
and rolls it over to mine. "I know you do," he says, reaching
for my hand.

"But it's a different kind of love than what I feel for Sam." I
wipe my eyes. "Drew is like a blue sky after a storm, but Sam

is the earth and the sun and the ocean. He's the reason for the storm in the first place."

"Not too many people have that kind of effect on us."

"So how am I supposed to tell Drew that he doesn't?" I shake my head. "He thinks I'm the love of his life. He thinks he's *mine*. I'm the most selfish person."

"You're not selfish. You lost the only love you'd ever known and then you picked up the pieces of your broken heart and you moved on. You're strong. You tucked Sam away for safekeeping, because you had to, and then you began building your life without him—a good life that included Drew. And sure, Drew's not the love of your life, but do you know how many people actually end up with their soulmate?"

"You did."

He flutters his eyes and shakes his head. "We're not talking about me." He puts his hand under my chin and says with certainty, "You did the practical thing, and there's nothing wrong with that. You built a life to be proud of with someone you love. That's far more than most people can say."

"And now it's about to come crashing down all around me. *God.*" I groan. "I should have told Drew about Sam. I had so many chances. I was just so afraid to hurt him."

"Sometimes it's easier to protect our loved ones with a lie than hurt them with the truth."

"How do I protect him now?" I sigh and shake my head. "I'm not strong, Sebastian. I leapt off that cliff today and kissed Sam knowing I wasn't doing the right thing for anyone except me."

"Then why did you stop?"

"Because I don't want to hurt Drew any more than I have to."

He presses his lips together and nods. "Case in point. You're not selfish."

"Weak argument."

"What about Sam?" he asks, swiveling in his chair.

"What about him?"

"Well, you're awfully concerned about Drew's feelings. Have you thought about how hard this must be on Sam?"

"Sam is . . . tough."

"I don't care if he's made of steel. If he feels the same way about you, he must be going through hell right now."

I drop my head to my hands and fight the tight feeling in my chest. The thought of hurting Sam is far worse than the thought of hurting Drew. I feel awful for even thinking that, but it's true. If they were in a burning car together, I would save Sam. I put my face back in my hands and mumble, "I'm a terrible person."

"No you're not." Bas pulls my hands away from my face. "You're a good person. And you're a kind person. You care about everyone around you. Now, maybe it's time to starting caring about you. What's right for you, Luc?"

"Sam. Sam is what's right for me. I know it in my bones. But what if choosing what's right for me means hurting everyone else in my life? How do I live with that?"

He drops his head to the side and asks, "Did I ever tell you about my Grandma Meg?"

I shake my head. "No."

"Margaret Monroe Monahan. She was firecracker. She died when I was in college."

"I'm sorry," I say, reaching for his hand.

"Before she died, she said something to me that changed my life."

I sit up in my chair and listen intently.

"As I sat on her bed, holding her hand, ready to say good-bye, with my girlfriend waiting in the other room—"

"Girlfriend?" I raise my eyebrows and he smiles.

"She looked at me and said, 'Honey, I want you to do something for me.' Of course, I told her I'd do anything. She said, 'I want you to be honest about who you are.' Now, I hadn't told anyone I was gay, especially not my family—I was having a hard enough time trying to come to terms with it myself—so I blinked and nodded, trying to figure out what she was talking about. But she just smiled and said, 'You're gay.'"

"How did she know?"

"We were always really close. I guess I was just more myself with her than I was with anyone else."

"Well, what did you say?"

"I didn't say anything, at first. I tried to laugh it off. But she knew. She looked me in the eye and said, 'You don't have to pretend with me, honey. I've known you were gay since you were thirteen years old.'"

I widen my eyes. "Did you know when you were thirteen?"

He crosses his arms. "I knew I didn't like girls the way that my friends did. I just didn't know what it meant exactly." He shakes his head and laughs. "Out of everyone in my family, my elderly grandmother was the only one who could see that I was gay."

"So what did you do?"

"I wept like a small child. It was like she had cut the string to a giant helium balloon I'd been holding on to all those years. It was an enormous relief. But it was also terrifying. At that point in my life, the idea of coming out to my family, and to my girlfriend of two years, was almost paralyzing. It meant admitting that I'd been lying to them. And it meant accepting that they might not forgive me."

"Sebastian."

"Honestly, if it weren't for the next thing she said, I don't know if I would have done it. But she looked at me and said, 'You listen to me, Sebastian. You only get one chance at this life. And it may seem like you have all the time in the world. But I'm at the end of the road and I know how fast it goes. Don't waste your life pretending to be something you're not. Be who you are. Be happy, angel.'" His eyes mist a little. "That's what she used to call me." He clears his throat. "That was the last thing she said to me."

I press my lips together and reach for his hand again. "Grandma Meg was a really smart lady."

He nods. "She was a pretty incredible woman."

"Thanks for telling me that."

"Lucy, telling my parents that I'm gay was the hardest thing I've ever had to do."

"How did you do it?"

"With a lot of courage. And faith. I believed what my Grandma Meg said to me that day. Telling my parents the truth was scary, but I wasn't going to spend my whole life pretending I was happy when I wasn't. Because the thought of lying in a bed at the end of my life knowing I'd never found true happiness was far scarier."

"But your parents understood? I mean, you guys are really close."

"Now. But it wasn't always that way. My mom was devastated because she thought I'd never be able to give her a grandchild." He laughs and shakes his head. "She prayed for me around the clock. And my dad couldn't even talk to me for a while. But yeah, they eventually came around, and in the end, they were asking for *my* forgiveness." He shrugs. "I think it was the hardest on my girlfriend. She thought it was her fault somehow, like she'd done something to turn me gay. We'd been dating for so long, I can see why it was confusing for her. But now she's married and has a baby. And I'm so happy for her. Because I know I couldn't have given that to her."

"Wow."

"I sometimes wonder, if my Grandma Meg hadn't made it her dying wish for me to be honest about who I really am, how many years of my life, and my girlfriend's, would I have wasted because I was too afraid to tell her the truth?"

"Sebastian, I can't imagine you being anyone other than you."

He stands up and pulls me out of my chair. "You're going to figure all this out, sweetie. You just have to be true to yourself. And keep harnessing all that emotion to create more amazing paintings like the one I saw today." He raises an eyebrow.

"I finished it," I say, trying to hide a smile.

His eyes light up. "Show me."

I lead him out of my office and over to the painting.

"Wow." He gazes at it. "It's really incredible. It may be your best work."

"You think so?"

He nods. "I love it. It's strong. Powerful. Provocative." He pulls his hand to his chin. "He looks determined, but I can't tell if he's winning the fight or losing it." He drops his head to the side. "But he won't give up. He'll take hit after hit if he has to."

I swallow hard, listening to his interpretation of the painting.

"And the way you layered the colors is really incredible. So . . . alive. And the lines here"—he points to the tattoos on his arm—"they're so fluid." He smiles at me. "You did good."

I smile back. "Thanks. Especially since you volunteered it for the exhibit."

"You're going to use it?" he asks excitedly.

I shrug and nod. "If there still *is* an exhibit."

"What are you talking about?"

I keep my eyes on the painting, afraid to look up and see the disappointment in Sebastian's eyes. "When Drew finds out about Sam—rather, when *Janice* finds out"—I let out a remorseful sigh—"it might be the end of the exhibit. You should probably be prepared for that."

"Then maybe you should wait until *after* the exhibit to tell Drew."

I look up at him, but I can tell he's not joking when I see

the serious expression on his face. "Sebastian, it's not until next week. I can't keep this from him that long."

"It's *only* a week. You've been working for this all year, Lucy. *We've* been working for this all year. How can you throw it away when we're this close? How can you throw away your chance to sell in New York?"

I chew the corner of my mouth. "New York isn't a guarantee."

"It will be when they see this," he says, staring at the painting.

I look at it again and think of everything we've done to prepare for the exhibit. All the late nights and months of planning. I think of New York and the possibility that it holds. My whole career hangs in the balance. I swallow down the lump in my throat and clench my fists. "Okay. I'll wait until after the exhibit. It's only a week," I tell myself. I may die of guilt, but I can wait a week to break Drew's heart. *It's not that long.*

Sebastian keeps his eyes on the painting and lets out a contented sigh. "It's going to steal the show. I wouldn't be surprised if you had an offer for fifteen thousand. Maybe more."

I pull my eyebrows together. "I'm displaying it, but it's not for sale, Bas."

"Pity. Well, it will definitely get you some attention if Sam shows up."

"Who said anything about Sam coming?"

"Lucy, you can't have a painting of him in the show and then not expect him to be there."

I hadn't thought that far. "If Sam comes to the exhibit, so will the media."

"Isn't that what we want?"

"I want people to take notice of my work, but that kind of attention is on a whole other level. And how will I explain it to Drew?"

He narrows his eyes. "Let's just worry about getting through dinner first."

My throat tightens at the thought of having Sam over for dinner, which is inevitable if I wait until after the exhibit to tell Drew. "Why the hell would Sam even want to come to dinner?" I huff. "Is he insane?"

Bas looks at me like I'm the crazy one. "He wants to size up his competition. He's a man. It's what we do."

"Well, I'd like to avoid it, but Janice isn't going to forget about it, is she?"

"Nope."

I roll my eyes and huff again. "Neither will Sam."

"You have two options. Tell Drew about Sam now and kiss your career goodbye. Or suck it up and have dinner with your fiancé and your soulmate, who fascinatingly aren't the same person."

I narrow my eyes at him. "That's not funny."

He pulls his mouth to the side and pinches his fingers together. "Just a little bit."

Chapter 13

Lucy

"Hello?" Sam's low, sultry voice answers the phone.

"Hey."

"Lucy?"

I'm quiet for a second. I've been fighting the urge to call him for the last twenty-four hours since he left me at the studio to sort out the ambiguous details of our future. But I couldn't wait any longer. I needed to hear his voice. "Yeah, it's me."

"Hang on a second." He says something to someone in the background, but it's muffled. "Hey," he answers again, his voice softer now.

"Is it a bad time?"

"No, I was in a meeting, but I stepped out."

"I'm sorry, I can call you later."

"It's okay. I can talk."

I'm quiet again.

"Are you okay?"

"Yeah, I'm okay."

"I'm glad you called. I thought I was going to have to use my resources to find your number." I hear the smile in his voice.

"Well, you have it now, so that won't be necessary."

"Good, because I can't go a whole day without hearing your voice."

"Sam—"

"I know, you need time. I'm trying to give it to you. But I don't want to wait for you, Lucy."

"I know."

"Where are you? I want to see you."

A mix of excitement and reluctance flashes hot across my skin. "Um, right now? I'm at home, but—"

"I'll be done here in an hour. I'll come get you."

"You want to come here? To my house? No."

He laughs quietly. "Okay, then meet me somewhere."

I close my eyes and shake my head. I doubt we can meet in public without him being noticed. But I need to see him too. I have to explain my decision to wait until after the exhibit to tell Drew. "I can come by your apartment later."

"Okay." I hear the satisfaction in his voice.

"Will you be home this afternoon?"

"I'll be there." I hear someone in the background. "Lucy, I have to go."

"Yeah, of course, your meeting. I'll see you later."

"Okay."

"Okay," I say, trying to hide the angst in my voice. "Bye."
I hang up, but my phone buzzes in my hand, startling me.

Janice.

I take a deep breath. "Hi, Janice."

"So, have you worked out the details with Drew yet?"

"The details?" My pulse races at the mention of his name.

"For dinner on Saturday."

"Oh, um, no. I haven't spoken to him about it yet." Because I'm hoping there won't be a dinner. "He's been really busy this trip."

"Well, I hope Saturday at eight is okay for everyone. I had Sebastian go ahead and add it to your calendar."

"I'll mention it to Drew when I talk to him." Which at the current rate will be when he gets home tomorrow. He's barely had time to respond to my text messages.

"Okay, well, be sure to tell Sam."

"I will."

"Saturday at eight."

"Got it."

"Oh, and darling, have you given any more thought to that gorgeous dress?"

"The dress. Right. I, um, I think that maybe I should see a few more before I commit." My face screws up with guilt, because I have no intention of trying on any more dresses.

"Well, okay. I'll see what else I can come up with."

I close my eyes and shake my head. I don't know who I'm more afraid of hurting. Drew or Janice.

"Bye, darling."

"Bye, Janice."

I slide my phone across the kitchen counter. I can't imagine having Sam here for dinner. I walk into the living room and scan the framed pictures on the shelves next to the fireplace that showcase the life I built without Sam. I think about what Sebastian said—how hard this must be for him—and I begin to take them down, one by one, stacking them in my hands.

I step back and eye the space. *Maybe Drew won't notice.* I shake my head and put them all back.

* * *

I pull into spot 322, surprised that the parking garage guard didn't ask for my ID. He just smiled at me and raised the gate to let me in. I park and get out, passing Sam's shiny black car on my way to the stairs that I take to the first floor.

When I walk into the lobby I'm greeted by the guard at the front desk. "Miss Bennett, it's good to see you again," he says, smiling at me.

I camouflage my apprehension with a smile. "Just Lucy."

"Okay, Miss Lucy. Is he expecting you?"

"Yes, I believe so."

"I'll let him know you're on your way up."

"Okay." I make my way across the lobby to the bank of elevators, my heels tapping on the marble floor as I go. I try to look at my reflection in the doors, but all I can see is a shadowy cast of black, my clothing color of choice this week, from my skinny-heeled zip-up booties to my moto leggings to my leather jacket. I did throw on a gray scarf to hide behind.

The elevator doors open and I step inside, followed by a

woman I wasn't aware was behind me. She presses the button
for the sixteenth floor, and I shrink under her watchful stare
as I press the button for the penthouse. Everyone in the building must know it's Sam's apartment.

She glances at my face and I feel my cheeks flame, but I
try to hide it with a polite smile. She gives me a small smile
in return, tucks her short brown hair behind her ear, and
pulls out her phone. She taps a quick message with her shiny
red fingernails and then presses her glossy lips together and
stares straight ahead. When her phone buzzes, she looks at the
screen and smiles, and it takes everything in me not to yank it
out of her hand to see what she wrote. She drops it back into
her expensive-looking purse, and I clutch mine tighter.

The doors open to the sixteenth floor and she glances at me
again with a patronizing look. "Have fun up there," she says
as she steps off the elevator, and I feel the blood drain from
my face.

She knows Sam.

The way she was looking at me, like I was pathetic... *He
must have girls up there all the time.* I can't help but wonder if
she has slept with him. The troubling thought fills me with
doubt quicker than it entered my mind. Here I am about to
give up my entire life, and for what? So I can become the subject of dirty looks and patronizing comments?

When the doors open to Sam's foyer, he's standing outside
his door waiting for me, wearing what looks like the remnants of an impeccably tailored suit, giving me his sexiest
smile. His collar is casually unbuttoned and his sleeves are
rolled up, but his belted pants and shoes are nothing less than

Armani perfection. My heart should be soaring, but right now I can't seem to pick it up off the floor.

He crinkles his eyes. "Hi."

I pry my tongue off the roof of my dry mouth. "Hi," I say, forcing a smile.

His eyes follow me as I walk inside before him. He catches my wrist and pulls me back, spinning me around to face him. "You look..." He presses his lips together. "I like this." He grins at my outfit and reaches for my hand. "You are so unbelievably sexy."

"That's not really what I was going for," I say, feeling him suck the oxygen out of the space between us. I grip his hand to keep my balance.

"Well, what were you going for then?"

"Concealment."

"Who are you trying to hide from?"

"You."

"You can't hide from me, Lamb." He pulls me close and looks into my eyes. "I see you." He nudges my nose with his, and I breathe in his warm scent.

No. "Stop." I push against his chest and scurry backward on my skinny heels, until I'm several feet away from him. "We can't." I swallow and shake my head. "I can't. We need to talk."

He scrapes his teeth over his bottom lip and rubs the back of his neck. Then he flashes his one-of-a-kind eyes at me. "Lamb."

No. I will not be seduced by his beautiful eyes, or his full lips, or the dimples in his flushed cheeks. And I will not fall into his arms every time he calls me *Lamb*. I march across his apartment to the kitchen and grab a bottle of water from the fridge. I twist the cap off and take a sip.

He follows me to within a foot of where I'm standing.

"No." I hold my hand up. "Stay there."

He raises his eyebrows at me.

"I need you to stay there...please." I take another sip of water.

He leans against the counter and watches me. "Do you mind telling me why?"

I put the bottle down and take off my scarf, which is now suffocating me. I know that I'm on the verge of creating a very big crack in the ice beneath my feet, but I need him to know. "Sam, what we did was...wrong."

He stares at me blankly, and I get absolutely no read on his thoughts, which is unnerving. "We kissed," he says, like it's no big deal, and I wonder if to him, it isn't. Considering his track record with women, it's probably a weekly occurrence. His eyes pierce mine, pulling me from my precarious thoughts, and his face turns to stone. "There was nothing *wrong* about it."

I hurt him. I chew the corner of my mouth. "You're right. It wasn't wrong. But that doesn't make it right, Sam. I'm still with Drew. And until I'm not, I can't go around kissing you."

"So what are you saying?"

"I'm saying that I want to tell Drew, before we...make out again."

He laughs softly, but I don't see an ounce of amusement on his face. "So then tell him."

I huff and shake my head, because he has no idea how hard it's going to be, no matter when I choose to do it. "You act like it's so simple."

"It is."

"Well, Drew might not think so," I say flatly.

His face falls again, but I won't apologize for caring about Drew's feelings. The thought of hurting him is crushing. My heart pounds in my chest for him. "I realize you don't care about that, but I do."

"So take your time, then."

My heart begins to beat faster, now out of anger. "You have *no* idea how hard this is for me, Sam."

"I don't know hard it is?" he asks with wide, disbelieving eyes. "Damn, Lucy. This isn't just about you."

I swallow down my anger and exhale a remorseful breath. "I know." I shake my head and give him an apologetic look. "I know it isn't. I'm sorry." I reach for his hand. "I'm going to tell him soon. After the exhibit next week."

He pulls his eyebrows together and asks, "Why then? Why wait until after the exhibit? Why not just do it now?"

"Because if I tell him beforehand, the exhibit might not happen. And, while I'm willing to give up my life with Drew to be with you, I can't give up my career." I give a halfhearted smile.

Before he can say anything, his phone buzzes on the counter and a green text bubble lights up his screen. He reaches for it and reads the message and starts swiping his thumb across the screen.

"Everything okay?"

He doesn't answer.

"Sam, what are you doing?"

"Checking Twitter."

I scrunch my face up. "You tweet?" I ask, trying not to laugh. I know he has an account, I've followed it for...a while. But the tweets are usually about his matches and various events. I can't envision Sam sharing deep thoughts about his morning coffee with the world, or caring about anyone else's.

"No. My manager handles my social media accounts."

"Well then, what are you doing?"

He pulls his hand to his face and rubs it over his jaw and chin. Then he turns the phone around and shows me the screen.

Who's the mystery girl in @samcolefights life?...Is boxing's most eligible bachelor @samcolefights off the market?...Breaking News: @samcolefights spotted with a mystery blonde.

I think I might actually throw up. "Oh," I say, trying to keep my voice even.

He calls someone and holds the phone to his ear. "Fix it. Now...I don't care, just fix it...Tell me when it's done." He ends the call and drops his elbows onto the counter.

"The woman in the elevator."

"What woman?"

"There was this woman in the elevator on my way up." All the thoughts she evoked before come storming back into my mind, making my pulse race. She obviously knows him. I'm guessing *intimately*. Jealousy fills my chest and oozes from the tips of my fingers, turning my fingernails into claws. "She looked me up and down and then told me to have fun up here, like I'm some kind of groupie," I say agitated, unable to hide my disdain.

"What did she look like?"

I cross my arms. *Need to sort through the catalogue?* "She had short brown hair. A lot of makeup. And an arrogant smirk on her face." I shake my head. "I guess you probably have women up here a lot."

"No, not really."

"I mean, I get it. Women probably throw themselves at you all the time. I just never really thought you'd be the kind of guy who parades them in and out of your bed like some kind of wannabe rock star." I hear the unflattering jealousy in my voice, but I don't care. I am jealous. I resent each and every woman who has ever captured his attention.

"You know that's not me."

"No, actually, I don't. What I know is that I see you photographed with a different woman every day of the week."

He raises an eyebrow and smirks. "I don't even have time for that to be possible."

I huff loudly and roll my eyes.

He stands directly in front of me and says firmly, "You're right, there are women who would probably love to be 'paraded' up here, to use your word. But not because they like me, or even know me. I figured that out pretty quickly," he says, shaking his head. "I don't bring strangers into my home, Lucy. So to answer your assumption...no, I don't have women up here a lot."

I pull in a slow breath and try to lasso the untamed emotion that broke through the fence and ran wild inside me.

"The woman you saw in the elevator...her name is Molly. She lives in this building. She's a friend. She was probably just wondering who you are."

Relief takes over and tugs hard on the reins. "She texted something to someone," I say, finding my way back to my original point. "I think it was about me."

He shakes his head and grumbles, "Molly."

"You think she's the reason for all those tweets?"

He shrugs and lets out a sigh. "That's how it usually works. Someone just has to plant the seed and the media goes nuts. Everyone wants the story and they want it first. But Molly wouldn't do something like that."

I'm a story? "Wow," I say, astonished. "I can't believe how cheap I feel." I take a sip of my water. "I'll be right back." I escape the kitchen to the nearest bathroom, where I sit on the lid of the toilet with my face in my hands.

"Lucy?" Sam knocks on the door, but I don't answer. "Lucy, the media makes up stories all the time. It's fine."

I stand up and open the door. "How? How is any of this fine? If they find out who I am...that I'm engaged! Well, there goes my career. How do you feel about Iceland? Is there boxing there? Because that's where I'm going to have to move after my reputation gets flushed down the toilet."

He grabs my hand and drags me back to the kitchen. He pulls a stool out from the island for me. "Sit down. I'm going to make you some tea."

"You know how to make tea?" I ask, smiling involuntarily.

"I'm not an invalid. I just don't cook."

"Tea would actually be perfect right now."

I take a deep breath and shrug out of my jacket while he fills a teakettle with water.

He sets it on the range and turns the gas on under it. "I'm sorry about Molly, but you really shouldn't worry. My manager will take care of it."

"What am I supposed to say if I see her again?"

"That she'd be right to stay on your good side, because you're from Brighton Park." He grins and winks.

"I try so hard to pretend that I'm not, then one condescending comment brings it all out." I drop my head and laugh softly. "Sorry about that. My reaction was less than ladylike."

He looks at me and smiles. "I loved your reaction. You don't have to pretend with me."

"Are you saying that I'm not a lady?" I laugh quietly.

He walks around the island and spins me around on the stool. He leans over me and pushes me back against the counter. "You are every bit a lady. And you are... breathtakingly sophisticated. But you'll always have a little of the Park in you. You can't polish that away." He grins and shows me his dimples. "It's part of you. And it's part of me. It's what makes us fight so hard for what we want." The whistle of the teakettle screams across the kitchen, demanding his attention, and he stands up straight, leaving me breathless and biting my smiling lip.

"Still, I'm sorry that I jumped to conclusions about your love life."

"The only love life I've ever had is you." He drops two tea bags into a couple of mugs. "Sugar?"

"Yes, please." I tuck my hair behind my ear. "I didn't like the way she looked at me."

"Molly looks at everyone that way." He hands me a mug and sits on the stool beside me.

"She's very pretty."

"Yes," he says impassively.

I sip my tea and consider asking a question I don't really want the answer to. But I have to know. "Have you two..."

"Yes," he says, just as nonchalantly as before.

I presumed the answer was yes, but hearing him say it so freely is shocking. I blink at him and nod, unable to find any words.

"She's a friend," he reiterates, as if that somehow makes it better.

"Do you sleep with all your friends? Or just her?" I ask, unable to hide the jealousy that's bubbled back up to the surface.

He creases his eyebrows and shakes his head. "She's someone I talk to."

I sip the warm peppermint tea in my mug. "Do you ever talk to her about me?"

"Sometimes."

I take another sip and accept the fact that Sam has an intimate relationship with the woman who just tweeted about me. "Do you *talk* to her a lot?"

His blank stare tells me that he does.

"When was the last time?" I ask, like some sort of masochist. "I'm just curious."

"Lucy, why are you doing this?"

"I just want to know."

He anchors his hands around his mug and looks at me. "Last week."

I can't hide the shock on my face. "Last week? Before or after I poured my heart out on your couch?"

"After."

"It was rhetorical," I whisper with what little air is left in my lungs.

"Lucy, you showed up out of the blue, ripped my heart out, shoved it in your pocket, and drove home to your fiancé. I didn't know if I'd ever see you again, and I was a little bit fucked up about it. So yes, I called Molly. Because unlike you, I have no one else."

I let out a slow breath and close my eyes, feeling like the world's biggest hypocrite. "I know. I'm sorry. I don't have any right—"

"You have every right." He drops his hands to his lap and looks at me. "You have every right. And I understand why that would upset you. But believe me when I tell you, I would trade every minute I've spent with Molly for just one fraction of a second with you."

I nod softly, feeling my emotions settle, but I can't shake the anxious feeling bubbling inside me. I chew the corner of my mouth and consider what I'm about to say. "Sam . . . I don't know if I'm ready for this."

"For what?"

"For women, or anyone for that matter, to look at me like I'm the scum of the earth just because I'm with you."

"You're not with me," he says, taking a sip from his mug.

I purse my lips and say seriously, "My life is easy, Sam. It's so incredibly different from where we grew up. I come and go as I please and people are nice to me. They actually think that I'm sophisticated, even if it is just a show. They treat me like I am. They respect me."

"I respect you."

"I know that you respect me, but I'm talking about every-one else. I just don't know if I'm ready to become a newsflash. I want people to take me seriously. I want to see my name on the cover of the *New Yorker* or *ARTnews* magazine, not *Us Weekly*."

"So what are you saying? You'd rather marry Drew so you can have a quiet life in the suburbs? All because of a stupid tweet?"

"It's not just that. It's everything that it represents. It's a world I'm not ready for." I close my eyes and exhale a breath that's laced with worry and uncertainty.

"It's a cop-out. You're just scared."

I open my eyes and he holds my stare.

"You're scared because you know that it's going be hard and you're going to have to say things to people that aren't easy to say."

I push my mug of tea away and stand up.

"Do you think it was easy for me to come see you at your studio after the fight in New York?"

"Sam," I whimper, feeling overwhelmed, because he's the one person I can't hide from.

He stands up and grabs my wrist. "Do you think it was

easy for me to walk away after we kissed, knowing you were going to back to him? Do you think it's easy for me to stand here now, wondering if you're really going to leave him or not? Because the thought of losing you again is fucking terrifying."

A sob bubbles out of me.

"I can't... I can't lose you again, Lamb." He lets go of my hand. "I don't know how many more rounds I have left in me."

I shake my head and wrap myself around him. "That's not going to happen."

He closes his arms around me, but he doesn't pull me against him. "You're starting to make me wonder."

I look up at his wary eyes and say resolutely, "I love you."

"Then be with me."

I press my cheek to his shirt. "Soon... I promise. The exhibit is only a week away."

His chest rises and falls against my cheek, but he doesn't say anything.

"It's important, Sam. The show might be my only chance of getting to sell in New York. I need it to go well. If I tell Drew beforehand, he or Janice could pull the proverbial plug. And I've worked too hard to let that happen. I know you don't want that to happen."

He unwraps my arms from around him and sits back down on his stool.

"This is all so much," I say, sitting down next to him. "I feel incredibly selfish. And you're right, I am scared. I've never been more scared in my life. I'm scared of what to tell

Drew, I'm scared of what to tell his mother, I'm scared of what they'll think of me. I'm scared that I'll be shunned by a community I've only just earned my place in. And I *am* scared that I'm going to be some kind of joke in the media. But most of all, I'm scared of hurting you." I place my hand on his arm and he closes his eyes.

"I've waited for you this long, Lucy. I can wait a few more days." He opens his unguarded eyes and they consume mine. "I'd wait for you forever."

His vulnerable words wrap around my heart, squeezing it so tight I can barely breathe. There's nothing I want more than to be with him, from this second on, until my last second on earth. I want to throw caution to the wind with abandon and find an island somewhere we can live on, just the two of us, for the rest of our lives. But that's a fantasy. Real life is harder and it's full of consequences that I have to face.

"You won't have to," I say tentatively. "Just one more week, that's all I need." One week isn't enough time to carefully shatter Drew's heart, but it's a deadline I can hold myself to. Maybe by then I will have figured out a way to process all of this and gather the courage I'm going to need to make the most seismic decision of my life.

"And when the exhibit is over, you'll be mine?"

I smile softly and nod. "Yes, officially."

He reaches for my hand and pulls me to my feet, so that I'm standing between his knees and directly in front his face. He wraps his hand around my hip and then rubs it across the small of my back. "What am I supposed to do with myself until then?"

"Well, first you're going to focus on getting better, so this can come off," I say, touching his cast. "And you're going to concentrate on your next match, so you can win," I say softly against his ear, "because you're a champion, and that's what champions do."

He exhales heavily through his nostrils, and I feel it on my cheek.

"And you're going to take care of whatever you need to take care of, so that we can start our life together." I press my lips together to fight the sudden onslaught of emotion. Overwhelming as it may be, the thought of starting a new life with Sam is every dream I've ever had. And now I'm standing on the verge of it being reality.

"I know you're scared right now, Lamb. But I promise that I will do everything I can to give you the life we always wanted." He smiles and shows me his dimples. "Forget this apartment. I'll buy you a house. The biggest one I can find."

I laugh softly and shake my head. "I'd live with you in a box."

"And I'll make you pancakes every morning," he says, just like he promised when we were kids.

"With bacon?" I add, remembering how much he loves it.

He smiles and nods. "And you can paint all the time. I'll build you a studio right inside our house."

I smile and think of the other dream we shared growing up. "And we'll have a family?" I couldn't imagine having kids with Drew, but I realize now it's because I wanted them with Sam. A strange rush of desire surges through me like a tsunami, and I'm shaken by the fierce need to have a family with him. Thoughts of him holding our baby girl, or boy, in the early morning light swirl through my head.

He nods and looks into my eyes, and I wonder if he's having the same vision. "Yeah," he says huskily.

I hold his face in my hands and whisper, "Even if none of that ever happens, I'll still love you." As I say it, I feel a pinch in my stomach. I want it all, so badly, but I can't shake the feeling of doubt that we'll never actually have it.

"It will happen," he says certainly.

I drop my hands and look away.

"Why don't you have faith in me?" he asks.

"I do have faith in you," I say firmly, looking up at him again.

"Good. Because I have faith in you." He pulls me closer, making me feel weak and strong at the same time. "If that's the life we want, that's the life we'll have. We're in control of that now. You and me. But it won't be easy and I can't do it alone." He wraps his hand behind my neck and rubs his thumb over my jaw. "Are you with me?" He gazes at me with pleading eyes, and all of my uncertainty and doubt falls away.

I am *so* with him. I don't care if it does shake the universe; I'll do it a hundred times for him. "I'm with you," I whisper, but before I can say anything more, his lips cover mine.

He stands up and pushes me against the counter, and kisses me passionately, pushing and pulling my lips with his and scraping them softly between his teeth.

Forgetting my virtuous resolve, I reach for his face and wind my hands into his hair, moaning quietly as he satisfies a place in my soul he carved out so very long ago. He lifts me up onto the cool marble counter and tugs my hips forward so that my thighs are pressed firmly against him as he rocks his hips up with a husky groan, gifting me with a morsel of pleasure when I feel him through his perfectly tailored pants.

"Sam," I mumble against his lips, but before I have to say anything else, he pulls away from me.

"I'm sorry," he pants.

I wait for the oxygen to return to my brain. "It's okay."

He unwraps my legs from around him and shakes his head. "No, it's not." He stands in front of me, his shoulders rising and falling with ragged breaths, and says, "I don't want to be something you feel guilty about and regret later."

"Sam." I reach for his shirt and pull him close to me again. "I want you. But please don't do that again until after the exhibit. Because I might not be able to stop the next time. And I *would* regret not waiting."

He drops his head and nods once, then he looks up at me with a grin. "One week. And then I want you every way I can have you. Without strings. Without doubt. Without hesitation."

"One week," I say with anticipation, "and then, the rest of our lives."

"It can't come soon enough."

Chapter 14

Lucy

"Lucy?" Drew calls from the kitchen. He walks into the living room, and I look up at him from my place on the couch. He looks exactly the same as he did when he left, but I feel like a completely different person.

"Hey," I say, fighting every bone in my body that's telling me to get up and tell him about Sam. "How was your flight?"

"It was good." He sits down on the couch by my feet and begins rubbing them through my socks.

"That's good." I force a weak smile and turn my eyes back to the TV, because it hurts too much to look at him.

"Everything okay?"

No. It's not okay. And I don't know how I'm going to keep pretending like it is. I tuck my feet under my legs and sit up straight. "Besides the fact that you were too busy to answer my phone calls while you were gone," I say coolly. Because the truth is, if he had answered my call after I kissed Sam, I would have already told him about it, and I wouldn't have to spend the next week lying in wait to break his heart. But then the guilt starts gnawing at me for even thinking that way. None of this is Drew's fault.

"What?"

I pause the TV and look at him. "It's just, I called you a lot and you barely had time to text me back."

He pulls his eyebrows together and sits up straight. "Because I was at the site, dealing with contractors all day, every day. And when I wasn't doing that, I was with the design team. And when I wasn't doing either of those things, I was sleeping, because the stress of it all is exhausting. I'm sorry that I didn't stop to check in on you. I just didn't realize you needed that level of attention."

I feel my face screw up at his backhanded apology. But before I get pulled into a fight, I remind myself that he shouldn't be apologizing at all.

"That didn't come out right. It's just, you know why I'm doing this...why I'm working so hard." He reaches for my face and rubs my cheek. "For us."

I turn off the TV and stand up. "It's okay. I knew what I was getting into."

"What is that supposed to mean?" He stands up and crosses his arms over his chest.

"Nothing. I'm just tired. I want to go to bed."

"What is it that you want me to do, Lucy? Stop working? Close my restaurants? Stay here and hang out with you all day?"

"No, of course not."

"Then what? You want me to call more? Text you ten times a day?"

"No." I shake my head. "That's not what I want."

"Then what do you want?"

I want *Sam*. "I just...want to go to bed."

"Lucy."

"Honestly. I'm just really tired. I'm not even mad. I'm sorry I gave you a hard time." I begin making my way up the stairs, but he follows me.

"You're really not going to talk to me about this? I mean, the last time we fought about it, you...you broke up with me."

I ignore the way my heart is pounding in my chest and say, "There's nothing to talk about. Really. I'm fine." I go into the bathroom and shut the door behind me, squeezing my eyes shut once I'm alone, but Drew stands on the other side of it.

"You don't seem fine."

"I am," I lie.

"You aren't acting like it."

I open the door, agitated that he won't let me be alone with my misery. "You know what, I'm not fine. I'm annoyed at your mother, as a matter of fact." As soon as I say it, I realize I've opened a whole new can of worms.

He pulls his head back warily. "What did my mother do?" he asks defensively.

"Nothing. She's just been a little overbearing with the wedding plans lately."

"She's just excited, that's all."

"I know," I say, nodding over the waves of guilt that are sloshing around inside me.

"Wouldn't hurt for you to show a little more enthusiasm about the big day."

"I thought we agreed that we didn't need to rush into it."

"Rush into it? You make it sound like some kind of risky business deal."

"You know that's not what I meant."

He narrows his eyes. "You're not getting cold feet, are you?"

"No." I pull my eyebrows together and shake my head, ignoring the frozen blocks of ice around my feet. "I just wish Janice was a little *less* excited, that's all."

"Okay, well, I'll talk to her."

"She also planned an impromptu dinner for us tomorrow night, which we're hosting, and you're supposed to cook."

He raises his eyebrows, and the corners of his mouth turn down. "Okay, so...I cook for people all the time." He shrugs. "What's the big deal?"

"The big deal is, she invited an old friend of mine, and I don't really feel comfortable having him over for dinner."

"Him?"

"Yes, *him*. Am I not allowed to have male friends?"

"Sure you are. It's just that you've never mentioned any of your old friends before, and the first one who shows up is a guy. Was he a boyfriend?"

"Yes," I admit.

"What's his name?"

"Sam."

"Is he from Brighton Park too?"

"Yes," I say with a defensive edge to my voice I didn't intend to have.

"And my mother invited him here, to our house?"

I slant my eyes at his insinuation.

"I understand why you're not comfortable with it."

I feel my blood run hot through my veins. "He's not some kind of thug, Drew."

"Well, what does he do?"

"He's a boxer."

He grins. "That's not a job. What does he really do, to earn a living?"

"He's a professional boxer. Maybe you've heard of him. His last name is Cole," I say, exasperated. "I hear he makes a pretty good living."

He holds his head back and squints. "Sam Cole," he says skeptically.

I raise my eyebrows and nod.

"Very funny. Who is he?"

"He's Sam Cole."

He blinks at me for several seconds. "You're telling me that you not only know Sam Cole, but he used to be your boyfriend?"

I raise my eyebrows and nod again.

"What the fuck, Lucy?" He puts his hands on his hips and starts pacing around the bathroom. He walks into the bedroom and paces a few more times with a determined look on his face.

"What is this reaction?" I ask, dismayed, not that I have any right to be.

"Are you serious?" He stops and shakes his head. "All this time...every match you've watched, every match you've made me watch with you, going to New York, for Christ's sake...and you didn't think to tell me? Don't you think that's a little strange?"

I try to lasso my heart, which is running wild inside my chest. If he only knew how many times I wanted to tell him about Sam. How many times I tried to tell him. I should have done it a long time ago. But if I had, who knows if I would have gone to New York to watch Sam fight. And if I didn't, I might not have ever seen him again.

"I didn't tell you because I thought you'd freak out. Clearly I was right."

"Well, Jesus, Lucy, that's kind of a big deal."

"Why? It's not like he's a Kardashian or something. He's from Brighton Park, remember?"

"Yeah, didn't he do time for dealing drugs or something?"

"That was a long time ago," I say over the tight feeling in my chest, "and he didn't do it. He was set up."

He gives me a dubious look that sparks my defenses and plays off the guilt attached to those words.

"He was," I say adamantly. "Sam didn't do drugs."

"And how exactly did my mother meet him?"

"He came by the studio earlier this week while she was there."

"So he just stopped by, out of the blue?" he asks suspiciously.

"Yes," I say, telling him the truth. I had no idea he was going to show up that day. "He heard about the exhibit and wanted to come say hi." Just not necessarily in that order. I shrug, hoping to slide the guilt off my shoulders. It doesn't work.

"Does he want to buy some artwork or something?"

"He mentioned coming to the show, so hopefully." That's a complete and utter lie. *I'm a liar.* I've just slipped on the slope of deceit. *It's for his own good,* I tell myself.

His or *yours,* my conscience argues.

Sebastian's, we both agree.

"Huh. Well, I can't say I've met too many friends from your past. Or too many famous boxers."

"Well, there's no need to start now. What you need to do is call your mother and tell her that this dinner is a bad idea."

"What? No way." He shakes his head and smirks. "I want to meet this guy."

"Oh, God. Seriously, Drew?"

He pulls his phone out of his pocket.

"Do not call your mom," I order.

"Hey, Momma," he says, grinning at me.

"Drew," I grumble through clenched teeth.

"Yeah, Lucy just told me about it. That sounds great... She's excited too." He widens his eyes at me. "Sure, I can make my signature dish... Yes, I'm sure he eats meat." He shrugs at me, but I don't respond. "Okay, see you tomorrow at eight... Love you too." He hangs up and grins.

"I'm glad you find so much humor at my expense."

He smiles and pulls me into his arms, but it doesn't comfort me at all. It only exacerbates everything that's wrong with this situation. "You're just so cute when you're flustered."

I push him away and he laughs. I march into my closet and grab my Chuck Taylors.

"Where are you going?"

"To paint."

"I thought you were tired."

"I was. But now I'm *flustered*, so I'm going to my studio to paint. I'll be home in a couple of hours."

He laughs again and falls onto the bed. "Don't stay too late."

* * *

I press the Bluetooth button on my phone and it rings through my speakers.

Once.

Twice.

Three times.

No answer. Disappointment settles over me, making me feel anxious. I was hoping to talk to Sam and persuade him to skip this absurd dinner.

I pull onto the dimly lit highway, finding my place in the center lane between the bright headlights of the car behind me and glowing red taillights of the one in front of me. Together we travel down the highway toward our destinations.

Fifteen minutes later, my phone rings through my speakers, startling me.

I glance at the dash. *Sam.*

"Hi," I answer.

"Hey. Sorry, I was in the shower when you called earlier."

I smile and raise an eyebrow thinking of him naked and wet. "I thought maybe you were asleep. I know it's late."

"You can call me anytime. If I'm asleep, I'll answer."

I nod but don't say anything.

"Is everything okay?"

"Yeah, everything's fine." I tap my thumb against my steering wheel. "Drew came home tonight."

He's silent for a second.

"Lucy, where are you?"

"I'm driving."

"Where?"

"I'm on the highway. I'm on my way to my studio."

"By yourself?"

"Yeah."

"It's almost midnight."

"I know, but I want to paint."

"Do you do that a lot?"

"Paint? Yes, quite often," I tease.

"Do you go to the studio at night?"

"Sometimes. Why?"

"Because it's not safe."

I laugh quietly. *Always the protector.* "Sam, I assure you, it's perfectly safe."

"You shouldn't be coming downtown at night by yourself."

"You live downtown."

"I live in a highly secured building."

"My studio is secure," I say, creasing my eyebrows. "I have an alarm." I can't help but feel a little uneasy now.

I hear a low rumble in the background. "What are you doing?"

"He was out of town. Where?" he asks, ignoring my question.

"Drew was in Philadelphia."

"Were you home alone all week?"

I press my lips together over a smile. "Yes. He travels all the time. I'm home alone more often than not. But I assure you, I'm quite capable of taking care of myself. I'm pretty independent," I say confidently.

"Do you have a house alarm?"

"Yes. And my neighborhood is gated. Why the sudden concern for my safety?"

"It's not sudden. I'm always concerned for your safety."

I smile. "Well, rest assured, I've reached my exit and I'm safely leaving the highway. I should arrive at my studio in"— I glance at my GPS—"six and half minutes."

"How long are you going to be there?"

"I don't know, an hour or so. I'll stop painting when I get tired."

"It'll be two a.m. when you leave. That's not safe, Lucy," he says firmly.

"Sam, my studio is on a quiet street in a good part of downtown, minutes from where you live, I might add. It's not like it's in Brighton Park," I point out, but he doesn't respond.

After a couple more minutes of trying to convince Sam of my welfare, I pull up to the curb in front of my studio. "You should know that I've arrived safely at my destination," I say assuredly, putting my car in park. I hold my phone to my ear while I unbuckle and open my door, but I freeze when a shiny black car roars up behind me.

"I see that."

I squint to see through the dark tinted windows. "Sam, is that you?"

Sam steps out of the car wearing black joggers and sneakers and a gray hoodie that's pulled up over his head. He holds his phone to his ear. "Yeah, it's me."

"What are you doing?"

He drops his phone into his pocket and walks over to me.

"Look, I'm fine. See"—I glance around the empty urban street that my studio is on—"it's safe."

He pulls his eyebrows together and reaches for my face. "He has no idea how precious you are."

"Sam, I'm fine," I say again softly. I glance around nervously, not because I'm afraid, but because I don't want anyone to see us together. Twitter is a far scarier place than downtown after dark. "Let's go inside."

He follows me inside and watches me turn off the alarm. He locks the door behind us, and I set the alarm again.

"Safe enough for you?" I smirk.

He follows me to the back of the studio.

"Lucy—"

"I know, the wolves..."

"You have no idea what kind of monsters are out there."

I turn around and look at him, but my smile disappears when I see the look on his face.

"There are terrible people out there who will do unthinkable things." His face is tortured by whatever thoughts are running through his mind. "I know, because I lived with them for three years. I was surrounded by them. Gates and alarms won't stop them."

"Sam." I reach for his sweatshirt and pull him close to me, and wrap my arms around him. I shudder thinking of what he saw and heard in prison.

"I will always worry about your safety."

I press my cheek his chest. "Okay. I'm sorry."

He hugs me tight. "He shouldn't be leaving you alone all the time."

I let go of him and walk to the couch to sit down. "I don't need Drew to protect me. He's not really the type anyway."

He sits down on the opposite end of the couch. "Well, what type is he?"

"I don't know. The too-busy-to-worry-about-me type. He works a lot."

"Then why did you agree to marry him?"

"Because I thought his work ethic was admirable. And he made me feel worthy of a life I didn't think I deserved. He encouraged me to follow my dreams and helped me turn my passion into a career," I say, glancing around the studio.

He rubs his hand over his mouth and jaw. "Sounds like the perfect guy."

"He is...on paper." I shrug. "But I've been trying to force a puzzle piece for a long time. I realize now that it will never fit, because he isn't right for me." I drop my head to the side. "Because he isn't you." I stare at him for a few seconds, deliberating over a truth I don't want to admit. But I finally do. "I still don't feel worthy of this life. Honestly, I'm not sure I ever will." I look around my beloved studio. "I've always felt like an imposter on borrowed time. None of this is really mine. And when I leave him, I lose it."

"Why do you think that?"

"Well, this studio was supposed to be a wedding present. One I only agreed to accept because I knew I could pay him back over time. But without a wedding, I doubt he'll still want to give it to me. And I wouldn't take it, even if he did."

"What if you bought it from him?"

I give him an impossible look. "I can't afford it. Even if the exhibit is a success, it would take years to earn back the money it costs."

"Then I'll buy it for you," he says, like it's no big deal, and I know that he would.

I smile at his sweet offer, but the thought of him spending his money on me so freely makes me uncomfortable. "What makes you think he would sell it to you?"

He moves closer to me on the couch, until our legs are touching. "Then I'll buy the whole damn building." He reaches for my hand and pulls me into his lap.

I lean against his chest and breathe in his clean scent. "You're so warm," I say, shoving my cold hands under his arms. He reaches between us and pulls the bottom of his over-sized hoodie up, capturing me in it, and tugging it down over my shoulders and arms so that I'm pressed against him inside of it.

I giggle and peek up at him and he kisses my forehead. I press my cheek to his neck. "How did you get here so quick?"

"I drove...fast," he admits.

"I know you want to protect me, but it won't do me any good if you kill yourself in the process."

"It was reckless, I know."

I wrap my arms around him inside his sweatshirt, and he shivers when I press my cold hands to his back. "Sorry," I say, but I don't move my hands. He's *so* damn warm.

He holds me tighter and rubs my back for a long silent minute.

"Was it awful?" I ask softly against his neck.

"What?"

"Prison," I say tentatively.

"Yes," he answers quietly without elaborating. I don't push him, but after a few silent seconds, he sighs and says, "Not all the time. Boxing was always good. And school helped keep my mind off it. But it's not a place I ever want to go back to."

"I'm so sorry."

"Don't be sorry, Lamb. You're what got me through it."

I close my eyes and try to hide from the guilt.

"You gave me a reason to go on. A reason to get into the boxing program. A reason to take classes. I could hear your voice in my head telling me to study." He laughs softly. "You always did know how to get me to."

"I'm sorry I didn't come," I whisper, remembering the betrayal I felt that kept me away and the subsequent sorrow that nearly destroyed me.

"There's nothing either of us can do to change the way things happened. Our paths went in different directions, but they were always meant to cross again."

I nuzzle his neck. "I really don't know how I would have made it through the rest of my life without you."

"Me neither."

I reluctantly shrug out of his sweatshirt and get up from the couch before my eager lips find their way to his. "We should probably thank Sebastian. He convinced me to go with him and Paul to New York to watch you fight Mario Sanchez."

He leans forward and rests his elbows on his knees. "You needed convincing, huh?"

I stand in front of him, looking down at his amused face. "It was one of the hardest things I've ever done. Because there was a chance that you'd see me and do one of two things: devastate my heart or devastate my life." I run my fingers through his hair, and he gazes up at me. "Thank you for not devastating my heart. My life will recover."

He reaches for my hand and rubs his thumb over the inside of my wrist. Then he stands up and looks into my eyes. "Thank you for not devastating mine."

My heart takes off in a wild sprint, and I have to bite my lip to keep from kissing him.

He drops his forehead to mine and exhales a warm breath against my cheek. "I thought you wanted to paint."

I press my burning lips together. "I did. But I guess I just needed to see you. I feel better now."

He holds his head back and looks at me. "Were you up-set?"

I realize I never explained *why* I wanted to paint in the middle of the night. "No, I was really more irritated than upset."

"About what?"

I let out a small sigh and roll my eyes, feeling my irritation return. "About this stupid dinner that Janice arranged." I cross my arms. "It's tomorrow at eight, by the way. Consider that your formal invitation."

He pushes his lips together over a smile, but his dimples give away his amusement.

"Why is everyone so gung ho about having this dinner? It's ridiculous."

He laughs at me.

"I think you two just want to size each other up."

"I guess that means you told him about me."

"Yes," I say softly. "I did. He's quite keen on meeting my pro boxer ex-boyfriend."

"Then I'd say your assumption is right." He grins.

"Sam, please, nothing good could come of it."

"I have to wait until after the exhibit to have you...fine, I'll wait. But I'm going to meet the guy you spent the last two years with."

My shoulders slump. I lost this battle before it even began. "Okay," I say, defeated.

"It's not only that."

I look up at him curiously.

"I'm really proud of you, Lucy."

"What?" My heart swells inside my chest.

"When I went to prison, you could have given up, but you didn't. You made something of yourself. *You* did that. No one else did it for you. I want to see the life you've built, even if it was with the wrong guy." He smirks.

I bob my head and smile softly. "Okay."

Chapter 15

Lucy

"Andrew, that smells amazing," Janice says, sipping her glass of prosecco. She leans against the kitchen counter, beaming with pride at her son's ability to make a perfect braised lamb shank. She's the picture of elegance in her ivory wrap top and matching ivory pants. She flips her shiny silver hair, showing off her sparkly diamond earrings.

I wonder if Sam even likes lamb. I giggle quietly to myself, just now realizing the irony of the dish.

"It really does smell fantastic," Paul says. "I think we need to come over for dinner more often." He smiles at Sebastian, who glances at me with apologetic eyes. As agreed, Bas hasn't yet filled him in on my predicament.

I busy myself wiping plates with a dish cloth and stacking them on the counter. I collect them in my hands. "You want to help me set the table?" I ask Sebastian, hoping for a few minutes alone with him.

"Sure." He grabs a pile of silverware off the counter and follows me.

"Anything I can do?" Janice asks, but I just smile and shake my head.

"I think we've got it."

"You sure?" Paul offers.

"Yep. Just enjoy yourselves."

Sebastian and I carry our tableware to the dining room and deposit it on the farmhouse table that Drew recently purchased.

"You have to admit, he's got great taste," Sebastian says, eyeing the table.

"Yes," I say, setting a plate in front of each tufted button chair.

He follows me around the table, carefully placing the silverware on either side of the plates. "Are you nervous?" he asks softly.

"Mm-hmm."

"Do you think Drew has any idea?"

I pause and look at him. "No," I say surely, which makes me feel even shittier about having Sam over for dinner. "What is wrong with me, Bas? How could I let this happen?"

"You didn't exactly have a lot of say in the matter."

"I don't know how I'm going to do this. I don't know how I'm going to be the person that Drew knows and the person that Sam knows at the same time."

"Just be yourself, Luc. It'll be fine."

"You don't understand. I'm different with Sam. Drew's going to notice. And if he doesn't, Sam's going to notice that I'm different around Drew."

"How are you different?"

"It's like my volume is set on low with Drew. But with Sam, it's all the way up. It always has been."

"So then find the remote and get somewhere in the middle."

I sigh and smile at Sebastian, not for his sage advice, but because he always gets my weird metaphors. "I need your help tonight, okay?"

"You don't have to ask. I've got you." He winks.

"You always do."

"Hey, who do you think will throw the first swing? My money is on Sam, broken hand and all."

"Bas! That's not funny."

"What's not funny?" Paul, asks, joining us. But before Sebastian can make up an answer, Paul holds one of Drew's goat-cheese-stuffed, bacon-wrapped figs to his mouth. "You have to try this."

Sebastian opens his mouth and closes it around the decadent appetizer. "Uh-muh-gawd," he mumbles as he chews. "Is it too late to change my bet?" he asks me.

I purse my lips and narrow my eyes.

"What bet?" Paul asks, but Bas just shakes his head and laughs.

"I need another one of those," he says, leading us back into the kitchen.

"Lucy, why don't you turn some music on," Drew suggests, mincing a garlic clove.

"Okay, what do you want to listen to?" I ask him.

Before Drew can answer, Sebastian says, "Why don't you put on that playlist you were listening to at the studio the other day? It was great."

"Okay."

"And make sure to turn the volume up," he says, smiling.

"Got it." I grab my phone and pull up the playlist Sebastian was referring to. I press play and a leisurely cover of Radiohead's "Creep" begins to play through the kitchen speakers.

"Why would anyone mess with a nineties classic?" Drew asks, keeping his eyes on his task.

"I think her voice is beautiful," Sebastian says, regarding the soft female voice that's crooning the lyrics to the somewhat dark song.

When it ends and James Arthur's "Always" begins to play, Drew glances up at me and grins. "I like this one," he says, seasoning the lamb shanks and sprinkling my heart with a pinch of salt. It shrivels as I listen to the song we danced to at Janice's charity ball two years ago.

The doorbell rings and my breath catches in my throat.

Drew remains focused on his task, Janice casually sips her sparkling wine, Paul looks at me excitedly, and Sebastian looks at me expectantly. But I'm frozen knowing that Sam is standing on the other side of the front door, waiting for me to invite him in to have dinner with my fiancé.

This is my punishment.

"You've got to answer it," Drew says, holding up his rosemary-and-olive-oil-covered hands.

"Okay." I inhale a quiet breath and force a smile to hide my apprehension.

Janice puts her glass down. "I'll get it," she says, giving me the push I need.

"No," I say, stepping in front of her. "I've got it."

I leave everyone in the kitchen and hurry to the foyer, glancing at my reflection in the large mahogany floor mirror that's leaning against the wall by the front door. I straighten my short floral-print skirt and run my hands over my waist where my black scoop neck sweater tucks into it. Then I smooth my hair, take a deep breath, and open the door to find Sam standing on my front porch against a suburban backdrop of two-story houses and well-established trees that line the dimly lit street. I see his shiny black car parked against the curb next to the mailbox, and it ties my stomach into knots. *Nothing about this feels right.*

His eyes trace me, from my high heels up to my face. "Relax, Lamb," he whispers, reading me like a book he memorized long ago.

I smile softly and inhale another quiet breath.

He crinkles his eyes. "Hi," he says, showing me his dimples, and my heart falls lazily into a hammock and swings back and forth to the tune of James Arthur's "Certain Things," which my playlist shuffled to just in the nick of time.

"Hi." I press my lips together, and the corners of my mouth turn up. "Come in." I hold the door open for him.

He walks inside and glances up at the crystal drop chandelier that's lighting the foyer.

"Drew picked it," I say, feeling compelled to explain away the lavish lifestyle I've been privy to since I moved in with him.

He nods and glances around the open space. "It's a nice house."

I shrug, unsure what to say.

"This is for you." He hands me a bottle of wine.

"Why thank you, sir. How very kind of you," I say in my best proper voice, trying to make light of the situation.

"It's a fairly customary gesture." He laughs softly and so do I.

"We've come a long way, haven't we?"

He looks at me with his unusual eyes and whispers, "Wait until you see where I'm going to take you."

My breath escapes between my parted lips as James Arthur croons the perfectly timed lyrics *"I'm certain that I'm yours"* through the house speakers.

I bite my lip and inhale a slow breath. *Be still my heart.*

"Should we go in?" he asks, glancing in the direction of the voices coming from the kitchen.

I bob my head apprehensively and eye the wine label on the bottle in my hands. Château Margaux. "Sam." I look up at him. "You didn't have to—"

"Sam, dear, I'm so glad you could make it," Janice says, joining us in the foyer, her heels tip-tapping on the marble floor.

"This is a four-thousand-dollar bottle of wine," I say quietly through my teeth. I recognize it from my days waitressing at La Pêche.

"Just take the wine," he urges, and steps around me. "Mrs. Christiansen. You look lovely," he says, charming her with his dimples.

She smiles and wraps her hand around his arm, pausing to feel his bicep. "Oh, wow, you are strong, aren't you?"

I give him apologetic eyes, but he just grins and obliges her.

"I have to be. It's kind of a requirement of the job."

"Yes, you must." She pats his arm and grins. "Come on, I want you to meet my son, Drew. He's making us an incredible dinner."

"Can't wait."

Neither can I...

I follow them to the kitchen, watching Sam walk with confidence in his tailored navy slacks and brown leather dress shoes. His fitted white button-down is tucked neatly into his belted pants, but his sleeves are rolled up casually, showing the tattoos on his forearm. If he's uneasy at all, you'd never know it.

"Drew, this is Lucy's friend, Sam," Janice says, before I have a chance introduce him.

Drew is standing at the sink, drying his hands on a dish towel.

I hold my breath and brace myself for the showdown. Just seeing the two of them in the same space is unnerving. Drew is handsome in his black slacks and blue button-down, but he pales in comparison to Sam, who is about the same height, but much bigger. Where Drew is trim and lean, Sam is chiseled and strong.

Sebastian stands beside me and puts his hand on my back. "Breathe," he whispers in my ear.

I inhale quietly and relax my shoulders.

Drew reaches out to shake Sam's hand. "Hi, I'm Drew, Lucy's fiancé," he says confidently. "It's great to meet you."

Sam wraps his hand around Drew's and they share a sturdy shake. "Sam Cole."

"Oh, I know who you are." Drew grins and glances up at me. "Lucy's a big fan."

Sam ignores Drew's tone, but it unsettles me.

"Don't get me wrong, I think you're great. I just don't have as much time to watch all the matches," he says, tightening the knot in my stomach.

Sam shakes his head and shrugs. "You either love boxing or you don't."

"Or you know the boxer," Drew says, glancing at me again. "I have to tell you, I was pretty shocked when Lucy told me she knew you."

"I just figured you wouldn't believe me," I say, eager to change the inevitable subject. I know there's no way around it, but I can at least try to steer the conversation in a more comfortable direction.

"I suppose you're right. I mean, it's not like you know that many people to begin with, Luc. Let alone a world champion boxer." He grins and shakes his head.

"Well, she knows me," Sam says flatly, changing the atmosphere in the room with the disparaging look on his face.

Drew gauges him and says, "So it seems."

"Sam, you remember Sebastian," I say, searching for the pressure valve.

Sam turns toward him and smiles, and his dimples light up Sebastian's face.

I know the feeling.

"Good to see you again, Sebastian," Sam says warmly, like they're old friends.

Sebastian beams. "Good to see you too, Sam." He puts his hand on Paul's shoulder. "This my husband, Paul."

Paul smiles and shakes Sam's hand. "It's great to meet you, Sam. I'm a huge fan. I watch all your matches. Seeing you fight Sanchez at the Garden was incredible."

"Thanks," Sam says humbly. "That was a memorable fight, for sure." He gives me a knowing look that calls the blood to my cheeks.

"I hope everyone's hungry. Dinner's almost ready," Drew says, inserting himself into the conversation again. "You like lamb, right?" he asks Sam.

"Actually, I love lamb," he says, flashing his beautiful eyes at me again.

"Can I get you something to drink?" Drew asks him, pulling the refrigerator door open. "I'm guessing you're a beer guy."

"Actually, Sam brought us a bottle of Château Margaux," I say, handing him the bottle.

He eyes the label, and the corners of his mouth turn down. "Well, that's one hell of a gesture."

"I thought a man of your tastes would appreciate it," Sam says.

"You've been to one of my restaurants."

"No." Sam shakes his head. "Haven't had the time."

Drew eyes him carefully. "Should I pour you a glass then?"

Sam stares at Drew and Drew stares back, and they engage in some silent exchange that dates back to the Paleolithic era. The growing tension between them is only intensified by everyone's watchful silence.

Where's that freaking pressure valve?

"No, I'll take a beer," Sam finally says.

Sebastian coughs and my eyes flash to him. He's trying, unconvincingly, to hide a smile.

Oh good, this is fun for him. I give him a sideways glance.

"Well, if you're going to open the Château Margaux, I'd love a glass," Bas says.

"I'll take one too," Paul adds, and the pressure slowly starts to release.

Drew hands Sam a beer, but I intercept it and twist the cap off it with a dish towel, seeing as how he has only one good hand. "Sorry," I apologize for Drew's tactlessness, wondering if it was intentional.

"Thanks." He winks at me, but thankfully Drew doesn't see because he's busy with the wine bottle opener.

He twists the cork out of the Château Margaux and casually pours eight hundred dollars per glass for Sebastian and Paul.

"It's a shame what happened in Las Vegas," Paul says, eyeing Sam's cast.

"Yeah, that was stupid mistake on my part."

"You're a southpaw, right, Sam?" Drew asks, and I push

my lips together to hide my amusement. Drew doesn't know the first thing about boxing. Whenever he does watch a match with me, he loses interest by the second round. He must have been studying up on his boxing terminology last night.

"What's a southpaw?" Janice asks.

"A left-handed boxer," Sebastian answers. "Sam's left hand is his dominant hand. His stance is different than an orthodox boxer because he puts his right leg in front." He glances at Sam and shrugs. "Sorry, it's the fan in me."

Sam grins and shakes his head. "No, that's right."

"So then how did you break your right hand?" Drew asks, holding his head back. I think he's genuinely curious. Still, I feel myself shrinking every time he opens his mouth. Maybe by the end of dinner, I'll have disappeared into oblivion.

"The most dangerous southpaws put their weak arm in front from time to time," Sebastian answers again. "It's the only way to strengthen it," he says in defense of Sam, and it makes me grin.

Sam smiles at Sebastian. "You know a lot about boxing."

"Yeah, I guess so. My dad has always been a big fan, so I grew up watching the greats."

"Well, I aspire to be like them." He sips his beer. "It takes focus." He pulls his eyebrows together and holds his cast up. "I wasn't focused the night this happened," he says, tugging on an invisible string that's tied tightly around my heart.

"When does it come off?" Paul asks.

"Tomorrow." He leans in to Sebastian and Paul. "I can't

fuckin' wait," he says quietly out of the side of his mouth, and they both laugh.

"I've never been able to watch men hitting each other in the face. It's just so...barbaric," Janice says, pressing her splayed fingers to her chest dramatically. She touches Sam's tattooed arm. "Doesn't it hurt?"

"Yes." He laughs and Paul and Sebastian join him. They're quite smitten with Mr. Cole.

It makes me smile.

"But lots of things hurt." He looks at me and my smile wanes.

"Well, I guess you probably had no choice but to fight when you were younger," Janice infers, and I feel my blood pulse through my veins before she even says, "growing up in Brighton Park."

I reach for the open bottle of wine and pour eight hundred dollars into a glass. "Just because we grew up in Brighton Park doesn't mean we were heathens," I say, keeping my voice steady, aiming to get my point across graciously.

"I'm sorry, dear, that's not what I meant."

"No, it's okay. I did fight. A lot, actually...so that Lucy didn't have to."

I smile over my first sip of buttery Bordeaux. It fills my head with vanilla and spice and berries and smoke. I press my lips together and savor the taste and smell, unsure which is more lovely.

"So you and Lucy...you go back a long way?" Drew asks, and I cringe.

Sam looks at me. "What were we? Eleven? Twelve?"

I push my lips together, thinking of how his shaggy hair hung over his eyes when I met him. I hated that house, but he made me feel so safe. "I was eleven," I say, smiling.

"Oh." Drew smirks. "When you said 'boyfriend,' I thought you meant, like a real boyfriend."

I see a hundred different thoughts flash across Sam's face, but he just smiles and says, "She was my family."

Janice exhales a dramatic breath. "Well, thank God she had you. I can't even think of our darling girl in a place like that."

"Yeah, well, she never belonged there," Sam says, giving me a knowing glance that I'm fairly certain Drew saw.

I turn my counterfeit eyes to Drew, hoping to convey my innocence, but I don't think he's buying it.

"Thank God she found a way out," Drew says provokingly, making my skin flush with anxiety.

Sam stares at him and I feel the tension rising in the room again, like a tank filling with water, threatening to drown me. "Thank God," he says flatly.

"Tell us how you got out, Sam." Drew pushes further.

"Drew, don't you need to check on dinner?" I ask. "It smells like it's ready."

"I, for one, am starving," Sebastian adds. He elbows Paul, whose eyes are glued to the two gunslingers.

"Me too," Paul says, eyeing Sebastian curiously.

"Should we go sit then?" I ask, clasping my hands together.

"Yes, let's," Janice says, tipping her glass up. She seems to be the only one in the room who can't feel the palpable tension. Must be the prosecco.

"I was arrested for a crime I didn't commit," Sam says, answering Drew's question. "And then I spent three years in a state prison. That's how I got out. But I'd say things worked out okay for me after that."

Drew smiles condescendingly. "Dinner's ready."

"Great," Janice says, flitting across the kitchen to refill her glass.

I narrow my eyes at Drew, hoping to convey the thoughts I can't say out loud. I've never seen him behave like this before, but apparently jealous and antagonistic are on his very short list of faults. "Come on, everyone, let's go sit down," I say, waving my hands toward the dining room. "I'll bring the wine. I think you've got everything else covered," I say quietly to Drew.

Drew puts his hands on the counter and gives me an apologetic look, but I ignore him and follow our party to the dining room.

"Sam, it's pretty incredible how quickly you dominated the boxing world after your release," Paul says. "That's something to be proud of."

Sam pulls his eyebrows together and nods. "Thanks."

"Lucy, I love the new table," Janice gushes. "I think I might get something similar after the remodel. Did Drew pick it out?"

"Yes," I say flatly.

"Drew has such a keen eye for design." She smiles. "It's in his blood. I wish Maurice had been more like that. I spent most of my marriage in the driver's seat. It would have been nice to ride shotgun every now and then." She puts her hand on mine. "Enjoy it, dear."

The look of disapproval on Sebastian's face makes me uncomfortable, but the look of disappointment on Sam's makes me want to run and hide.

"So tell me, Sam, is there anyone special in your life?" Janice asks, placing her napkin in her lap.

"Yes," he says matter-of-factly, and I stop breathing. I think Sebastian has too.

"She must be a lucky girl."

He shakes his head and says, "I'm the lucky one." His eyes flash to mine and my heart starts pounding.

Drew enters the room, carrying several steaming dishes. I've always been amazed at how he balances them on his hands and forearms. He places them in the center of the table. "Okay, we've got rosemary-braised lamb shanks, brown-butter-roasted potatoes, and asparagus ribbon salad. It's family style tonight, so please, help yourselves."

"Thank you, darling. I can't wait to dig in," Janice says, picking up her fork.

I give him a small smile, hoping that he's reined in his male bravado. "Everything looks great, Drew. Thank you."

"It looks amazing," Paul says. I watch him cut a piece of lamb and put it in his mouth. He closes his eyes as he chews.

I can't help but smile. I've always loved seeing how people react to Drew's food for the first time. He's an incredible chef.

Sam takes a bite and nods. That's probably the closest thing to a compliment Drew is going to get from him.

It's quiet for a minute besides the clinking of silverware as everyone eats. I relish in the relaxed atmosphere, no matter how short-lived it may be. For the moment, everyone seems to be enjoying their meal.

I sip my wine, savoring the way the warm, buttery notes complement the lamb. I swirl my glass, watching the burgundy liquid coat the crystal, thinking how this will probably be the last time Drew cooks for me. I glance up at him and he smiles, all of his ego falling by the wayside. I look at my glass again and take another sip. *What is he going to think when he looks back at tonight after I tell him about me and Sam?* I take another sip and try to swallow down the giant lump in my throat.

Sebastian subtly raises his eyebrows at me. He must notice me struggling with my thoughts about the not-too-distant future. "Lucy, I'm sure everyone would love to hear about the exhibit," he says, pulling me back into the here and now, which isn't much better.

"Yes, Lucy, tell us. Are you ready for next week?" Janice asks. "You must be getting so excited."

I take a deep breath and answer, "Yes, we're both very excited," I say, looking at Sebastian. "I think we're almost ready."

Sebastian puts his napkin down and reports, "The RSVPs have been tallied, the guest list has been finalized, all the featured artwork is set up—"

"Are you coming, Sam?" Janice interrupts Sebastian excitedly.

"That's right," Drew says, sitting back in his chair. "Lucy said you were interested in buying some artwork." He sounds genuinely interested. Maybe he's trying to redeem himself.

Sam raises an eyebrow at me.

Yes, I lied!

He takes a sip of his beer and puts it down on the table. "There's a piece I've got my eye on."

Drew puts his elbows on the table and gives Sam a hard look, but before he can say anything, Sebastian says, "The only thing we have left to do is confirm the menu with you, Drew."

Drew's ears perk up to that. "Well, there's no time like the present."

"Actually, I've had some last-minute thoughts about the menu," I say, squinting, because I know how much Drew loves when I change my mind at the last minute.

He looks at me warily. "What kind of thoughts?"

"Well, you know how I wanted to have fun with the food since it's an art show?"

"Hence the mac and cheese you requested," he says flatly, because I finally wore him down and got him to agree to a less refined menu.

"Mac and cheese?" Janice reproaches, unable to hide the look of disapproval on her face.

"With lobster and gruyère," Drew clarifies. "Served in martini glasses, of course," he says, placating her.

Sebastian looks at me over the rim of his wineglass. "What were you saying, Lucy?"

"Oh, just that I thought we could add some color to the menu by serving little stacks of macarons for dessert... in a rainbow of pastels," I say, smiling at him, "from fuchsia to violet. And those paint palette cookies we saw in the window display at Canicci's. I know they could fill an order within a week's time."

Sebastian grins and bobs his head. "I love it."

"And there's this drink I saw that looks like a rainbow," I say to Drew excitedly. "It reminded me of the watercolors I used to paint with when I was little. That should be an easy addition, right?" I smile when I see Sam smiling at me.

Drew's mouth is covered by his folded hands, but when he drops them I see the concerned look on his face. "Luc, we should probably serve champagne."

"Of course. But I want the rainbow drink too."

"It's an art show, Lucy. Your first art show. I thought you wanted people to take you seriously. Icing cookies...rainbow drinks?" He pulls his eyebrows together. "That just feels a little bit like a kindergarten orientation, don't you think?"

I feel my cheeks flame.

"If she wants the drink, let her have the drink," Sam says, putting his napkin on the table.

I feel the blood drain from my face. "Sam, it's fine," I say, masking my embarrassment.

Drew stares at him and shakes his head. "I wouldn't expect you to understand."

"What does that mean?" I ask, in defense of Sam.

"Nothing." Drew puts his napkin on the table and sits back in his chair.

"I think it means that it's time for me to go," Sam says, backing his chair away from the table.

Janice holds her hand up. "No, of course it doesn't." She

looks at Drew. "Tell us what you meant, darling." She prompts him to explain away his comment.

He lets out an exasperated breath and looks at me. "It means that just because he brings a fancy bottle of wine to dinner and drives a hundred-thousand-dollar car doesn't make him sophisticated. For crying out loud, he fights for a living, like a damn dog."

"Andrew!" Janice admonishes.

I watch Sam get up from his chair, the look on his face calm yet terrifying. His eyes meet mine and I shake my head. I know what he's capable of when he's angry.

"I think I should go." His voice is deep and controlled.

I glance at Paul's and Sebastian's shocked faces and see the embarrassment on Janice's. I shake my head at Drew with shock. "What is wrong with you?" I grit through my teeth.

"Lucy, honey, you didn't grow up with this...lifestyle. And that's okay," he says, looking at me like I'm some kind of injured puppy. "But the people who will be at your show did. They'll expect a more sophisticated menu. Trust me on this."

Sam rounds the table and my muscles tense as he approaches Drew. "She's not a child."

Drew stands up and my blood races through my veins. "I'm well aware of that."

"Sam, just go," I say, stepping in front of him.

His shoulders rise and fall to the rhythm of my racing heartbeat.

"Sam, please."

He looks down at me and I'm gutted by the look in his eyes.

I'm sorry, I mouth.

He walks away, dragging my heart on the floor behind him.

Drew reaches for me. "Lucy."

"No." I push his hand away and go after Sam. I pull the front door open and run down the steps after him. "Sam," I call, but he ignores me. "Sam, stop," I say, catching up to him just before he gets in his car.

He closes the door and slams his fist down on the shiny black roof, making all the muscles in his forearm ripple, but he doesn't look at me. He drops his head and takes several deep breaths.

"Sam, please, just talk to me." I tug on his sleeve.

"What are you doing with that guy, Lucy?"

I pull my eyebrows together, unsure whether the question is rhetorical. "He's not normally like that."

"Bullshit."

I shake my head and repeat, "He's not."

"Because you always do whatever he tells you to? Because you never challenge him? Because he doesn't let you forget where you came from?"

"What? No. He's good guy, Sam. And he's never been anything but wonderful to me."

"Is that what he's programmed you to think? That he's this great guy you don't deserve, who will give you whatever you want? Jesus, Lucy." He shakes his head and gives me a serious look. "Has he put his hands on you before?"

"What? No!" I exclaim, ignoring the pit in my stomach. *Where is this coming from?*

He watches me carefully, looking for any cracks in my resolve.

"He isn't that kind of guy, Sam. You don't know him," I say, defending Drew now. "He was just, I don't know, threatened by you tonight. It didn't help that you were prodding him every chance you got."

He folds his hands on the roof of his car and drops his head between his arms.

"I'm sorry for what he said to you. It isn't true."

He looks at me again, the anger gone from his eyes now. "Of course it's true."

I blink at him, unwilling to participate in his self-deprecation.

"Lucy, I'm not sophisticated," he says, patting his chest. "I was raised in the system without parents, without privileges. I saw drug dealers every day. I stepped over needles on my way to school. And I spent three years wearing a jumpsuit in a state prison."

"Sam—"

"And I fight. Like a fucking dog, because nobody ever gave us anything. I fight so that we can have a life like this." He throws his hand up at the house. "I fight so that one day, our kids won't have to."

"I know," I breathe.

"He's right. I have more money than I know what to do with. But I'll never be sophisticated, because that's not me. I'll never be like him."

"I don't want you to be."

His face screws up. "I don't know."

"What don't you know? I was raised in the system too. I didn't have privileges either. I saw the same drug dealers and stepped over the same needles. We're the same, Sam."

"Then why do you care so much about these people?"

"Because these people care about me! That's how it works," I say, frustrated.

"You sure about that? Because they didn't seem to care about anything you had to say in there."

"That isn't true. You just don't understand them."

"Oh, but you do?"

"Yes," I say, exasperated, "I do!"

He shakes his head and huffs. "I forgot, you speak upper-class now."

I feel a sharp pinch in my heart. "Screw you," I say, blinking back tears.

He stares at me with a face of stone, but he doesn't say anything.

"They are the *only* ones who cared about me when I was struggling to get started. They did everything they could to help me. They're the reason I'm even having this exhibit."

"You've mentioned that."

I shake my head, because I'm so frustrated with him I could scream. "You don't have to accept it, Sam, but Drew loves me. And I'm going to break his heart when I tell him about us," I practically yell.

"Then maybe you shouldn't."

My heart pounds inside my chest and a hot flash of panic pricks across my skin. "What?"

"You've got it all, Lucy. A great guy, a great career, a great house." He chews the corner of his mouth. "What have I done for you?"

I shake my head and say firmly, "Don't do that."

He rubs the back of his neck and closes his eyes. "It's my fault." He drops his elbows on the roof of his car. "*I* was supposed to get you out of Brighton Park. *I* was supposed to give you a better life. *I* was supposed to protect you."

"This isn't your fault, Sam. Life just had different plans."

"I'm so proud of you, Lucy. I really am." The corner of his mouth turns up into a small half smile, but it doesn't hide the pain in his voice. "I mean, this"—he glances up at the house—"it's more than we ever could have dreamed of when we were kids. But this life, this guy"—he gives me a disheartened look—"it's changed you."

I shake my head and insist, "No it hasn't, Sam. I'm still the same."

"How could you be?" I see the defeated look in his eyes, and it fills me with fear.

"I'm the same," I say through clenched teeth, tears filling my eyes now.

"The fact that you can't see it tells me you're not."

"Sam, what are you saying?"

"I'm sorry I let this happen."

"Sam." I step closer to him, but I resist the urge to touch him, knowing several pairs of eyes might be watching me.

His face screws up and he closes his eyes. When he opens them again, they're filled with fire. "Kiss me," he says urgently.

"What?" I ask, feeling my emotional wave pool shift inside me.

"Kiss me," he pleads.

"That's not fair. You know I can't."

"I'm not testing you, Lucy. I just want you to kiss me."

My knees soften and my hands begin to shake. "Why are you doing this?"

"Please, Lamb. Just kiss me, right here, right now. And then go inside and tell him about us."

The air leaves my lungs in a painful rush, and the street lamps begin to sway.

"Come home with me," he begs.

My heart beats painfully against my ribs. "I—I can't," I cry. "You know why I can't."

He closes his eyes and drops his head. "Yeah. The exhibit. *Drew.*"

"Sam, please...don't do this."

He opens his car door but pauses before getting in, propping his arm on the edge of the door. "Go on." He nods toward the house. "Go back to him."

I wrap my arms around my stomach to hold myself together, but a sob bubbles up out of me anyway. "I'm sorry."

He drops down into his seat and shuts the door, but not before I see the pain on his face.

When the car roars to life I rush to the window and press my hands against the dark glass. "Sam."

He begins to pull forward but stops when I don't move.

"Sam, please." I tap the window desperately.

He lowers it just enough for me to see the heartbreak on his face again. "Lucy, move back," he says roughly.

"No," I grit through my teeth.

"Lucy," Drew calls from the front porch.

When I look over my shoulder at him, Sam peels away and takes off down the road.

I wrap my arms around myself and inhale a shaky breath, but when Drew calls my name again, I wipe my eyes and march back to the house. When I reach him, I pause and say firmly, "He is my friend and you insulted him. And you embarrassed me." I shake my head with disappointment and step around him to find three very alarmed faces waiting for me inside.

"It's okay," I answer the question in Sebastian's worried eyes.

"Are you sure?"

"Yeah." I nod. "But I think it's probably best for everyone to go home."

Bas pulls me into a tight hug. "Call me," he whispers.

I hold on to him and let out a quiet sob, but quickly swallow it down. "I will."

He releases me and leads Paul through the front door, passing Drew without looking up at him.

Janice tucks her purse under her arm. "Lucy, please pass my apologies along to Sam, should he ever speak to you again." She stands directly in front of Drew and says sharply, "Your behavior tonight was unacceptable." She presses her lips together tightly and continues through the front door and down the steps.

Drew watches her get in her car, and then closes the door and leans against it. He puts his hands in his pockets and looks at me with heavy eyes. "I'm sorry."

"Don't," I say quietly.

"I am." His face is soft and unguarded.

I wipe my eyes. "Do you think you rescued me like some kind of stray dog?"

"What? No."

"That's what you think of us, me and Sam."

"I don't think that about you, Lucy. I love you," he says firmly, stirring my emotions. "I'm sorry for how I acted tonight. I've never really felt insecure about us before. But he's a lot to compete with."

Just tell him and get it over with. Go to Sam.

I close my eyes and ignore the thought.

"It was childish, I know. And, I realize, pretty stupid. I'm just glad one of his hands was in a cast. But I saw the way he was looking at you."

My pulse pounds in my ears.

Rip the Band-Aid off now.

"You don't see the way men look at you like I do. He couldn't keep his eyes off of you. I don't care if he's the president. I'm not going to let another man come into my house and stake claim on something that isn't his."

My face screws up reflexively. "You know I'm not a piece of property, right?"

"Of course. You know that's not what I meant." He takes a few steps toward me.

"Don't." I hold my hand up, wanting to keep my distance from him.

"I know you're mad. You should be. I was a jerk."

"He's like family to me, Drew." He's *everything* to me.

He furrows his brow and shakes his head. "I realize that you have a history with him, Lucy, but you're not kids anymore. I don't know if I want you striking up a friendship with him."

Sam's presumptions about Drew echo in his patronizing tone.

"Well, I'm sorry you feel that way, but you can't tell me who I can and can't be friends with." Maybe it's a wasted effort, but after the way he spoke to me at dinner, I'm not about to let him start telling me what I'm *allowed* to do.

The corners of his mouth turn down. "No. I can't tell you who you can be friends with. But I will tell you when I don't want you hanging around men who want to fuck you."

My mouth pops open and I feel the disgust make its way onto my face.

"I know that's crass, honey, but it's the truth. I could see it all over his face."

"He's not some random guy I met at a bar," I say, feeling like I need a shower.

"Dammit, Lucy, I don't want you seeing him!" he shouts, unsettling me further. He closes his eyes, inhales a deep breath, and runs his hand through his hair. When he opens his eyes again, his face is relaxed. He reaches for me, but I take several steps back. "I'm sorry, I didn't mean to scare you."

Screw the exhibit. It's not worth it.

"Drew, I—I have to..." I look up at his dark blue eyes and steel my heart, but my unwilling tongue won't cooperate. "I—I..."

"Lucy, I'm sorry. I didn't mean to yell at you like that."

When I see the remorse in his eyes, I search for sympathy, but I find only doubt. Suddenly, everything I thought I was so sure about before becomes a question. "Is this what it would be like?" I ask, shaking my head.

"What?"

"If we got married."

"If?" His face grows serious. "Lucy, what are you talking about?"

"You just thought that because I'm so grateful for everything you've done for me, I'll do whatever you say? And when I don't, then what? You'll just scream at me until I fall in line?"

"What? No."

I close my eyes and exhale a somber breath as I let go of the life I used to see with him.

I let go of the exhibit.

And then a new dream takes their place.

Sam.

"Drew." I open my eyes and focus on my steady, sure heartbeats. "I don't want to get married," I say certainly.

He puts his hands on his hips, and his chest rises and falls in hurried breaths, but his face is smooth and unreadable. "Lucy, you're, um, you're just upset. You're not thinking clearly."

I give a small, apologetic smile and shrug. "Yeah, actually, I am. For the first time in weeks."

"No, you're not." He swallows hard and says, "You're just mad because I was rude to—"

"Sam?" I huff a quiet breath and shake my head. "Drew, Sam isn't just some old friend."

He clenches his jaw tight and looks away.

I wait for him to say something, but when he doesn't, I reach for him. "Hey," I say softly, trying to get him to look at me.

"Why don't you, uh, why don't you go ahead and go to bed?" He keeps his eyes off me and makes his way into the kitchen.

"Drew, we need to talk about this," I say, following him.

"You're tired." He reaches for his bottle of bourbon and slides it across the counter. "And you've got a lot on your plate right now. Let's just get past the exhibit and then we can talk about the wedding. Okay?" He opens the cabinet and pulls down a glass.

"Do you really think that's a good idea?" I ask, watching him fill the glass with bourbon.

"Don't worry about the mess in here," he says, bringing the amber-colored liquor to his lips. He takes a long sip and puts the glass down. "I'll clean up."

I watch him with wary eyes, but he quickly busies himself with the pots and pans he left on the stove.

"Drew."

"Go on," he says without looking up at me. "Go get some sleep."

I exhale a frustrated breath, because there's no talking to him now. "Okay."

Chapter 16

Sam

"Hey, Jimmy."

"How's it going, champ?" He steps out of his security booth.

I drop my head back against the headrest. "I've had better nights."

He pulls the waist of his pants up and leans against my car window. "How's the hand?"

"Fine. Cast comes off tomorrow."

"You gonna be ready for Ackerman?" he asks skeptically.

Beau Ackerman is the reigning super middleweight champion of the world, and now he's vying for my title. Cocky fucker couldn't stay in his own weight class. Some people think he might actually have a shot since I broke my hand, but I plan to disappoint them.

"I'll be ready."

"All right." He smiles and steps back. "Have a good night, Sam." He raises the gate and I pull forward into the parking garage.

I circle the ramp up to the third level and park, but I don't get out. I look at the empty spot beside me, imagining Lucy's car there. She should be here with me right now. I grip the steering wheel and try to ignore the ache in my stomach. I turn the car off, get out, and head inside my building.

"Sam," Terrance calls as I pass the security desk in the lobby.

I stop and walk over to him. "Hey, man, how's it going? Haven't seen you in a few days. Everything okay?"

"Yeah, my wife had a baby girl a couple of days ago."

"No kidding?"

He pulls his phone out of his pocket and holds the screen up for me to see. "Isn't she the most beautiful thing you've ever seen?"

I smile and nod. "Yeah, she's gorgeous. What's her name?"

"Jasmine."

"I like that."

"I call her momma sunflower, so it just fit, you know?"

"Is that her?" I ask pointing to the picture.

"Yeah, that's my sunflower. My day one."

I smile over the ache in my heart. "You're a lucky man."

"Don't I know it."

"Well, congratulations." I shake his hand.

"Thanks, Sam. You have a good night."

"You too, Terrance."

I continue across the lobby to the elevators. When I step

inside, I hear heels tapping on the lobby floor. Just before the doors close, a small hand with red-painted fingernails appears between them, and they open again.

"Hey, Sam," Molly says, smiling up at me.

I look down at her big brown eyes, wishing there was a way she could help me that didn't involve sleeping with her.

"Hey," I say flatly, staring straight ahead.

"What's the matter?" she asks, eyeing me carefully. "Everything okay?"

I pull my eyebrows together and shake my head. "Not tonight, okay, Molls?"

"Sam, whatever it is, you can talk to me."

I give her a sideways glance, because she knows as well as I do that talking just leads to sex. "Not tonight."

She raises her eyebrows and faces the elevator doors. "Okay."

I glance at my casted hand, feeling like a chained dog. All I want to do is put on a pair of gloves and beat the hell out of a punching bag. The doors slide open to the sixteenth floor, and she begins to walk out, but I grab her hand and pull her back. "Wait." I'm too wound up to sleep. If I go inside my apartment, I'm just going to climb the walls. "Take a drive with me."

"A drive?"

"I could use the company."

The corners of her mouth turn up. "I thought you said not tonight."

"I just want to go for a drive, Molly. Do you want to come with me or not?"

She studies me carefully. "Yeah, Sam, I'll come with you."

"Okay." I press the button for the lobby and my mind wanders to Lucy. She's with *him*. *What's the difference?*

The doors open to the first floor and Molly follows me out.

"Sam, Miss Pritchett," Terrance says curiously as we pass him.

"Hold down the fort," I say to him as we walk outside.

I lead Molly to the parking garage stairwell, and she proceeds up the stairs before me. I can't help but look at her ass in the red leather pants she's wearing. It's in my face the whole way up to the third floor. "You could take someone's eye out with those boots," I say, wondering how she doesn't topple over in them as we climb the last few steps.

"Your girl had on something similar, if I recall."

I ignore her and follow her to my car.

"Are you going to tell me who she is, Sam?" she asks, sliding into my passenger seat.

I start the engine and back out of the spot. "Why, you need something new to tweet about?" I glance over at her. "That was pretty fucked up, what you did that day."

The corners of her mouth turn down. "I don't know what you're talking about."

"You insulted her on the elevator and ten minutes later my Twitter feed was blowing up. I think you know exactly what I'm talking about."

She closes her eyes and shakes her head. "I'm sorry." She sighs. "I texted someone who I thought was a friend and I guess she tweeted it."

"It was fucked up," I repeat.

"You're right. It was. But it was a mistake. You know I would never do something like that to you." She drops her chin and then peeks up at me. "Forgive me?"

She'll never let me hear the end of it if I don't. I look over at her and nod. "Yeah, okay."

"So, who is she?"

I grip the steering wheel and stare straight ahead. I don't want to talk about Lucy right now.

"All right, I'll guess. She's...your sister. No, no." She shakes her head. "You don't have any siblings." She narrows her eyes and smirks. "That you know about."

I give her a slanted look.

"Okay, she's...your lawyer." She bites her bottom lip and shakes her head. "Mixing business with pleasure...*not* a good idea. Been there."

"She's not my lawyer."

"Why won't you just tell me who she is?"

"It's complicated."

"You should probably know by now, I'm good with complicated."

I give her an incredulous look and she frowns.

"Just because I'm a trust-fund baby doesn't mean that I'm shallow and pretentious."

"I didn't know that."

"That I'm shallow and pretentious or that I'm a trust-fund baby?"

"I've never thought you were shallow or pretentious. I didn't know about the trust fund."

"Yeah, well, my dad owned a pharmaceutical company and he made a lot of money before he died."

I glance over at her. "I'm sorry, I didn't know."

"It was a long time ago."

"So, is that how you started your company?"

"Well, I got a bachelor's degree in graphic design and a master's in marketing first." She narrows her eyes at me. "Prerequisites for running a graphic design firm."

"That's not what I meant."

"I know. And yes, it helped." She looks out of her window. "I barely remember him. Except, well"—she shifts in her seat and smiles—"when I was little he called me peanut. He would come home from work, which sometimes seemed like days later, and say, 'Come here, peanut.' Then he'd throw me on his shoulders. I remember that. I always loved that."

"What happened to him?"

"My mom."

What? "She killed him?"

She laughs quietly. "No." Her smile fades. "She got cancer."

"Jesus, Molly. Why didn't you tell me any of this before?"

She shrugs. "It was so long ago. I was only seven, so..." She picks at the corner of one of her red fingernails. "He was heartbroken when she died, so I'm told. He started drinking. And then one day, he ran his car into a tree. He died on impact."

I'm not sure what to say, so I don't say anything.

"He wasn't in his right mind. He didn't mean to leave me. He just loved her so much..." Her voice trails off and she stares out of her window again.

We ride in silence for a few minutes, until we're on the outskirts of the city. But when we pass the graffiti-covered *Welcome to Brighton Park* sign, Molly looks at me and asks nervously, "Where are we going?"

"We're both orphans, Molly. The only thing that really differentiates us is circumstance. You were left with a trust fund, and I was left with all this." I raise my hand and gesture at the dimly lit projects we're driving past.

She squirms in her seat. "I can't believe you grew up here."

"Well, not far from here." I glance at her concerned face. "Don't worry, I'm not going to stop. I just like to drive through sometimes, remember where I came from."

"Why would you want to remember a place like this?"

"Her name is Lucy. We grew up here together."

She stares at me for several seconds. "Wait. The woman in the elevator? *That* was Lucy? *Your* Lucy?"

"The one and only."

"But she was so..." She shakes her head. "*She's* from Brighton Park?"

"I know. You wouldn't know it by looking at her, but believe me, there was a time when she wore secondhand clothes and dyed her hair pink with Kool-Aid packets." I think about the day she came into my life, with her tangled hair and shy smile.

"When did you reconnect?"

"A few weeks ago."

She gives me apologetic eyes. "Oh, Sam, I hope I didn't—"

"No. I talked her off the ledge after she saw the tweets."

She nods and looks down at her lap. "So is that why you wanted to take a drive instead of going up to your place?"

I reach for her hand and give it a squeeze. "You'll always be my friend, Molly. Just not that kind of friend. Not anymore, okay?"

She pulls her hand away and tucks her hair behind her ear. "Isn't she engaged?"

"For now."

"And you're you expecting that to change?"

"I don't know. Yes," I say, frustrated by the events of the evening.

"And if it doesn't?"

"Then I'll wait."

"For how long?"

"I don't know, Molly. Forever," I say, irritated.

"Wow," she whispers. "You really do love her."

"Life would be a hell of a lot easier if I didn't," I say, winding the steering wheel to pull into a gas station.

"What are you doing?"

"I just have to get gas."

"Is it safe?"

"I know the tenant, Marcus. He's been working here since I was a teenager. It's safe."

She glances around the well-lit gas station. "Do you think I could use the restroom?" She scrunches her nose.

I nod. "Marcus keeps them clean."

"Okay." She gets out and hurries across the parking lot.

I insert my credit card into the gas pump and begin filling my tank. I watch the numbers climb on the meter for a few minutes until they reach twenty-three gallons, and then I hear Molly's heels tapping across the parking lot again. I look up and she gives me two thumbs up, but then she freezes and her face falls.

"Give me your wallet," a gravelly voice says from behind me.

I turn around and see a man in a dark hoodie standing behind me, holding a gun.

"Give me your wallet!" he shouts.

I reach for my wallet and pull several hundred dollars out of it. "Here, just take the money."

He takes the cash and shoves it in his pocket. "I know there's more. Credit cards too. And your car."

I shake my head and rub my hand over my chin. "You're not taking my car."

He points the gun at my face. "Are you crazy?"

"Just give it to him, Sam!" Molly cries.

I take a step toward him. "Do you know who I am?"

"The bullets in this here gun don't give a fuck who you are."

"You think I'm scared of a gun?" I shake my head. "I've known guys like you my whole life."

He looks down at my arm. "You got some tattoos, so you think you're tough, huh? You don't know me. Cocky rich boy in your fancy clothes on the wrong side of town. In your fancy car with your fancy lady." He looks over my shoulder at Molly. "I bet she tastes real good."

"Sam."

I take another step toward him and grit through my teeth, "Put the gun down, take the money, and walk away."

"Nah, you ain't scared. But she is." He points the gun at Molly.

She screams and falls to her knees.

I step back and hold my hands up. "Okay, man. Just leave her alone. She didn't do anything. If you want to shoot somebody, shoot me." I pull my key fob out of my pocket. "Here, take the car."

He ignores me and starts to walk toward Molly.

"Hey!" I shout, and he stops. When he looks over his shoulder at me, I throw a hard left hook at his face, and he falls to the ground. But not before firing his gun. The blast sounds through the empty gas station and rings through my ears.

I look down at the man out cold on the pavement and kick the gun away from his hand. Molly is still crouched down on the ground. She looks up at me, but her face is sheet white.

"Molly." I run over to her, and she reaches for me with a bloody hand. *Oh, fuck.*

"Sam! You okay?" Marcus shouts across the parking lot. "I called the police."

"We need an ambulance. My friend was shot."

He runs back inside.

"I was shot?" Molly asks weakly.

I lift her arm and try to find the wound, but all I see is blood. "Yeah, but you're going to be okay. Help is on the way." I hear sirens getting closer.

"Sam?" I hear the fear in her voice.

"You're going to be okay."

"Something's ... wrong," she slurs and falls limp in my arms.

"Molly? Molly?"

Several police cars pull into the gas station, followed by an ambulance.

"She needs help!" I yell to the officers getting out of their squad cars with their guns drawn. "She was shot."

One of the officers lowers his gun and kneels down beside me. "Is she breathing?"

"I don't know. I think so. She just passed out."

Several EMTs surround us and begin checking her vitals. I try to lay her down, but one of them looks at me says, "Don't move, Mr. Cole. We'll move her."

I stay still while they transfer her onto a stretcher. "Is she going to be okay?" I ask as they wheel her over to the ambulance.

"We're going to do everything we can to make sure that she is."

A second team of EMTs huddle around the shooter.

"What about him?" I ask one of the officers.

"He'll be treated for his injuries and charged with attempted armed robbery and attempted murder, if that's what happened." He looks at me inquisitively.

"It is."

"Mr. Cole, can you come with me, please?" He walks toward his squad car, and against every fiber of my being, I follow him.

After providing detailed answers to his scrutinizing questions, he pats my back and gives me permission to follow the ambulance to the hospital. "You better get that hand checked out," he says, which only at the mention begins to ache.

I flex my fingers in and out a few times. I think it's okay, but I need to have it looked at just in case.

The officer gives me his card. "I'll be following up soon, Sam."

"Okay, thank you."

"Take care of that hand, champ."

* * *

"Hi," I say to Molly, who is blinking up at me from her hospital bed.

"Hi," she croaks.

"How are you feeling?"

She swallows and closes her eyes. "Thirsty."

I hand her a cup of water from her bedside table, and she reaches for it with a shaking hand. "Here." I hold it to her mouth and she takes a sip.

She inhales a deep breath and groans. "Ow."

"Do you need me to get the nurse?"

"No." She shakes her head and clicks a small device in her hand. "I need morphine." She smiles weakly and I see that the device is connected to her IV.

"The nurse said you were shot in the side, but the bullet didn't hit any organs. You were really lucky."

"Yeah." She shakes her head. "I can't believe I got shot."

"Molly, I . . . I'm so sorry."

"It's okay. It's not your fault."

"I should have never taken you there. It was stupid."

She reaches for my hand. "Thank you for what you did, Sam."

"I don't know, maybe if I didn't hit him, you wouldn't have been shot."

"Or maybe I would have, at close range."

I shrug and nod.

"How's your hand?"

"A doctor looked at it and said it's fine." I make a fist and only feel a slight ache in it now.

She closes her eyes. "Good."

"The nurse said your aunt is on her way?"

"She's flying down from Chicago. She's going to stay with me until I'm better."

"That's good."

She yawns. "What time is it?"

"Three."

"In the morning?"

"Yeah."

She looks at my bloodstained shirt. "You should go home and get some sleep. And burn that shirt." She scrunches up her nose and gives me small smile.

"I can stay until your aunt gets here."

She shakes her head from side to side. "No. I'm fine. Go."

"Are you sure?"

"Mm-hmm."

"Okay."

"And, don't worry about me tweeting anything. I can barely hold my phone right now." She laughs quietly.

"TMZ already took care of that for you."

Her eyes widen a little. "What? They did?"

I nod and she closes her eyes again.

"There were a lot of people around tonight. It was inevitable."

"Have you talked to Lucy yet?"

"No." I can't even begin to think of how I'm going to explain this to her.

"Please tell her how sorry I am for that day in the elevator."

"I will."

"She must be a pretty incredible woman."

"She is."

She closes her eyes and whispers, "I hope everything works out for you, Sam."

"Me too."

She lies quietly.

"Molly?" I whisper, but she doesn't answer. Hopefully the morphine kicked in.

I lean over her and gently kiss her forehead before I leave.

Chapter 17

Lucy

I wake to the smell of bacon and look over at Drew's side of the bed. It's still made from the night before. He didn't come to bed. My heart sinks, because I know there's more than breakfast waiting for me downstairs. There's a man waiting for answers. Answers I tried to give him last night. I close my eyes and sigh. I should have tried harder.

I sit up and grab my phone, blinking until my blurry eyes adjust to the daylight, and I see three missed calls from Sebastian. He texted too.

Sebastian: OMG. Are you okay? Call me.
Me: Yes but I can't talk now. I'll come over after I shower.
Sebastian: Ok

I throw my covers off and climb out of bed, lured by the smell of coffee and bacon. I pass the guest bedroom on my way downstairs and find the guest bed slept in and unmade.

"Good morning," I say to Drew, who is standing over the sink.

"Good morning," he says over his shoulder.

I take a seat at the island. "Did you sleep okay?"

He nods and turns around. "I thought maybe we could use a little space last night. And I know how much you like when I come to bed smelling like bourbon." He smiles softly.

"You didn't have to sleep in the guest room."

He shrugs and says seriously, "That bed's actually really comfortable."

I nod and watch him make a cup of coffee. "Drew, I think we should talk about last night."

He hands me the cup. "I meant what I said, Lucy. You need to spend the next few days focused on the exhibit. Not on us. And I need to focus on my work too. A problem came up with the permitting this morning, and I'm going to go back to Philly to handle it in person."

"You're leaving again?"

He looks at me and says, "I heard you last night, okay?" He puts his hand on mine. "But right now, I think the best thing for both of us is a little space. That way you can focus on making the exhibit a success. Because no matter how muddy the waters are between us right now, I'm not going to let it interfere with the biggest night of your career. Not when you've worked so hard for it."

"Drew." I close my eyes and exhale a tentative breath.

He walks back over to the stove and makes a plate. "Here,

have some breakfast." He puts the plate in front of me, but there's no way I can eat with my stomach in knots.

"I'll be back in a few days. Then we'll get through the exhibit and talk about it," he says, giving me a small, sincere smile. "Okay?"

"Okay."

* * *

I knock on Sebastian's door, and he answers with record speed, like he was waiting on the other side of it.

"Hey." I walk inside and drop my purse on the bright yellow tufted bench that's pushed against the wall in the foyer. Paul and Sebastian's apartment is the picture of midcentury modern perfection. Straight, clean lines are contrasted by smooth, curved angles, and warm neutral tones are accented with vibrant pops of color. It's 1955 meets today, and I love it. "Where's Paul?" I ask when I don't see him.

"I sent him away when you said you were coming over."

"Sebastian. You didn't have to do that."

"We were out of groceries anyway. I hope you're not hungry."

"No." I shake my head. "I ate." I picked at my bacon anyway. But I did finish my coffee.

"Oh, good. I've been really worried about you. Are you okay?" He takes my hand and pulls me into the living room.

I sigh and fall onto the sofa. "I don't know."

"Have you talked to Sam?"

My heart sinks at the mention of his name. "No." He was

so upset when he left last night. I just want to give him some space today. It seems to be a common theme, but maybe it's the best thing for all of us. Honestly, after everything that happened last night, I need some time to regroup.

"Well, I'm sure the story was grossly exaggerated."

"What story?" I ask, raising my eyebrows curiously.

His eyes narrow and then widen. "Are you joking?"

"No," I insist, trying to slow the thoughts that are suddenly storming my mind. "What story?"

"Didn't you see the news?"

"No," I say, practically shouting at him now. I was a little preoccupied.

He inhales a deep breath and says gravely, "Sam was involved in a shooting last night."

"What?" My pulse races and my vision blurs around the edges. Suddenly the developments with Drew seems insignificant. "Oh, my God. Is he okay?" I scramble for my phone as tears flood my eyes.

"He's fine. He wasn't shot."

I stifle a cry.

"But he got mugged at a gas station."

I fumble with my phone, trying to unlock it. "I have to call him."

Sebastian reaches for my arm. "Lucy. He was with a woman."

My eyes flash to his, and when I see the pity in them, I know that it's true. "What?"

"She's the one who was shot."

My heart turns inside out and hides from a pain so big it could destroy me.

Sebastian puts his hand on mine, which I realize is shaking. "She's okay."

Should that give me some sort of comfort?

"Who is she?"

"According to the news, her name is Molly Pritchett."

My heart stops beating altogether.

"She owns a graphic design company and..." Sebastian's voice fades away. All I hear is the strangled sound of my breath catching in my throat.

"Lucy?"

I look at up him.

"You okay?"

I stand up and shake my head. "No. I am not okay."

He reaches for me, but I pull my hand away.

"She's the woman from the elevator in Sam's building. The one he admitted to sleeping with. The one who tweeted about me!"

"No." His eyes get big. "Are you kidding? Of course you're not." He grabs my hand and pulls me back down onto the couch.

"Why was he with her, Bas?"

"I don't know, sweetie."

I grab my phone and search for the story.

Sam Cole Shooting: Girlfriend Shot.

Sam Cole's Girlfriend Shot in Mugging.

I put my phone down when I see a picture of his car. "Girlfriend?"

"You know it's not true."

"When did it happen?" I ask, knowing Bas has already read every article.

"Ten thirty."

"Where?"

"Brighton Park."

I exhale a silent breath and drop my head to my hands. "This is my fault." I cry softly.

"What? Honey. No."

"He was so upset when he left last night. He begged me to go with him. He begged me, Sebastian. And I told him no." I go grab a tissue. "I was so worried about Drew and the stupid exhibit, I just let him go."

"The exhibit isn't stupid," he says, reining me in. "Drew, however..." He gives me a slanted look.

"I don't know what got into him last night," I say, wiping my eyes.

"I do. *Sam.*"

"How could I do this to him?"

"How could you do what to who?"

"Drew! I told him that I didn't want to marry him last night."

"Wait. What? You did?"

"Don't worry, he's in denial or something. He won't talk to me about it until *after* the exhibit."

Sebastian listens quietly, but I see a thousand thoughts cross his face.

"He said the only thing he wants me focused on right now is the exhibit, because it's the biggest night of my career and he doesn't want anything to mess it up."

"Oh," Sebastian says, pulling his dark eyebrows together behind his clear-framed glasses.

I put my face in my hands and cry, "And all I can do is worry about is Sam."

"Because you love him."

"I thought he loved me too," I say, wiping my eyes.

"Sam does love you."

"What if something changed? Maybe something clicked in him last night."

"I'm pretty sure that's not how it works."

"I really hurt him, Bas."

"Then you should call him."

"And say what?"

"Hi, Sam. How are you? I'm glad you didn't get shot!"

"He knows I've seen the story. Why hasn't he called *me*?"

"Technically you haven't seen the story. And, I don't know, maybe he has PTSD from a man waving a gun around in his face."

I give him an doubtful look.

"Okay, maybe he's sleeping."

"It's one o'clock in the afternoon."

"Maybe he was at the police station all night."

I shudder at the thought.

"I'm sure there's an explanation, Luc."

"And what if there's not? What if I lost Sam before I even got him? Or worse, what if this whole time he's been someone I didn't want to believe he could be? I mean, it would explain why he was in Brighton Park that time of night. Maybe he's involved in something."

Sebastian stands up. "Okay, I think we're getting ahead of ourselves. Until you know the whole story, stop jumping to conclusions."

I go to the foyer and grab my purse.

"Where are you going?"

"To clear my head."

"I'll come with you."

"No."

"Lucy."

"I want to be alone."

"I don't know if that's a good idea."

"I'm fine, Bas. I just need to be alone for a little while."

"Okay," he says, reluctantly. "But please check in with me later. Don't forget and turn me into a crazy person running around the city looking for you."

"I won't."

"Everything's going to be fine," he says unconvincingly.

"I hope you're right."

He shrugs one shoulder. "I usually am."

Chapter 18

Lucy

It takes me only ten minutes to get to my studio from Sebastian's downtown apartment. When I park my car, I drop my head to the steering wheel and peer inside my studio through the giant windows. Painting is usually my go-to fix, but as I gaze at my dark studio, I can't find the motivation to go inside.

I see the reflection of an airplane in the glass, angling up into the sky. When it disappears, I look up and try to find it again. I see it and pull forward, rounding the corner to keep it in view. I drive several blocks and then turn again. And again.

Before I know it, I'm halfway to the airport and approaching Brighton Park.

I look at the rundown houses as I pass them, thinking of Sam and what happened somewhere near here last night. I check my gas gauge. I have a full tank. I didn't mean to end up here, but it's a straight shot to the airport, so I keep driving, watching the planes angling up into the sky as I get closer. I think about Sam and what life was like for us here. It was a hard life. At least that's what everyone says. It's what they think. But not me. Life was so much easier when we had nothing to trap us, to hold us back, to tangle us up. We just had each other. No strings. No binds. Just us. And we were happy.

I see a group of girls on the side of the street coloring the cracked sidewalk with chalk. They look up when I pass them, and I see the envy their eyes, the same envy I had at their age whenever a nice car drove down my street. But what they don't realize is that I also envy them.

I follow the service road that circles the airport and find a place to pull off at the far end of the runway, on the *right* side of the barbed-wire fence. I turn my car off and open the door just as a plane takes off. I get out and watch it fly over me. I forgot how loud it was this close. I close my eyes and let the roaring engines take me back to when I was sixteen.

My phone vibrates in my hand, and I open my eyes. *Sam.* I fumble to answer it. "Sam," I shout over the noisy engine.

He says something inaudible.

"I can't hear you, hold on." The plane disappears, taking the noise with it. "Sam?"

"Hey," he answers tentatively.

"Are you okay?" I ask, needing to know that he really is.

"Yeah. I'm fine. Are you?"

"Yeah." Physically, anyway. Mentally, not so much.

"Where are you?"

I chew the corner of my mouth. I wanted to talk to him, to hear his voice, to know that he was really okay. But I'm overflowing with fear and frustration and anger. I want to know what really happened last night, but I don't think I can take hearing it right now.

"Lucy, where are you?" he asks again, as another plane flies over.

I press the phone to my ear and shout, "Sam, now's not really a good time."

"Lucy, please," I hear him say when the plane is gone. "I need to see you."

I close my eyes to block the tears that rush to them, but it doesn't work. They leak onto my face anyway.

"Please, Lamb. Just tell me where you are."

"I'm really glad you're okay," I say over the lump in my throat, and hang up the phone.

He immediately calls back, but I don't answer. I toss my phone on the seat and shut the door.

Another plane screams overhead, and I watch it fly over, but the view isn't the same standing up, so I climb onto the hood of my car and lean back against the windshield. I cross my outstretched legs and let the bright November sun warm me inside my jacket.

A few minutes later, I watch another plane fly across the cloudless blue sky. And another a few minutes after that.

I begin keeping count.

Five planes later, a car roars up next to mine, startling me. *Sam?*

I sit up as he gets out and hurries over to me.

"Sam, what are you doing here? How did you—"

"Why weren't you answering?" he asks desperately.

I shake my head, still wondering how he knew I was here. "I—" I close my eyes. I can't look at him. I swing my legs over the side of the car and slide off the hood.

He stands in front of me. "Lucy, please."

"What were you doing with her, Sam?"

He shakes his head. "It's not what it looked like."

"Really? Because it looked like you were involved in something sketchy at night in Brighton Park with a woman you've admittedly slept with." I exhale and ask the question that's been burning inside me since I left Sebastian's apartment. "Were you...buying drugs?"

"What? No, I wasn't buying drugs! I've never touched drugs. Dammit, Lucy, when are you going to believe me?"

"I don't know what to believe," I shout.

"Just let me explain." His beautiful eyes implore me. "Please."

I lean against the car and give him my attention as another plane flies over.

He inhales a deep breath and runs his hand through his hair, and the muscles in his arm flex beneath his painted skin. When it's quiet again, he rubs his scruffy chin and tightens his square jaw. "You hurt me last night." His eyes water and it nearly knocks me down.

My heart comes out of hiding, where's it's been since Sebastian uttered the words *He was with a woman*, and it practically leaps out of my chest, wanting to comfort him.

"Sam—" I close my eyes, feeling overcome with guilt and regret. I know that I hurt him.

"I didn't mean to hurt you back," he says hoarsely. "That's not why I was with Molly." Hearing him say her name makes me nauseous. "But I know that it did hurt you. And I'm sorry."

I look at him and shrug. "It's my fault." *My own selfish fault.* "I was so worried about Drew and the exhibit..." I exhale a sorrowful breath. "I'm sorry. I didn't mean for everything to get so screwed up."

"It's not screwed up."

"Then why were you with her?" I ask desperately.

"I was really upset when I left you last night. I was angry. I just needed something to take my mind off it." He shrugs. "She was there."

I press my lips together and nod, accepting my punishment.

"We just talked."

"You talked? In your car?"

"Would you rather I took her up to my apartment?"

I let out a weighted breath. *No.*

"I thought taking a drive was a better alternative. We just talked," he says again.

"About what?"

"You."

I close my eyes and shake my head.

"It's true." He gazes at me with honesty in his eyes, but I'm not ready to accept it.

"Why, so she can tweet something else about me?"

"She didn't do that. She admitted to texting someone, probably because she was curious about you, and maybe a little jealous, but she didn't put anything on Twitter. She wanted me to tell you that. She's really sorry about it. She didn't know who you were."

I cross my arms and look down at my feet. "Is she okay?" I ask softly, allowing myself to feel sorry for her.

"She will be."

"What were you doing driving around Brighton Park that late?"

"I just wanted to feel close to you." He gazes at me and I exhale the last of my resentment.

I know exactly what he means. That's how I felt driving here.

"Why did you wait until a few minutes ago to call me? What were you doing all morning?"

He holds up his right hand, which is no longer casted.

"You were getting your cast off," I say, shaking my head, thinking of the anxiety I've had all day. *Couldn't that have waited?* "I know you wanted it off, Sam, but considering last night's events—"

"It had to come off before I saw you."

"Why?"

"Because I knew that when I saw you, I'd have to do this." He takes my face in his hands and kisses me passionately as another plane rumbles over us. He pushes and pulls my lips with his, and the scruff that surrounds them scrapes wonderfully against my skin, leaving it tingling and my lips swollen when he parts them. He caresses my tongue with his, healing the places in my heart that were falsely convinced of betrayal all day. A cry of relief bubbles out of me, and Sam responds

with a moan. I no longer care about anything else. *He* is all
that matters.

He tugs my lips between his teeth once more, then he
kisses me softly and rubs his thumb over my cheek as the
noise from the plane disappears.

"Damn that felt good," he whispers, balling his right hand
into a fist. He steps back and looks at me. "I'm sorry, I know
you told me not to kiss you. But after last night..."

"It's okay," I breathe, trying to remember why I invoked
that rule in the first place. When I remember, I press my tingling lips together and reach for his right hand. I turn it over
and touch his palm. "Is it better?"

"It is now." He laces his fingers with mine and gazes at me.
"I didn't mean to hurt you."

"I didn't mean to hurt you either," I say, looking into his
beautiful eyes.

He rubs his thumb over the back of my hand. "I'll wait for
you, Lucy. If you need more time, after the exhibit, you can
have it."

"No." I shake my head and shrug. "I already told Drew."

"You told him? What did you say?" His impatient eyes
search me for the answer.

"That I didn't want to get married."

"You did?" he asks, unable to hide the relief in his eyes.

"Yes."

"Is that *all* you told him?"

"Well, I tried to tell him about you and me, but he didn't
want to hear it. I think he believes I'll change my mind if he
gives me space. He wants to wait until after the exhibit to

talk about everything. He said that I've worked too hard to let anything get in the way of it."

He nods thoughtfully. "Well, that's one thing we agree on. He shouldn't get in the way of it. And neither should I."

"Does it even matter anymore?"

He drops his chin and gives me a pensive look. "Yes, it does."

"Sam, last night after you left, I realized the only thing that really matters is *you*."

"Lucy—"

"When I was driving here, passing the streets we grew up on, all I could think about was how simple life was back then. How good it was. I didn't have a fancy house or a car or a studio. I had you and that was all I needed."

"You didn't have those things, but you wanted them."

I shrug. "I have them now. And without you, they're meaningless. Without you, the studio, my paintings, my career... none of it matters."

He shakes his head. "Forget everything else. I can buy you a house and a car and a studio. But I can't buy back all the hard work you've put into your career, and into this exhibit."

"Sam."

"I'm not going to let you do anything to mess it up, not when it's only a few days away. You, Lucy Marie Bennett, are going to earn your spot in New York."

I bite my bottom lip, disappointed that it's no longer tingling, and nod reluctantly. "I don't want to hurt you anymore."

"So don't." He shows me his dimples, and my heart

searches for a chisel and stone to carve the following vow into: *I will never hurt you again.*

"You know Drew's not going to be thrilled to see you at the exhibit," I say warily.

"So does that mean I'm invited?" He fights a smile, and the corners of my mouth turn up.

"It would be a shame if the star of the show wasn't there for the unveiling of his painting."

"You're going to use it?" He smiles freely now.

"It should draw quiet the crowd."

"Well, I guess I better be there, then."

I laugh softly, but my smile wanes. "Sam, you tend to bring out the worst in Drew. He made it clear last night that he didn't want me to see you again."

"Why, what did he do? Did he hurt you?" He scans my face.

"No." I shake my head, ignoring his absurd assumption. Although I did see an unfavorable side of Drew last night. "He just said that you couldn't take your eyes off me all night." I raise an eyebrow at him.

"I can't help it." He shrugs. "It's like breathing."

"Yeah, well, he noticed."

"It doesn't help that I can't touch you until after the exhibit." He balls his right hand into a fist again, like he's fighting some carnal urge to touch me now that it's out of a cast.

I reach for his arms and wrap them around my waist. "Well, maybe you could kiss me again," I say, throwing caution to the wind, desperate to feel his lips on mine again. "Just once more."

He grins and shows me his dimples. "I'm not kissing you again until you're mine."

I give him an incredulous look. "But you just did."

"In a moment of weakness." He crinkles his eyes. "But I won't do it again." He drops his hands and leans against the car beside me.

I press my lips together and try to savor the kiss, which I can no longer taste, knowing it will be my last until after the exhibit. Maybe even longer, depending on how everything goes with Drew.

I sigh quietly and frown.

Without looking at me, he loops his pinky with mine and grins, and his dimples send my heart soaring like the plane flying over us.

I gaze up at it and tug on his hand, pulling him toward the front of my car. He smiles and climbs up onto the hood after me, and we lie back against the cool windshield.

Seconds pass before he reaches for my hand again.

I squeeze his hand tight when another plane roars over us. When it's gone, I let out the breath I was holding, along with all the stress from the last twenty-four hours. I feel Sam's body relax too, and it fills me with a sense of peace and calm. I inhale another deep breath, savoring the comfort I feel lying beside him with the warm sun on my face.

I drop my head to the side and look at him staring up at the blue sky. "How did you know I was here?"

He looks at me and I lose myself in his eyes. "You

can't hide from me, Lucy. Not anymore. I'll always find you."

"Promise?"

"If I have to use every resource I have."

The corners of my mouth turn up. "Good."

Chapter 19

Lucy

I stand in front of the floor-length mirror in my bedroom, admiring my sparkly reflection. I put my hands on my waist and feel the tiny gold beads and crystals that cover the top half of my dress. A strip of black silk separates it from the long black taffeta skirt that touches the floor. I turn around and look at my bare back, and tighten the black silk ribbon that's tied behind my neck.

I love this dress.

I swing my long, slicked-back ponytail and smile. I spontaneously stopped into the salon and had the bottom third of it dip-dyed pink for the occasion, and I think I love it even more than my dress.

"Lucy?"

"Upstairs," I call to Sebastian, who is picking me up for the exhibit.

Drew is already at the studio with his staff getting the food set up. After three days in Philly, he returned home upbeat and determined to make the exhibit a culinary success. But I'm not so sure the space apart did me any good. It only exacerbated the fact that tonight is now the pendulum upon which our relationship swings. And I'm somewhat convinced he's still completely unaware, which only adds to the cloud of anxiety that's been looming over me all day. I wanted tonight to be about my work, but it's been irrevocably tangled up with Drew and Sam, and I have no one to blame but myself.

Sebastian walks into my bedroom, looking debonair in his snug black tux and indigo bow tie.

We both gasp at the same time when we see each other.

"Sebastian, you look so handsome!"

He eyes every inch of my dress and then turns me around so he can see the back. He widens his eyes and smiles. "Holy bananas, you look so hot."

"Really?"

"I mean it. If I were straight, you'd be in trouble."

I laugh. "Sebastian."

"I love everything about this." He holds his hands up in front of me. "The dress. Your hair!" He touches the pink end of my ponytail. "Your eyes. Those lips!"

I press my Ruby Woo red lips together and smile.

"You're channeling your inner Gwen Stefani."

"Well, I'll take that as a compliment."

"Wait until Sam sees you."

I smile with nervous excitement. I haven't seen Sam since

last week, which was intentional on all counts. I decided to use the space Drew gave me to focus solely on the exhibit. And Sam has been with Joe and Tristan getting ready for a fight in Quebec tomorrow night. Other than a few text messages from him, which were undoubtedly the highlight of my week, my days were filled with event planning, to-do lists, dread, and guilt. Not necessarily in that order.

"Are you ready? We should get going," Sebastian says, glancing at his watch.

"Yeah, just let me grab my shoes." I go to my closet and step into my black Christian Louboutin stilettos. "Is Paul downstairs?"

"No. He said he had a pit stop to make, so he's going to meet us there."

"Oh, okay." I kick up one of my red soles for Bas to see.

"Fancy."

"I thought a little retail therapy might make me feel better about breaking Drew's heart."

"Did it?"

"No. Not at all."

"Well, at least you'll look good doing it."

* * *

It's dusk when we pull up to the curb in front of my brightly lit studio, where Sebastian is promptly greeted by a valet. We rented a nearby parking lot and hired a valet service to assist with parking. I just hope we have a big enough turnout to justify it.

We walk inside and the waitstaff stops and looks up at us from their tasks.

"We're not guests, but we are in charge, so get back to work," Sebastian teases, and several of them smile before returning to their jobs.

"I love your dress," one of the waitresses says as I pass her on my way to find Drew.

"Thank you."

"And your hair." She smiles with wide eyes.

"Thanks," I say, smiling at her.

"Lucy," Drew calls from behind the macaroni bar, where he's busy wiping out martini glasses with a dish cloth.

"Hi," I say, smiling at him. I hold my hands behind my back and sashay from side to side in my dress.

"Hey, can you grab the other box of champagne flutes from your office? I put them in there this morning so no one would break them."

I stare at him for several seconds, waiting for him to compliment my dress, but he doesn't seem to notice. He's in *the zone*. "Yeah, sure."

"Be careful not to break any of them. I don't have extras."

"Okay." I head to my office, glancing around the studio as I go, checking the vibe and feel of each strategically positioned piece that I pass. I stop in front of the painting of Sam that's now hanging on the wall beneath a track of lights that are shining on his powerful body, highlighting his handsome face and unusual eyes. I smile thinking of how everyone might react to it. Hopefully not the same way Drew did. He was fairly underwhelmed by it.

I sigh and my shoulders fall under the weight of the worry that seems permanently affixed to them lately.

"What's wrong?" Sebastian asks, walking up behind me. "It looks great. Everything looks great."

"What am I doing, Bas?" I ask, keeping my eyes on the painting.

He stands beside me and stares at the painting for a few seconds, before saying, "You're hosting your first art exhibit."

"I feel like a fraud."

"You're not a fraud. You're incredibly talented."

I press my lips together and shake my head. "They're all going to know. Maybe not tonight, but sooner or later, they'll know."

"So they'll know. And they might even care for twenty-four hours. But then they'll move on."

"Maybe we should take it down," I say, gesturing to the painting. "It feels like I'm just rubbing it in Drew's face."

"No," he says firmly.

"Drew doesn't even know that Sam's coming tonight. Maybe I should call Sam and tell him not to come."

"Lucy, the show starts in a half hour. He's probably already on his way."

"I don't know what I was thinking," I say, unlocking my phone to call him.

"You were thinking that the love of your life might like to be part of a night that will likely be one of the biggest nights of your career."

I pause and look at him.

"And you were thinking that using his painting in the

show would be a beautiful way to honor everything he's accomplished and the man he's become for you... a way to say thank you for being patient and waiting while you navigate this unfamiliar road."

"Yes, but..." I cover my face with my hands and try to shake off the frustration of my self-inflicted predicament. "If I do that for Sam, I hurt Drew."

He drops his head to the side and looks at me.

"But if I protect Drew, I hurt Sam," I say, reading his not-so-subtle thoughts.

He raises his eyebrows and nods.

"These choices suck." I huff.

"Is there really a choice?"

"I don't want to hurt Drew any more than I have to, Bas."

"Well, life's not that easy. There's a cost for the things we want. That's what makes them worthwhile." He sighs. "There's no 'buy one, get one free' here, Luc. If you want Sam, you have to be willing to pay the price."

"You mean, be willing to hurt Drew."

He shrugs. "Yes."

"And be willing to risk my career. And be willing to give up my nice, *normal* life."

"Yes, to all of the above."

I let out a heavy sigh. "And I'm just supposed to be okay with hurting Drew because that's the breaks?"

"Of course not. You should care that it's going to hurt Drew and it's probably going to hurt Janice too. And that's going to suck. And people are going to have opinions about it and that's going to suck too. It's not going to be easy. But *that's* the price. That's what you have to be willing to pay for Sam."

I swallow hard and nod, accepting a truth I know I'm going to have to face.

"Isn't he worth it?" Bas asks.

"Of course he is."

"Okay then, there's no choice."

I exhale a deep breath. "I just want tonight to be over with. I think I'm going to tell Drew about Sam as soon as it is. If he'll listen." The thought of ending things with Drew fills me with anxiety. Not because I'm second-guessing my relationship with Sam. But because it means giving up the safe, expected life I've come to know. And the foster kid deep inside me panics at that. It's like jumping off a high dive. I want to jump. But it goes against every self-preserving bone in my body.

I look at the time on my phone, eager to get it over with. "Three hours. The show should be over by then, don't you think?"

"Hey." He looks at me. "This is your night. Be here. Okay?"

I blink at him and nod. "Okay."

"Let's just focus on the show for the next few hours before you take your running leap off the cliff."

I nod at Sebastian, whose uncanny way of knowing exactly how I feel helps ease my anxiety. "Okay."

The corners of his mouth turn up. "Smile. You look too good not to."

I smile automatically.

"And don't forget...Sam's not the only one you get at the end of all this." He reaches for my hand. "You've got me too."

I squeeze his hand. "I'm pretty lucky."

Drew calls my name.

"Shoot. The champagne glasses." I hurry to my office and pick up the box that's sitting on my desk. I carry it in my outstretched arms, wrapping my fingers around the corners of it tightly.

"I can carry it," Sebastian says, walking beside me.

I tighten my grip on it. "I've got it."

"Lucy," Drew calls again.

"I'm coming," I say, stepping on the hem of my dress. I stumble forward. "Shit!" The box wobbles in my hands. I try to balance on my heels, but it's a losing battle. Sebastian grabs my arm, keeping me upright, but the box continues its trajectory to the floor, landing with a crescendo of shattering crystal.

I gasp and assess the damage. "Shit! Shit! Shit!"

Drew walks over to me and stands with his hands on his hips, staring at the crushed box on the floor. He closes his eyes and shakes his head.

"I'm sorry, I tripped."

"It's fine," he says calmly, but he doesn't look calm. "Are you okay?"

"Yeah, I'm fine."

"Sebastian, do you think you could you help Lucy clean this up? I've got to go put my tux on."

"Sure, we've got it."

Drew heads to my office to get changed, and Sebastian gives me a crooked smile. "You okay?"

"Yes." I reach for the box.

"Here, let me help this time," he says, reaching underneath the box to help me carry it to the back.

A few minutes later, Drew steps out of my office looking handsome in his black tux. I walk over to him and straighten his bow tie. "You look great."

He looks at me and sighs.

"I'm sorry about the champagne glasses. I didn't mean to drop them."

"I know you didn't."

"It'll be fine. We can just use the other eight hundred and one glasses you brought." I smirk.

"You can't serve champagne in a martini glass, Luc."

"Well, what about the box you already unpacked?"

"Each box holds fifty champagne flutes. It's not enough."

"You really think everyone will come?" I smile with anticipation.

"Janice Christiansen is nothing if not persuasive. I think you'll definitely need another box. I'll be back," he says, pulling his keys out of his pocket.

"What? Where are you going? People are going to start showing up any minute now."

"The staff knows what to do. I'll be back in no time. Don't worry."

"But I need you here," I say, panicked. These aren't my people. These are *his* people. Janice's people.

"You'll be fine." He stretches his neck and looks behind me.

I glance over my shoulder and realize he's looking at my ponytail.

He pulls his eyebrows together, and the corners of his mouth turn down. "When did you do that?"

I reach behind me and pull my hair over my shoulder, touching the pink end of my ponytail. "This morning."

"Isn't it fabulous?" Sebastian says.

"It's something," he says, amused, concerned, maybe a little worried about my mental well-being. "I'll be back soon."

I follow him through the studio. "Please hurry."

"I will." He turns around and smiles at me before he leaves. "You look great, by the way."

I purse my lips over the smile he evokes. "Thank you."

Sebastian scans the list in his hands. "Done, done, done..." He looks at me. "Wait. The music," he says, smiling with what I can tell is nervous excitement. It excites me too.

I widen my eyes and nod. "Hurry."

He disappears to the back and a few seconds later, Ben Howard begins to croon the lyrics to "Keep Your Head Up" through the studio speakers. I smile and close my eyes and let the airy melody flow through me. When I open them, Sebastian is walking toward me, singing along to the cheerful song.

He smiles and takes my hand. "Keep your head up, keep your heart strong...no, no, no, no...keep your mind set, keep your hair long..." He spins me around, and I laugh. "My, my darlin'...keep your head up, keep your heart strong..." He puts his hand behind my back and pulls me against him, and we sway back and forth to the music, laughing and singing along.

He spins me again, and I swing my ponytail, shouting, "Keep your hair long!"

He squeezes his eyes shut and shouts, "My, my darlin'."

We dance until the song ends and when it does, I feel like there's light pouring out of me. I smile and hold his hands. "I love you, Bas. I don't know what I'd do without you."

He pulls me into a hug and kisses the top of my head. "I love you too. Now let's have some fun!" He spins me out of his arms. "This is our night! We deserve it!"

I smile and agree, "Okay!"

"Quick, before everyone gets here. Let's have a toast."

I bob my head and follow him over to the bar, where the bartender promptly greets us. "What can I get you?"

"Champagne"—Bas glances at me and smirks—"in two martini glasses, please."

The bartender gives him a funny look, but serves the champagne in martini glasses as requested.

Sebastian raises his glass. "Here's to a successful *and noticeable* night. And...to keeping your hair long." He winks.

"Cheers to that." We clink our glasses and sip our champagne.

A few minutes later, several people file into the studio, including a few of the artists whose work is on display tonight.

"My people," I say relieved, remembering that they aren't socialites. Most of them are struggling just to make ends meet, just like I was not that long ago. We leave our glasses on the bar and cross the studio to welcome them.

Sebastian pours on the charm and encourages everyone to look around. "Please, help yourselves to a drink. And be sure to try the lobster macaroni. It's to die for."

The waitstaff buzzes around with trays, offering drinks and

hors d'oeuvres as more people make their way inside the studio. As soon as the door closes behind them, another group walks in.

I look at Sebastian with wide eyes and see the satisfaction in his.

Janice walks in on Paul's arm, dragging him from person to person as she schmoozes her way through the room.

"Should I go rescue him?" Sebastian asks.

"If you care about him, yes."

We make our way over to them, and Janice smiles when she sees us. "Look who I found."

"Thanks for returning him to me," Sebastian says, taking Paul's hand. He kisses Janice on the cheek. "You look fabulous," he says, eyeing her crimson gown. It sweeps over one of her shoulders and hugs her slender body.

"Thank you, Sebastian."

I lean in to hug her and she squeezes me tight. "I'm so proud of you," she says quietly against my ear. "Have fun tonight." She releases me and I swallow down the conflicting feelings of gratitude and sorrow. She steps back and looks at my dress. "Darling, you look absolutely stunning. This dress is incredible," she says, spinning me around to look at the back. "Oh." She gasps.

I look over my shoulder. "What? What is it?" I reach for the zipper at the small of my back, but it's secure.

"Your hair. It's...pink."

"Oh, yes. I, um..."

She raises her eyebrows and smiles softly. "You're an artist," she says, surprising me. "You express yourself through color."

I nod. "Yes."

"It's gorgeous," Paul says, spinning me around again to look at it.

"Thanks." I turn around and admire his fitted indigo tuxedo. "You look great."

He smiles graciously and Sebastian beams. "He's perfection."

"So what was the pit stop you had to make?" I ask curiously.

"Ah." He reaches inside his tuxedo jacket. "Just a little something to commemorate the night." He hands a small box to Sebastian, whose eyes light up when he sees the personalized cuff links inside.

"Oh, I love them," he gushes, and hugs Paul. "Thank you."

"Here, let me help you put them on," Paul says, and I smile watching them.

"Lucy, where's Drew?" Janice asks.

"He went to get more champagne glasses. I accidentally dropped one of the boxes he brought."

"Oh, dear." She touches her diamond necklace and presses her lips together into a tight smile.

"Lucy?"

I turn around and see an unexpected face with short brown hair and glossy lips smiling at me.

"I don't know if you remember me, but—"

"Molly," I say, but it comes out like a question.

Sebastian's head snaps up.

"I know you must be really busy tonight, but I was hoping to talk to you for just a minute. If that's okay?"

"Um, sure. Yeah." My eyes flash to Sebastian, who offers little help.

I walk with her across the studio, glancing down at her tight black cocktail dress.

"Your studio is really beautiful."

"Thank you."

"I love art." She smiles shyly. "I'm a graphic designer, so it's in my nature."

"I didn't know that."

She tucks her hair behind her ear. "I thought maybe Sam would have mentioned it."

I tense automatically upon hearing his name and stop walking. "He didn't."

"I hope he passed along my apology."

"Yes."

"Good." She drops her head. "I really am sorry for how I behaved that day in the elevator. And for the media stories that ensued. I never meant for that to happen," she says sincerely.

I nod and begin walking again. "Are you feeling better?" I glance down at the place on the side of her flat stomach where she was shot.

"Oh, yeah. I'm much better now. I mean, it's still pretty sore, I won't lie. But I was going stir-crazy inside my apartment. Your show was just the reason I needed to get up and put on some real clothes." She laughs softly and admits, "Sam thought it might be a good idea." She smiles and shakes her head. "He really loves you, you know."

My smile wanes and my heart races.

"Like the way girls dream about being loved."

Part of me is irritated that she knows anything about the way Sam loves me, but the other part is delighted to hear her say it.

"It's not a wonder why. Besides the fact that you're beautiful and have *really* cool hair, you are talented, girl!" She laughs and shows me a beautiful white smile.

I laugh uncomfortably and smile back.

"Seriously. I had a chance to look around, and I'm really impressed with your work."

"Thank you."

"I was wondering if you might be interested in doing some work for me."

"For what?"

"I own a graphic design company. I'm guessing Sam didn't tell you that either."

"No." But I did *read* about it.

"Well, I've been looking for an artist who can breathe some new life into our designs, and what I've seen tonight is exactly the kind of thing I've been looking for."

"I don't know anything about graphic design," I say, shaking my head.

"That's okay. You don't have to. You just have to create the artwork. Draw, sketch, paint. Whatever you like. My developers will do the rest."

"Oh. Well, um . . . I don't know."

"Look, you don't have to decide tonight." She reaches into her clutch and pulls out a business card. "Just think about it, okay? Then call me," she says with wide eyes.

I take the card from her. "Okay."

"All right, that was longer than a minute. I don't want to keep you. But I'm really glad that I got to meet you, Lucy. Good luck tonight."

"Thank you."

She smiles and I watch her weave in between tuxedos and cocktail dresses all the way to the door. I head to my office to put her card away, and when I walk back out into the studio, I hear a commotion and see everyone gathering around the entrance.

Sebastian appears beside me. "Sam's here."

My heart speeds up on cue as Ben Howard's "Only Love" plays through the speakers. The crowd thins as he makes his way inside and walks over to me.

"Wow," I breathe.

"Yeah." Sebastian sighs.

Sam's eyes meet mine and he smiles, charming me and the rest of the room with his dimples. He's wearing a perfectly tailored black tuxedo that looks like a million bucks, he's freshly shaven, and his hair looks as if it was professionally styled.

"Does he have a stylist?" Sebastian whispers to me.

"No. I don't know. Maybe."

The closer he gets, the less oxygen seems to go to my brain. I giggle just before he reaches me, and Sebastian nudges my arm. "Don't forget that everyone's watching," he says quietly.

I nod and try to compose myself.

"Sam, it's great to see you," Sebastian says, reaching out to shake his hand. "So glad you could come."

Sam raises his eyebrows and smiles. "You too, Sebastian." He leans in to him and says quietly, "Just be yourself. They'll lose interest in a few minutes."

Sebastian smiles and nods.

"Lucy, you remember Tristan," Sam says, gesturing to the man standing beside him. He's tall and well built, almost as well as Sam, and is wearing an equally impressive suit. His dark, almost black hair is styled perfectly over his handsome face, and his blue eyes shine when he smiles at me. I remember him as if I saw him at Joe's yesterday.

"Lucy Bennett, I can't believe it," he says in a deep, almost unrecognizable voice.

"Tristan," I say, smiling at him. "I can't believe it either." I reach up to hug him, and he wraps his arms around my waist, squeezing me tight. "It's so good to see you."

"You too, beautiful. Congratulations on all this."

"Thank you."

Sebastian clears his throat, and I promptly introduce him. "Tristan, this is my good friend and *amazing* assistant, Sebastian Ford."

Tristan gives Sebastian a firm handshake. "Tristan Kelley. Nice to meet you."

"Nice to meet you too," Sebastian says, unable to hide the enthusiasm in his voice. "Sebastian Ford."

I lean in to him and whisper, "I already said that."

"Right." He smiles and bobs his head.

Somebody has a crush on Tris.

"And this is my manager, Miles Angelo," Sam says, introducing us to a thick man with olive skin and jet-black hair that's slicked back.

Sebastian shakes his hand and so do I. "It's nice to meet you, Miles," I say. "I've heard a lot about you."

"I've heard a lot about you too, sweetheart." He looks at Sam and says to him, "If you would have told me she was this pretty, I wouldn't have given you such a hard time about her."

I push my lips together over a polite smile. *A hard time about me?*

Sam drops his chin. "That's not true. Don't listen to him."

Miles slaps Tris's shoulder. "Come on, I'm gonna go get a drink."

"I'll come with you," Sebastian says.

"Do you want to get something to drink?" I ask Sam.

"No, I don't drink before a fight."

"Oh. Right." I smile and glance around the room at all of the faces that are watching us. "Come with me," I say to him, and lead him to the back of the studio.

As soon as we're away from everyone, he reaches for my hand. "Wait. Stop."

I turn around. "What? What's the matter?"

He lowers his eyes to my dress and slowly brings them back to my face. "God, you're beautiful."

My shoulders relax and I smile.

"I mean it." He steps toward me, closing the space between us. "You are the greatest work of art in here tonight." His warm breath falls on my parted lips, and I quickly inhale to taste it on my tongue. He reaches for my ponytail and brings it over my shoulder. "I love this." He shakes his head and smiles. "You have *no* idea how much I love this."

I smile at the seductive tone of his voice, and my anxiety disappears, replaced by the longing and desire I've been suppressing since the moment he pressed his lips to mine in this very spot. I swallow hard and try to ignore it. "So, um, what have you been doing all week?"

"Thinking of you."

I fight a smile and say casually, "I thought you were training for your fight against Beau Ackerman tomorrow night."

"Yeah, well"—he laughs and scrapes his teeth across his bottom lip—"I'm ready for that now too."

"What else are you ready for?"

He gazes at me and says, "You." He crinkles his eyes, and I see the excitement and anticipation in them. "Us."

"Me too."

"Lucy, Drew's back," Sebastian says, popping his head around the corner, and my face falls.

Sam raises his eyebrows and gestures for me to go before him.

I follow Sebastian through the studio and immediately see Drew behind the bar, setting up the champagne glasses.

"You might as well get it over with," Sebastian says.

I nod and continue toward Drew with Sam on my heels. "Behave," I say to him, and he grins.

"You made it." I smile at Drew, but he only glances up from his task for a moment.

"Lucky for you, I decided to come back."

Humor. *Good.*

"Well, I'm glad that you did."

He glances up again and sees Sam standing beside me, and all humor subsides. He stands up straight and asks rather rudely, "What is he doing here?"

Some part of me hoped that Drew might act differently around Sam tonight, that he might suck up his insecurities for my big night. It was a senseless notion—one I had no right to hope for.

"It's good to see you too, Drew. Everything looks really great tonight."

"Lucy, can I talk to you for a minute, please?" Drew asks me, ignoring Sam, who tenses beside me.

"Yeah, sure." I glance up at Sam and follow Drew. "Drew, please, this night is important and I know you wouldn't do anything to ruin it. Sam is my friend and I invited him here."

"And I thought I told you, I don't want him to be your friend."

"Yes you did. But that's like telling the sky not to be blue. He *is* my friend. He's more than that, he's family," I say, trying to make him understand, as if it will somehow soften the imminent blow. I clear my throat and say softly, "I invited him here, Drew. I want him here. So please respect that."

"Is this your way of getting back at me for dinner the other night?"

"What? No."

"Then what, Lucy?" He drops his head to the side and gives me a devastated look. "Do you really not want to get married anymore?"

My throat begins to close. *Not here.*

He puts his hands on his hips, and I see the panic spread across his face. "Is there...is there something going on between you two?"

I stare him like a deer in headlights, frozen by the words I need to say but can't. Not yet. *Not now.* "Drew—"

"Miss Bennett?"

I look over my shoulder and see a portly-looking man holding a camera. "Yes?" I manage, trying to keep my voice even.

"I'm Whalen Michaelson, from the *Atlanta Journal*. I was wondering if I might take some pictures of you."

"Of me?"

He nods and says brightly, "Yes."

"I'd love to get a few shots myself," another man says, holding up his laminated *Atlanta Daily* badge.

"Oh, um." I turn around and bob my head. "Okay."

"Perhaps Mr. Cole wouldn't mind getting in a few with you?"

"Oh," I choke out, "I don't know."

"Surely he'd be willing to pose for a few shots in front of his own painting," Whalen Michaelson suggests.

I pull my eyebrows together and look for Drew, but he's gone.

"It is him, isn't it?"

"Um, yes, but—" Maybe it's my imagination, but it feels as if everyone in the studio has formed a concentrated circle around me. I glance around at the unfamiliar smiling faces.

"I'd be happy to," Sam says over my shoulder, smiling at the reporters.

I look up at his handsome face, and I'm disconcerted by how calm he is, a stark contrast to how I feel.

"Great. Shall we?" Whalen Michaelson gestures toward Sam's painting.

I feel Sam's hand gently brush the small of my back, urging me to go before him, and I force my stiletto-clad feet to carry me over to the painting.

"Okay, Mr. Cole, Miss Bennett, if you could stand together here..." He positions us beside the painting and looks through his lens. "A little closer."

Sam reaches around my waist and pulls me closer to him, making every muscle in my body clench tight.

"Perfect."

Sam slowly pulls his hand back, trailing it along the waist of my dress, and gently caresses the small of my back with his thumb. I let out a slow breath and try to calm my pounding heart.

"What is it called?" one of the guests asks.

"Is it for sale?" someone else asks.

I shake my head and smile. "No, it's not for sale."

"Pity. I would pay top dollar for it," another man says, raising his rainbow martini, and everyone laughs.

"And the name?" Whalen Michaelson prompts.

"Oh." I look at Sam and then look at the painting. *"Lionheart."*

Sam looks at me as if no one else is in the room, and for just a moment, I forget that there is.

"It's called *Lionheart*," I say softly to him.

"Sam, how do you know Lucy?" someone asks.

"We grew up together," he says, crinkling his eyes at me. "We go way back."

"Two hundred and fifty thousand," Drew says, stealing my attention away from Sam.

"What?" I look at him like he's lost his mind.

"For the painting. It's two hundred and fifty thousand," he says again, raising his amber-colored drink to the man who asked if it was for sale.

"No." I shake my head and look at Sebastian with wide eyes.

"Like Lucy already said, it's not for sale," he says, helping me.

"Two hundred and fifty thousand," the man agrees.

"Two seventy-five," another man counters.

"No!" I shout, then quickly cover my shock with a smile.

"Anyone for three hundred?" Drew asks, ignoring me.

"She said it's not for sale," Sam says calmly, leaving my side to stand in front of Drew, which I know is a bad idea. A *very* bad idea.

I quickly follow behind him. "Sam."

Drew swallows down the last ounce of bourbon in his glass. "What are you, her bodyguard now?"

"If I need to be."

I roll my eyes at Sam and his unnecessary security detail. "Drew, I know you're upset right now, and I'm sorry." I groan, feeling my emotions slosh around inside me. "But you can't sell my painting."

"Upset? Why would I be upset?"

I swallow hard and whisper, "I don't know."

"Oh, honey, I think you do know. I think you both know,"

Drew says, loud enough for the people around us to hear, and my cheeks flame when their eyes light up with curiosity.

Not here. I give Sebastian a panicked look, and he successfully diverts everyone's attention by introducing one of the artists whose work is on display.

"Follow me," he says to the crowd, leading them to the far corner of the studio to see her painting.

Sam raises his hand to Drew's chest. "Maybe we should take this to the back, so we don't disturb Lucy's guests."

Drew looks at Sam with disdain. "I don't care who you are or how well you think you know Lucy. You need to stay the hell away from her."

"Drew, that's enough!"

Sam takes a step toward him and stands two inches from his face. "When *she* tells me to stay away from her, I will. But I don't see that happening anytime soon."

"Sam, stop it!"

Drew shoves his glass into my hand, and I take it mechanically, paralyzed by what I'm watching unfold before me.

This is it. It's over. The show. My career. It's all coming to a head right here, right now, in the middle of my studio. And I can't do anything to stop it. I close my eyes. *I probably deserve it.*

Sam hovers in front of Drew. "What? You want to hit me?"

"Sam," I scold, but he ignores me. He doesn't even hear me. There's too much testosterone pumping through his veins.

He opens his arms wide and holds his hands out, inviting Drew to hit him. "Come on, hit me."

"Drew, don't!" I'm no longer concerned about the show or

the guests who have started to migrate toward us again. Sam could kill him.

Drew pulls his fist back and throws an impressive right hook at Sam's face, and everyone around us gasps, including me.

"Sam!" I reach for him, but I'm quickly blocked by Miles and Tris, who are both shouting at him and pushing him back.

Sam smiles at Drew. "Is that all you got?"

"That's enough," Miles says, pushing Sam back.

Drew lunges at Sam again, and I reach for his arm. "Drew, stop it!" He yanks his arm away, but it comes back at me, knocking me to the ground.

Sam breaks through Tris and Miles, and grabs Drew's collar.

"Sam, don't!" I scream when he pulls his fist back, and he freezes. "Please," I beg. "Don't hit him."

His chest rises and falls, but he lets go of Drew's collar. He holds his arms out, like before. "Hit me again," he growls at Drew.

Drew shakes his head and steps back.

"You wanna fucking hit me. Hit me!"

Miles steps in front of Sam and shouts in his face, "Are you kidding me right now? Are you fucking kidding me?"

Tris takes the opportunity to grab Sam's arms and pull him back again.

"Get him in the car!" Miles shouts, pushing them toward the door. "You gotta be fucking kidding me. Get in the god-damn car!" he shouts at Sam as Tris pushes him through the door.

I watch Sam climb into the back of a black SUV and disappear behind the dark tinted windows. It pulls away from the curb, leaving me standing in the middle of my studio, surrounded by a sea of alarmed faces.

Drew steps toward me.

"No." I shake my head and walk calmly to my office, but he follows me.

"Lucy, talk to me," he pleads, once we're alone.

"What do you want me to say?" I spin around and glare at him. "I'm so angry at you right now."

"Yeah, well, the feeling's mutual."

"You tried to sell my painting, Drew! What is wrong with you?"

"What's wrong with me? How about the fact that you don't want to get married, for starters?"

"I tried to tell you a week ago and you wouldn't listen to me," I say.

"Because I thought you'd come to your senses!"

I shake my head and bite my trembling lip. "I have. Which is why I can't marry you." I shrug and say tearfully, "It's over, Drew."

"Over? How can you say that?"

I swallow the painful lump in my throat and cry, "I'm sorry."

"You're sorry?" He shakes his head and stares at me. "How could you do this? After everything I've done for you. After everything we've—You're just going to throw it all away?"

"You *have* done so much for me. But that was never why I was with you."

"Then why?"

I blink at him and shake my head. "Because I loved you," I say wholeheartedly. "I *love* you."

"You love me?" He huffs a short laugh and closes his eyes. "Damn, Lucy, you sure have a fucked-up way of showing it." He turns around and opens the door.

"Drew, where are you going? We need to talk about this."

"I'm done talking." He walks out of my office and closes the door behind him, leaving me to wallow in my despair and self-loathing for the next thirty minutes, afraid to show my face to anyone who might still be lingering around the studio.

Someone knocks on the door, and I get up from my chair to open it.

"Sebastian." I look over his shoulder. "Where did Drew go? Is he still here?"

"No, he left. Everyone's gone. Are you okay?"

"No." I plop back down in my chair, and my dress puffs around me. I prop my elbow on my desk and put my face in my hand. "I guess the show was a failure, huh?"

"Actually, you sold twelve paintings, over half of which were yours."

I sit up straight. "I did? Really?"

"And I think there was enough buzz around Sam's painting to get the attention of the modern art curator at the Met," he says, grinning.

"Funny."

"Not funny. I'm being serious."

"Sebastian."

"You had an offer for two hundred and seventy-five *thousand* dollars. That's insane."

"That is insane. Do you think he was insane?"

He laughs. "I think everyone was much more impressed with your work than your love life. Several of the guests said it was one of the best shows they'd been to." He arches an eyebrow. "Maybe in part because of the entertainment at the end. But I think, mostly because of your talent."

I huff a disbelieving breath. "Entertainment for them, torment for me." I groan. "That was awful."

"I know."

"I want to be so mad at both of them, but I did this. It's not their fault."

Bas tilts his chin to the side. "Ehh, it's a little their fault. I'd say more Drew's than Sam's. He did try to sell your painting."

I groan. "What am I going to do, Bas? Drew won't talk to me, and Sam leaves for Quebec in the morning. I can't let him go after what happened tonight."

"No." He shakes his head. "Not unless you'd like to see him get hurt again."

"Sebastian."

"Well, you remember what happened the last time he was distracted by the likes of you."

I bob my head and stand up. "What should I do?"

"Go to him. Right now. Come on." He takes my hand. "I'll drive you to his apartment."

Chapter 20

Lucy

I direct Sebastian as we make the short drive through the city to Sam's apartment. "Just pull up there," I say, pointing to the curb in front of the entrance to his building. My hand hovers over the door handle, ready to open it when he stops.

He parks in front of the large glass doors outside of the lobby. "Want me to wait?" he asks as I gather my dress and hurry from the car.

I turn around and shake my head. "No."

"Good luck," I hear him say as I dash inside.

I turn around and give him a small wave through the glass door.

"Miss Lucy."

I stop in front of the guard. "Hi." I smooth my long black skirt. "I'm sorry"—I flash an apologetic smile—"I don't think I ever got your name."

"Terrance."

"Hi, Terrance." I smile at him. "It's good to see you again."

"Good to see you too," he says warily, glancing down at my dress. "Sam was dressed up fancy tonight too." I smile automatically, but he shakes his head and says, "He sure was hot when Mr. Miles brought him home, though."

"Oh, um." I pull my eyebrows together. "Yes."

"Does he know you're coming to see him?"

I shake my head and he studies me for a moment, but then he nods toward the elevators and says, "Go on. I'll let him know."

I flash a small smile and dash across the gleaming marble floor toward the bank of elevators. "Thank you, Terrance," I call across the empty lobby, and my voice echoes off the walls.

"Slow down, Miss Lucy," he calls back.

When the elevator doors open, I hurry inside and press the button for the penthouse. I'm whisked up to the twenty-fifth floor in record time. *Thank you*, I say to the universe, which clearly understands the importance of me seeing Sam right now. I hold my breath for the millisecond it takes for the doors to open again, anxiously waiting for him to appear on the other side of them, but all I see is his empty foyer.

The door to his apartment is cracked open.

I exhale my anticipation, in exchange for a lungful of apprehension, as I step out of the elevator. I press my hand to his door and push it open. "Sam?"

I walk inside his dark apartment and follow the orange glow coming from his living room. I find him standing in front of the fireplace, still partially dressed in his tux, with his hands on the matte-black mantel, gripping a lowball glass. His sleeves are flipped up and his open collar is hanging loosely around his neck.

"Hey...what are you doing?" I ask tentatively.

He sips the clear liquor from his glass and sets it back down on the mantel.

I put my hand on his back. "Are you okay?"

"I'm sorry," he says, staring at the fire.

I wrap my hands around his thick arms and rub them over his broad shoulders and down his wide back, savoring the way he feels through his crisp white shirt. "It's okay. You don't have to be sorry."

He sighs quietly.

"Hey," I say against his shoulder, "look at me."

He turns around and his eyes grip me. "It was all for nothing." He clenches his jaw tight, and the tiny muscles flex where it hinges. "I ruined your show." His skin glows in the light of the fire, and the flames cast a shadow on the cleft in his chin, making it hard to focus on what he's saying. "I'm sorry," he says, squeezing my heart.

I reach for his face. "Sam, you didn't ruin anything. Believe it or not, the night was a success."

He gives me a dubious look.

"We sold twelve paintings."

"Really?"

"Yes." I smile and see the relief in his eyes, but it's fleeting.

"It's already in the media, Lucy."

I assumed it would be. I drop my hands and sigh. "So what?"

"So what?" He raises his eyebrows. "They know your name now. It's not just me in the headlines. They're speculating. About us. About Drew." He shakes his head. "There were a lot of people there tonight."

I swallow down the sick feeling in my stomach. *That's the price.* I look at his handsome face and stand a little taller. *I'll pay it ten times over if I have to.* "And?"

He exhales an incredulous breath. "Don't you care?"

"No." I shake my head. "Not anymore." I reach for his face again. "Right now, the only thing I care about in the entire world is you." I rub my thumb over his cheek where Drew hit him. "Are you okay?"

His face softens and the corners of his mouth turn up into a small, amused smile, but then he reaches for my hand and says sincerely, "I am now."

I smile, glancing at the glass on the mantel behind him. "What are you doing drinking before a fight?"

He shrugs. "It didn't seem that important when I thought I wrecked the biggest night of your career."

"And now that you know you didn't?"

"Maybe a little more important again."

I push the glass down the mantel until it's out of reach. "Are there *other* things you shouldn't do before a fight?" I ask, trailing my fingers over the buttons on his shirt, desperate to feel his healing lips on mine.

"Like what?" he asks, low and husky.

I reach for his hands and lace my fingers with his. "I'm yours, Sam." I gaze up at him, and the fire I've worked so hard to control finally breaks free and blazes through me, burning me from the inside out, sending embers soaring into the space between us.

His chest rises and falls with a quiet groan that fans the flames higher when I see the look in his stormy eyes. He slowly trails his hand up and down my back, sending goose bumps across my bare skin, and I savor the feeling of his firm stomach pushing against me each time he inhales. "I've wanted to do that all night," he whispers, steeling the last bit of breath from my lungs. He brings his hands to my face, and I part my eager lips to welcome his, but he doesn't kiss me. "You're mine," he says achingly, and I see the question in his eyes.

I nod fervently and answer, "Yes."

He presses his mouth to mine and kisses me desperately, pushing and pulling my lips with his, the way that I love, the way that leaves them tingling and wanting more. He rubs his hands up and down my back, finding the zipper at the top of my skirt, and tugs it down, groaning into my mouth when his fingers brush over my black lace panties. He reaches inside my dress and squeezes my lace-clad bottom, pulling me against his hips.

I moan into his mouth, wanting to absorb him through every pore in my body, but he releases me and reaches for the silk bow that's tied behind my neck. He pulls the ends until they fall loose and chase my sparkly gold dress to the floor, which settles around my feet in a puff of black taffeta.

I stand weak-kneed on my stilettos as Sam gazes down at my nearly naked body, and I'm silently begging him to touch me *anywhere*. He reaches for my ponytail and brings it over my shoulder, letting his hand slide down the length of it over my aching breast, which he resists with a quiet groan as his fingers follow the curve of my arm, leaving a blazing trail on my skin that I feel everywhere.

He raises my hand above my head and says softly, "Turn around."

I carefully step out of the cloud of black taffeta at my feet and slowly spin around under his tattooed arm, feeling his fiery eyes ignite every place on my body they meet.

He wraps me in his arms and pulls me close to him again. "You're so beautiful," he breathes, and I melt in his arms. He presses his lips to mine and kisses me again, and I know that the only reason I'm still standing is because he's holding me up.

He lifts me off my feet and I wrap my legs around his waist, crossing my red-soled heels behind him. I shove my hands into his hair, undoing the work of whoever styled it, and kiss him urgently as he carries me to his bedroom on the other side of the wall.

"A double-sided fireplace," I mumble into his mouth, surprised to see the orange flames glowing against the walls.

"Uh-huh," he mumbles, uninterested in the matter. He drops me onto the plush duvet that covers his giant bed and crawls over me, kissing me slowly, caressing my tongue with his, and soothing a place deep inside me that only he can. He kisses my jaw and neck, holding my hands by my shoulders as he slowly drags his lips to my breast, and I welcome the warm rush of desire that surges through me. His mouth covers my nipple, and he moans softly against it, sending vibrations to the deepest part of my body. He continues with hot, wet kisses all the way down to my hip, pressing his hand against my stomach when I arch my back. He wraps his other hand around my knee and trails kisses along the inside of my thigh.

"Sam," I whisper, desperate for him to extinguish the flames just inches from his mouth, but he moves farther down my legs and kneels between my feet.

He carefully removes my shoes, and I press my bare feet to the bed, feeling the soft duvet under my toes as he kisses his way back up my legs. He hooks his fingers in my panties and pulls the black lace over my hips, pausing to press his lips to the burning place between my thighs, igniting the flames with his warm breath, before dragging the lace the rest of the way down my legs, leaving me naked and squirming beneath him.

He presses his hands to my thighs and covers me with his mouth, giving me the sweet relief of his soft lips and warm tongue. I look down and see him gripping my thighs in his strong hands, still wearing the remnants of his tux, the muscles flexing in his tattooed forearm when he stretches it over my stomach, and the fire sears down my legs. He looks at me with his beautiful eyes, and the flames engulf my entire body.

I grip the duvet in my fisted hands as waves of pleasure rock through me, bringing my back off the bed beneath his hand. He groans against me, shattering me into a million pieces, and the world falls away for a few blissful seconds.

When I open my eyes, he's kneeling at my feet, unbuttoning his shirt. He kicks his shoes off and they tumble onto the floor behind him. I sit up and smile, but his face is even more intense than before. His hungry eyes pierce me and reignite the smoldering fire inside. I kneel in front of him and push his shirt off his broad shoulders and down his arms, taking in the sight of his sculpted torso glowing in the light of the fire. I press my fingers to the tattoos that cover his chest and softly kiss his neck, dragging my lips up to his jaw. My hands roam freely across his stomach, feeling his muscles flex under my touch as my fingers follow the defined V that points below his pants. I unbutton them and pull his zipper down, feeling the heat radiate off him when I tug them down a little.

He reaches for my face and kisses me, but my eager hands remain diligent. I reach inside his pants and rub his erection, and he groans softly against my cheek.

"I want you," I whisper, tugging his pants down past his hips.

He kisses me hard and lays me back on the bed as he shrugs out of his pants and positions himself between my legs. He runs his hand along my thigh and bends my leg over his hip, and I rock my hips up, feeling him between my legs. "Sam," I beg.

He rubs himself against my entrance, and I bite my lip, anticipating the feeling of him inside me, a feeling that could never be replicated. He exhales a warm breath against my parted lips and pushes into me, sending electricity coursing to every nerve ending in my body. I cry out, but he covers my mouth with his, muffling the sound as he slowly pulls out of me and pushes back in, filling me up and satisfying the ache deep inside. *Ohh.* He eases out of me again, and I gasp at the sensation, at the heavy fullness of him when he glides back in. I press my hips up against his, needing to feel every familiar inch of him.

He drops his head beside mine and I breathe in his warm scent as he gifts me with the heavy, full sensation again, before he pulls back, leaving me aching and wanting more. He sinks into me again, deeper this time, making me gasp and hold him tighter as I rediscover the puzzle piece that's been missing for so long. He reaches for my hands and pulls them above my head, lacing our fingers together as he rocks into me, again and again, synchronizing his movements to our slow, deep kisses, like a familiar dance we perfected long ago.

"I love you," I whisper against his lips.

He rolls over and sits up, pulling me into his lap without breaking our connection, and I sink down on him until our hips are flush. I wrap my arms around him and close my fists in his hair, and he loosens my ponytail until it falls in silky strands down my back. "I love you too"—he shoves his fingers into my hair and grumbles against my ear—"so fucking much."

I laugh softly, but when he lifts me again, we both fall silent at the sensation. He lifts me again and I slide back down, exhaling shallow breaths against his lips. Up and back down. Up and back down. Again and again, like waves on the ocean, bobbing up and down together, our tongues dancing to the slow rhythmic motion.

I lean back in Sam's arms and he kisses my breasts, softly tugging my nipples between his lips until the heat begins to take over again, crawling up my thighs and burning between my legs as my breasts swell under his tongue. He leans forward, until I'm practically lying on the bed, and I rock my hips against his, trying to extinguish the fire. "Sam," I cry, begging him to put out the flames.

He lays me on the bed, leaving me empty and aching as he crawls over me. But when he sinks into me again, I feel the relief through my whole body. He moves in and out of me faster, pushing deeper, sending electricity to the tips of my fingers and the ends of my toes. *Oh, yes.*

He groans and pulls out of me again, leaving me gasping for air, but before I can beg him for mercy, he rolls me onto my stomach and pulls my hips up off the bed a little. He lies on top of me, pressing me against the bed under his welcome weight, and I grip the duvet in my fists when I feel his erection sliding between my thighs. He pushes into me, groaning against my ear when I push back against his hips. He grips my hands and begins to move in and out of me, satisfying me in a whole new way.

I close my eyes and exhale a silent breath through my parted lips, savoring the way he's pressing *every* single part of my body against the bed each time that he moves. "Ahhh," I cry as he pushes me over the edge without warning, sending me soaring through a beautiful familiar blackness that consumes my body and leaves me trembling beneath him.

He rolls me over and kisses me hard, and plunges into me again, making me cry out each time he thrusts into me, grinding his hips against mine.

"Sam," I say when I can't take it anymore, but his mouth covers mine and the fire consumes me once more, leaving me writhing beneath him as he comes, groaning against my lips.

I lie beneath him, waiting for the feeling to come back to my fingers and toes, but without oxygen it's not likely. "Sam"—I gasp for air, which I can't find because he's lying on top of me with his full weight—"you're crushing me."

He rolls onto his back and gives me a small, satiated smile that makes my heart fall dreamily into a bed of flowers. He pulls me over to him, and I drape myself across his chest like an overcooked noodle. He wraps his heavy arm around me, and we lie quietly for a while until I begin to drift off.

"I can't go back," he says softly, pulling me from the early stages of sleep, which my body is now demanding.

"Hmm?" I hum against his chest.

"I lived without you for a really long time, but I can't go back to that now."

I open my drowsy eyes and look at him.

"I can't live without you, Lamb. Not anymore." He gazes at me and I see our entire lives painted in his eyes.

I put my hand on his worried face. "You don't have to."

He pulls me back down on his warm chest, and after a few minutes, or maybe even seconds, I drift into a peaceful, dreamless sleep.

Chapter 21

Lucy

I wake from the best sleep I've had in as long as I can remember. I stare at the ceiling in Sam's bedroom, knowing exactly where I am and not wanting to be anywhere else. I sit up in his comfy bed, holding the soft duvet under my arms, and look at the blue sky through the giant windows. The autumn sun is filling the room with soft light. I smile and stretch my arms above my head, and fall back against the plush pillows.

"Sam?" I call, smiling, knowing he must be somewhere nearby. After a few seconds and no answer, I sit up again. I listen for the shower but don't hear anything coming from the bathroom. "Sam?" I call again.

No answer.

I get up and look down at my naked body, briefly contemplating my options before yanking the sheet off the bed and wrapping it around me. I walk through the living room, glancing around the open apartment. "Sam?"

I find him in the kitchen standing in front of the stove, working diligently over a frying pan. There's a mess of bowls and batter-covered utensils lying on the counter beside a box of pancake mix. He picks up the box and studies the back of it carefully.

"Hey," I say, smiling at the sight of him freshly showered and shirtless.

He turns around, spatula in hand, and smiles at me. "Hey."

"What are you doing?" I ask, feeling my heart swell with every beat, because I already know the answer.

"Making pancakes." He smiles shyly and it takes everything in me to fight the sudden onslaught of tears. "I'm trying to anyway." He laughs softly. "I don't have any bacon."

"Next time." I walk over to him, wrap my arms around him tight, and eye the perfectly golden pancakes in the pan. "You're doing a great job."

He smiles proudly. "I made coffee if you want some."

I pull the sheet tight, tucking it under my arms, and pour myself a cup.

"Sugar's over there," he says, pointing to a small bowl. "And there's half-and-half in the fridge."

I grab the half-and-half and pour it into my coffee until it clouds under the surface, then I stir in some sugar and carry it to the island, where I perch myself on a stool.

I sip my coffee and watch him slide the pancakes onto a plate.

He turns off the burner and carries it over to me. "I'll get the butter and syrup," he says, rounding the island again. He returns a few seconds and sits beside me.

"Plates and forks?" I suggest, pressing my lips together over a smile.

"Right." He jumps up again.

When he returns, I wrap my hand around his wrist and kiss him softly. "Thank you for making me pancakes."

He smiles and his dimples go straight to my head. "You're welcome." He sits down beside me again and we help ourselves, slathering our warm pancakes with butter and drizzling them with syrup.

I take a bite and smile as I chew. "It's really good," I say over my mouthful.

By the time I've finished my plate, Sam is on his second helping. I sit back and sip my coffee and watch him clean his plate. When he's through, he puts his fork down and turns toward me on his stool. He reaches for my face and tucks my hair behind my ear. "This," he says, gazing at me.

I smile softly and set my coffee down when I see the look in his eyes.

"I want this," he says longingly. "Every day."

"Me too," I breathe, igniting the familiar fire in his eyes.

He reaches for my face and pulls me off the stool, kissing me passionately until the sheet unravels from around me and falls to the floor. I press my naked body against him and melt into his kiss, tasting the sweet syrup on his lips.

"I can't." He gasps, releasing me.

"Oh...okay," I say quietly, nodding over my disappointment as the oxygen reaches my tingling limbs again.

"It's not that I don't want to, Lamb." He gazes down at my naked body. "Believe me, I do. But I can't. Not right before a fight."

I blink up at him and smile. "I can wait."

He scrapes his teeth over his bottom lip. "Promise?"

"Just be sure to save a few rounds for me. Okay, champ?"

He nods his head and grins. "Okay." He picks up the sheet and wraps it around me. "I have a surprise for you," he says.

"You do?"

He crinkles his excited eyes. "I want you to come to Quebec with me."

My breath catches in my throat. "Quebec?"

"Yeah. I want you to come to the fight."

I look up at his smiling face and try to lasso my frantic heart. "I, um, I'd have to look at flights," I say, trying to sort through the details of the impending day in my head. *Maybe I could... No, I have to go talk to Drew.* I have to explain everything. He deserves that much. It could just be a gut feeling, but I think it might take a while.

"That's the surprise. It's all taken care of. You just need your passport and some clothes. We can swing by and get them on the way to the airport." He grabs his phone off the counter and looks at the time. "Miles should be here any minute to pick us up. The flight's at noon."

"What? No," I say, feeling my face scrunch up. "Sam, I—" I feel like I can't breathe. "I can't get on a plane right now."

His face falls. "Why?"

Because I need to work out the details of my broken engagement with Drew. I have to pack my things. I have to find out what he plans to do with the studio.

"Don't you want to see me fight?"

"Yes. Of course I do."

"Then what's the matter?"

I hold the sheet around me and walk to the bedroom, where I aim to find some clothes to put on. "Do you have a T-shirt or something I can borrow?" I ask as he watches me from the doorway.

He pulls a shirt out of his dresser drawer and hands it to me. "Here."

I put it on. "Where are my panties?" I ask, frustrated.

"They're around here somewhere," he says, scanning the floor.

I march past him to the opposite side of the room, where I find them on the floor and pull them on. I pass him again and plop down on the bed.

"Lucy, what is going on?"

"I can't go to Quebec with you, Sam."

He inhales a deep breath, and I watch the muscles in his torso flex all the way down to the V. "Why?"

My phone buzzes on the floor, and I immediately wish I hadn't gotten up to bring it in here last night. Sam picks it up, pausing to look at the screen before handing it to me. "I guess I got my answer." He tosses it on the bed beside me and walks into the bathroom.

I pick it up and look at the screen, and my heart shrinks inside my chest. It's filled with text messages and missed calls from Drew and Janice.

Drew: I'm sorry about last night

Drew: Where are you?

Drew: Please come home

Drew: I'm worried about you.

Drew: We can work this out

Janice: It's normal to have cold feet, but I know you and Drew can work this out.

Janice: There's still plenty of time until the wedding.

Janice: Don't forget about the cake tasting this week.

It buzzes again. Low battery.

I toss it on the bed and get up. "Sam." I find him in the bathroom, leaning over the sink, gripping the counter. I put my hand on his back and say softly, "Sam."

He turns around abruptly. "Why?" he asks urgently, and my heart aches at the strangled sound of his voice. "Why did you tell me it's over with him?"

"It is over. I ended it with him last night."

"Well, I don't think he got the message."

"Which is why I can't go to Quebec with you. I need to go talk to him."

"I'm done sharing you, Lucy."

"I never asked you to share me," I say, swallowing my frustration. "I'm yours, Sam. I've always been yours."

"Don't." He drops his chin and shakes his head. "Don't say that again, until you really are. *Without* strings. *Without* hesitation."

I exhale a silent breath. Nothing hurts like the pain inflicted by Sam. "Okay. I'm sorry," I whisper, and walk back into the bedroom.

I look through the giant windows at the city below and touch the cold glass. "I told him it was over," I say, when I feel Sam standing behind me. "Maybe I should have gone home to him last night to make sure it got through to him, but"— I turn around and look into his sad eyes—"I wanted to come home to you."

He exhales a heavy breath. "Come with me to Quebec, Lamb."

Someone knocks on the door.

"It's Miles," he says, giving me one last pleading look before he goes to let him in.

He returns a few seconds later. "Lucy, please just come with me. We'll worry about everything else later. It doesn't matter."

"I can't do that, Sam. I have to talk to Drew. I owe him an explanation. He deserves that much. Everything will be settled by the time you're back."

He grabs his shirt off the bed and slips it on. "So go talk to him then," he says, reaching for his duffle bag. "I'll tell Miles to cancel your ticket."

"Sam."

"I have to go, Lucy," he says, deflated.

"I don't want you to leave like this."

"Then come with me."

"I can't," I say, feeling overwhelmed.

"Sam, we have to go," Miles shouts across the apartment.

"I've got to go," he says flatly. "Stay as long as you need. Terrance can arrange a car for you. His number is on the inside of the keypad by the front door."

"Sam." I reach for him and wrap my arms around his waist. "I love you."

He drops his bag and wraps his arms around me. "I love you too," he says quietly.

"I'll be watching tonight," I say when he releases me.

He picks up his bag again and nods. "Bye, Lucy." He walks out of the room.

"Bye, Sam," I say softly, feeling the words leave my body with a wave of anxiety. When I hear the door to his apartment shut, the apprehension consumes me.

What am I doing?

I pick up my phone to call Sebastian, but the battery dies and it powers down. *Shit.* I look around for a phone charger, hoping to find one plugged into the wall behind one of the nightstands, but I don't see one. I sit on the bed and open one of the drawers, where I find one and quickly plug it in. I connect my phone and lay it on the nightstand to charge, but something catches my eye inside the drawer—an envelope with my name written on it. I pick it up and see several more stacked beneath it, all with my name written on them.

I open the unsealed envelope in my hands and pull out several pieces of folded notebook paper that are filled with Sam's handwriting. My chest falls heavily as I begin to read them.

* * *

Sam, Twenty-One Years Old

I close my eyes and try to block out the noise in my cell block. I imagine Lucy. I see her face and focus on her pale blue eyes.

When everything is quiet, I pick up my pen and begin writing.

Lucy,

It's been three years since I've seen you. I worry about you all the time. I don't know where you are. Are you okay? I know you may never get this letter. I don't even know where to send it. Did you graduate? Did you leave Brighton Park? Did you go to college? I pray that you did. I pray a lot these days. I pray that I'll get out of here soon. I'm up for parole in a couple of months. I can't believe I'm even saying that. I didn't want my life to be like this. I'm sorry.

I got my GED. I've been taking college classes too. I'm about to get my associate's degree. Can you believe it? That's the only good thing about this place. That and the boxing program. Since I've had good behavior I've been able to participate in it and I've actually won all of my matches.

I'm so lonely, Luc. I miss you so much. I miss everything. We never had much but here I have nothing. Without you I have even less.

Please be okay. Please have faith in me. I can change this. I can make it better. I'm not like our parents. I don't belong here. I'm doing everything I can to get out early. My lawyer thinks I have a good chance. I just want to see you. I want to hear your voice.

Are you ashamed of me? Is that why you haven't come? I understand if you are. When I get out I'll do everything in my power to change that. I'll make you proud of me again. I'll do good things. I'll show you that I'm still the person you thought I was. You've known me since I was twelve. You know my heart. You know who I really am.

I love you, Lucy. I love you and I always will. Even if you can't find faith in me again. Even if you never come back to me. I love you. You made me better. You made my life better. I don't know who I'd be if it weren't for you. You made me want to be a good person. You taught me that it doesn't matter where you start. You taught me the importance of an education. You taught me to love. You were the first person to love me and I'm forever grateful for that.

When I close my eyes tonight I'll see your face and I'll dream of your voice like I always do. It's the only thing that comforts me in this awful place. I hope you've found comfort too wherever you are. And I hope that you're happy.

Sam

* * *

Lucy

I fold the letter with shaking hands and carefully place it back in the envelope, crying quietly over the pain of losing him all those years ago, over the pain he must have been in when he wrote it, over the loss of who we were before, and the lives we lived after. An abandoned sob bubbles out of me and echoes through his quiet apartment, reminding me why I'm alone, and I sit up straight in the bed. I wipe my eyes and reach for my phone, which has turned back on now.

"Sebastian."

"Hey. How did everything go?"

"I need you to come get me," I say urgently.

"Why? Where's Sam?"

"He left for Quebec."

"Is everything okay?"

"It will be."

"Lucy, what's going on? Are you okay?"

"I'll explain when you get here. I'm fine. Just hurry."

"Okay, I'll be there as soon as I can."

"Could you bring me some clothes?"

"Sure. Let me just grab my cape and I'll be right over." He musters the smallest laugh out of me.

"Terrance is the guard downstairs. I'll tell him you're coming up. It's the twenty-fifth floor."

"Which apartment?"

"His apartment is the twenty-fifth floor."

I hear a quiet gasp.

"Sebastian."

"Okay, got it. Hurry. Bring clothes. Terrance. Twenty-fifth floor."

"Yes. See you soon."

"Okay, bye."

I hang up the phone and hurry to the keypad by the front door, where I dial Terrance's number and plug my dying phone into the nearest outlet to keep it charging. "Hi, Terrance, this is—"

"Miss Lucy."

I pause. "Yes."

"Sam gave me your number. For security reasons," he explains. "He wanted to make sure you could reach me while you were staying with him."

"Oh, okay," I say, nodding with approval as if he could see.

"He said you might be needing a car this morning. Is that why you're calling?"

"No, but—"

"Is everything okay?"

"Yes, everything's fine. I've arranged for my assistant to pick me up. He's bringing me a change of clothes, so I was hoping you wouldn't mind letting him up."

"What's his name?"

I give him Sebastian's information and then head for the bathroom where I proceed to take the fastest shower of my life.

* * *

I turn my head to listen for the front door, but when I don't hear anything, I turn the hair dryer back on. It's one of the few things I found in Sam's bathroom that might help me look more like a human than a drowned rat. I run my fingers through my hair, separating the pink and blond strands as the dryer whips them around my face. I hear something again and turn the dryer off.

Knocking. Definitely knocking.

Sebastian.

I hurry to the front door, holding my towel securely under my arms. "Hey," I breathe when I open the door and see him carrying a multitude of bags that will hopefully improve the state of my appearance. I take a quick inventory. Dry-cleaning bag, drugstore bag, my makeup bag from the studio...and coffee. I sigh in relief. "You're my hero."

He smiles and walks in, casing the apartment with abandon. "Oh, my God, this place is incredible," he gushes.

"Yeah, I know, it's great. Now come on." I take the coffee from him and drag him to the bedroom. "We have to hurry."

"Wait," he says, laying the dry-cleaning bag over the back of the couch in the living room. He gazes at the stone fireplace and his eyes wander to the giant windows that enclose the space.

"Sebastian."

He turns his attention back to me. "Sorry. What were you saying?"

I raise my eyebrows. "That we need to hurry."

"Why? What's going on?"

I shake my head and try to explain. "Sam wanted me to go to Quebec with him and I told him no."

"Why did you do that?"

"Because I think I should probably give Drew his ring back before I go flying off to another country with Sam."

"Okay, it's Canada, not the South of France."

I drop my head to the side. "I need to finish things with Drew the right way, Sebastian. I've screwed so many things up, but I need to take responsibility for my actions. Sam and I have a second chance, and I want to start our future without my engagement to another man hanging over our heads."

"Okay. But if Sam's going to be in Quebec for the next couple of days, what's the hurry?"

"The fight starts at seven. I want to be there."

"You're going to Quebec?"

I shrug. "I've made Sam wait long enough, don't you think?"

Sebastian's eyes dart around like he's connecting points on a graph. "Okay, well, have you looked at flights yet?"

"No."

"Take this," he says, handing me the drugstore bag and my makeup. He pulls out his phone and starts tapping the screen. "Go." He urges me toward the bathroom. "Wait, take your clothes," he says, handing me the dry-cleaning bag.

"Bas—"

"I know, you couldn't live without me. It's true. Now get your butt in that bathroom and get dressed!"

I smile, feeling hopeful, and hurry to the bathroom. I open the dry-cleaning bag and find my black ripped-kneed skinny jeans, a white cami, and my soft gray oversized cable-knit sweater. I shake the bag and find my black suede lace-up ballet flats at the bottom of it. I throw on my clothes and rummage through the drugstore bag, finding deodorant, toothpaste, and a toothbrush. *He really is the best.* I grab my brush and a hair tie from my makeup bag and pull my hair up into a messy ponytail. Then I rub on some tinted moisturizer, brush on some mascara, and dab my lips with gloss.

I step out of the bathroom feeling refreshed and ready. *Kind of.* Sebastian is still tapping away on his phone. "Okay," he says without looking up. "I've got two tickets out of Atlanta at 1:18."

"Two tickets?"

He looks up at me. "You're crazy if you think I'm letting you leave the country by yourself."

I press my lips together over a smile. "It's just Canada, re-member," I say, smirking.

"We have a two-hour layover in Toronto, so we won't actu-ally get to Quebec until seven."

"Seven? That's too late," I say, panicked. "The fight starts at seven."

"That's the best I can do, Luc. We'll just have go straight to the arena from the airport."

I take a deep breath and nod, grateful that he'll be with me. "Okay."

"That's a much better look for you," he says, eyeing my outfit.

"Thanks." I smile and drop my hands to my hips. "A friend of mine picked it out. He's got great taste."

"You're just lucky that I had some of your dry cleaning in my car. And those shoes, which have been rolling around in my back seat for weeks." He picks my dress up off the floor where it fell off me last night and clears his throat. "You know, you could have at least laid it across a chair or some-thing." He gathers it in his hands. "A dress like this deserves better."

"I'll remember that next time."

He shakes his head at me. "Are you ready?"

"As I'll ever be."

Chapter 22

Lucy

Sebastian and I are both quiet on the drive to my house, until the silence makes me anxious. "Can you turn on the radio?" I ask, pulling my thumbnail to my mouth. I scrape my teeth back and forth over the edge of it.

"Yeah." He turns the radio on, but the soft tempo and soulful voice pouring from the speakers doesn't help.

I gaze out of my window and see a plane angling up into the clouds that now blanket the sky. I let out a heavy sigh, thinking of Sam, imagining that it's his plane.

"We could go straight to the airport instead. Flee the country and whatnot," Bas teases.

"Don't tempt me."

He pats my bouncing knee. "You're going to be fine, Luc. Just think, in a couple of hours you'll be on your way to see

Sam." He glances at his watch and I know that I'm going to have to hurry or we'll miss the flight.

He pulls into my neighborhood and my heart pounds with both apprehension and determination. I take a deep breath as he navigates the tree-lined street, and I feel the angst grow with every familiar driveway we pass. By the time he pulls up in front of the house and puts the car in park, I'm frozen.

My pulse pounds in my ears when I look up at the house and think about everything I'm about to give up.

Sebastian turns to me and takes one of my hands in his. "Don't waste another second because you're afraid, Lucy. Be brave." He gives my hand a reassuring squeeze, and I swallow down the trepidation that's creeping up my throat.

"Okay." I open the door and step outside, welcoming the cool breeze that blows against my heated cheeks.

"I'll be waiting right here," he says as I shut the door.

I give him a weak smile and make my way to the house, stepping on the brown papery leaves that cover the ground as I go. By the time I reach the front door, the fall air has wrapped around me and creeped inside my sweater. I rub my arms and pull my keys out of my bag. I can't remember the last time I used my key to open the front door, but it occurs to me I probably never will again. I push the door open and walk inside.

"Drew?" I call up the stairs.

He walks out of the kitchen wearing sweats and messy hair. "Where have you been?" Concern, relief, anger, and sadness each take their turn on his face.

I stare at him for several seconds, thinking of everything I need to say to him, but as he looks at me, my feelings slide off my shoulders without my saying anything at all. The truth lands at his feet, and his face falls.

"You were with him."

"Drew—"

He runs his hands through his hair, and I see the realization in his eyes. "Did you sleep with him?"

Tears roll down my cheeks as I look in his eyes and answer honestly. "Yes."

He stares at me for several stunned seconds before exhaling. "Wow." He staggers over to the stairs and sits down on the bottom step.

I ignore the giant pit in my stomach, pick up my heavy feet, and go sit beside him.

"I know you said you didn't want to get married, but I didn't think—I thought—" He looks at me with watery eyes and huffs. "You didn't even give me a chance."

I drop my head to the side and give him a rueful look, because it wouldn't have made a difference. "I'm sorry."

"Was this a onetime thing, or..."

"Yes. I mean, we haven't...since we were kids."

He huffs a quiet breath and shuts his eyes.

"But I kissed him," I admit, snipping the string to the balloon of guilt that's been tied to me ever since.

He looks at me with disappointment in his eyes.

"I wanted to tell you about it. I tried to. Right after it happened, I called and called, but you wouldn't answer." I close my eyes and shake my head. "That's no excuse, I just...I wanted to tell you. It's been eating me up inside. But I didn't know how to tell you that I love him. That I've always loved him. Even when I tried not to. And I'm sorry for hiding that from you. I should have told you a long time ago. I just was afraid."

"Of what?"

"Of losing everything that's good in my life. The studio, my career...*you*." I shake my head and say solemnly, "The last thing I ever wanted to do was hurt you."

He drops his chin and asks roughly, "So is that why you never told me about him before?"

I nod and look in his eyes. "Yes, because I love you too, Drew."

"Just not enough."

I swallow the hard lump in my throat. "No. Not the way that you deserve."

"What I deserve? What I deserve is a fiancée who wants to get married, who doesn't flinch at the mention of a wedding dress." He shakes his head. "I knew you were getting cold feet before all this. I just wish I knew why."

"Drew, there's a part of my life I've never told you about. An ugly part that doesn't fit into a memory box or a photo album. A part that I worked very hard to try to forget about. And I did, for a long time. When I met you, I was so lost. But you were like a candle flickering in the night, leading me out of the dark. You opened my eyes to a world that was big and bright and full of promise, a life that gave me hope. You helped me find purpose and showed me how to pursue my passion. You picked up all my broken pieces and made me whole again. You loved me."

"I still do." He looks at me with tears in his eyes. "I did those things because I love you," he says, lassoing my heart and tugging it hard. "From the moment I saw you, I knew you were different. The way you spoke, the way you moved, the way you shielded your eyes from everything around you. Maybe nobody else saw it, but you couldn't hide your scars from me. They were deep and they were beautiful. Just like you."

"Drew," I cry, feeling a shift in the earth beneath me.

"I know that you have a history of people leaving you. Your dad and then your mom, the way that she did. Sam left you too. But I want to be the one who stays."

A cry bubbles out of me.

"I know I don't have your history the way he does. But I know you, Lucy. I know us. And I know what we can be together. Just give me a chance."

"Drew."

"You don't have to do this, Lucy. I forgive you, okay? After everything that happened last night and the way that I left, I understand why you went to him. But I forgive you," he says, piercing my heart with his desperate eyes.

I inhale a shaky breath and look at his face, full of forgiveness that squeezes my heart. I reach for his warm hand and hold it in both of mine. "I'll always love you, Drew. You gave me a life I never knew before and you taught me to chase my dreams. You believed in my talent and helped me start my career, and I will always be so grateful for that. And for the two years we spent together." I smile softly and squeeze his hand. "I love how hard you work for your future. And I know that one day, you're going to find the right person to share it with."

"Lucy."

"That person's not me, Drew. My heart belongs to Sam. I could go on pretending that it doesn't, but eventually, maybe years from now, you'd realize it. And I won't let that happen. Because you deserve to be happy. I think we both do."

Chapter 23

Lucy

"You know you can't take all of this," Sebastian says, closing his trunk over the mound of clothes I deposited in it.

"We'll sort it out when we get there. Can we just go, please?" I beg, rounding his car to get in. I open the door and plop down in the passenger seat, trying not to look up at the picturesque house I called home for the last year, but my traitorous eyes steal one last glimpse of it. As soon as Sebastian pulls away, I let out a breath that's accompanied by a quiet sob.

"Oh, honey," he says, reaching for my back.

"I just can't believe it's over," I say, wiping my eyes.

"I know it wasn't easy for you."

"Do you think he'll be okay, Bas?"

"Drew, yes. Janice, however..."

My shoulders slump. "I'll reach out to her when we get

back, try to apologize. But I have a feeling Drew will forgive me before she does."

Sebastian glances at the clock on the dash. "You don't have time to worry about it now. The flight leaves in an hour."

"Just hurry, okay?"

"Well, maybe we wouldn't be so rushed if someone didn't decide to empty her entire closet into my car."

"I wasn't sure what the protocol was. I just grabbed everything I could carry. It didn't help that Drew's heartbroken eyes were glued to me the whole time. I think I was having an out-of-body experience."

"Did you ask him about the studio?"

"No." I sigh and shake my head. "I couldn't. It's too soon."

"Well, Drew's a good businessman. Whatever he decides, I'm sure it will be well thought out over weeks, if not months. You have time to consider your options."

I drop my head back against the seat rest and look at him. "Sam offered to buy it."

"Well, that seems like a pretty good option."

"I can't let him do that, Sebastian. What would that say about me?"

"That your boyfriend's a millionaire." He smirks.

I shake my head at the notion. "I wouldn't feel comfortable."

"You could sell the painting of Sam, buy the studio on your own," he offers, giving me a sideways glance.

"That isn't an option either."

"I know. I was just throwing it out there." He taps his

thumb against the steering wheel as he drives, and says quietly, "Two hundred and seventy-five thousand dollars."

"Right now, there are more pressing matters. What am I going to wear to the fight? I can't go in this," I say, pulling on my sweater.

"I made arrangements."

"You did?"

"I'm nothing if not resourceful. While you were inside, I was scouring the Toronto airport for clothes on my phone. Luckily, there are a few high-end stores near our gate. They're holding a dress for you and a suit for me."

"You never cease to amaze me."

"I just hope your shoes from last night are somewhere in that crumpled pile in my trunk. They'll look great with what I bought you."

"Underneath it, actually."

"Oh, good."

"What about tickets to the fight?"

"I've got it covered."

"Did Paul pull some strings at work or something?"

"No, I called Miles."

"Miles? Sam's manager, Miles?"

"Yes. He gave me his business card last night, so I called him."

"Wait a minute. How did you call him? Aren't they on their way to Quebec? Was Sam with him? Of course he was." I answer my own question quicker than I asked it. "Does he know you called? Does he know that we're coming? Was he okay? Is he upset?"

"I don't know, Lucy," he says, stopping me. "He didn't pick up."

"Oh."

"I left him a message. I asked him to leave the tickets at will call, but told him not to tell Sam because you wanted to surprise him."

"You don't think he should tell him I'm coming?"

"We don't need him distracted," he says, raising his eyebrows.

"Right."

"Now, let's get this show on the road," he says, taking the exit for the airport. "Just pray that the security check line isn't long."

Thirty minutes later, we're running through the Atlanta airport.

"Excuse me. Pardon me," Sebastian says, weaving through the crowd of people.

I follow on his heels as closely as possible, keeping my head down to avoid their annoyed, judging looks. *Yes, we're late for our plane because I was busy breaking off my engagement.*

"Come on," Sebastian says, taking my hand as he jogs through an open path. "Gate F5, up there on the right."

"Do you think we'll make it?"

He looks at his watch as he runs, impressing me with his coordination. "We have five minutes before they close the gate. Run faster."

When we reach the gate, I drop my hands to my knees and suck in as much oxygen as I can, but Sebastian is barely out of breath. *Sam was right, I need to get to the gym.*

"Boarding passes, please," the stewardess says.

We hand them to her and enter the jetway.

"I can't believe we made it," I say, feeling the blood return to my legs.

"Me neither," Sebastian says, smoothing his hair.

* * *

"Ladies and gentlemen, welcome to Québec City Jean Lesage International Airport," the pilot says over the speaker as we taxi to our gate. "Local time is 7:02 p.m. and the temperature is thirty-five degrees. Grab those jackets."

I look down at my exposed thighs and give Sebastian a worried look. He obviously wasn't considering the temperature in Quebec when he chose my sleeveless black cocktail dress.

"Bienvenue à l'aéroport international Jean Lesage de Québec," a female voice says.

"They speak French here," I say, shaking my head.

"And English," Bas reassures. "We'll be fine."

"I'm going to freeze in this," I say, glancing down at my exposed shoulders.

Sebastian takes his suit jacket off and hands it to me. "Put this on until we get there."

I shrug into it as we make our way down the narrow aisle.

Sebastian already has his phone to his ear before we exit the plane. "Thanks, we'll be outside in about ten minutes," he says to the Uber driver.

"It's twenty minutes to the arena, Bas. The fight might be over by the time we get there."

"You headed to the Ackerman fight?" a burly man behind me asks.

"The Cole fight," Sebastian answers.

"By looks of that first round, it'll be the Ackerman fight," he says, staring at his phone.

"Why, what happened?" I ask, panicked.

"Sam Cole's finally met his match, that's what happened."

I glare at the man, but Sebastian grabs my elbow and pulls me into the busy airport. "Let's go."

I run beside him, feeling my ponytail swing back and forth to beat of my heels tapping across the floor. Since we already cleared customs in Toronto, it doesn't take long to reach the exit. I wrap Sebastian's jacket around me before we step outside, but it doesn't block the chilly Canadian air that wraps around my bare legs and creeps up my ruffled skirt. Thankfully, my dress has a high neckline, so I'm not completely exposed to the elements. But *holy crap*, it's cold.

Sebastian spots our Uber and ushers me into the back seat.

"You are going to the Ackerman fight, correct?" the driver asks in his French accent.

"The Cole fight," I grumble.

"Yes. Please hurry," Sebastian says, showing me the time on his phone. It's 7:15. "We're obviously running late."

"I will turn it on for you," the driver says, changing the channel and turning up the volume on his radio.

And that's another hard blow to the head for Sam Cole, the commentator says, and I grab Sebastian's hand.

"It's okay, he can take it," Bas tries to reassure me.

If you're a Sam Cole fan, this is not easy to watch... No, another announcer says, *this isn't the Sam Cole we're used to seeing fight... And that is the end of round three... A smiling Ackerman is showing the world that Sam Cole isn't the only champion in the ring tonight.*

"Can you go any faster?" I ask.

"I am going as fast as I can. It is not much farther."

Three excruciating rounds later, he pulls up in front of the arena. Sebastian tips him and we run from the car to the will call window.

"We need two tickets," I say urgently to the man behind the window.

"Miles Angelo," Sebastian interrupts. "Can you check to see if he left tickets for us, please?"

"What's the name?"

"Sebastian Ford."

"Or Lucy Bennett," I say.

"IDs please."

We hand him our IDs, and he picks up the phone and speaks to someone. He slides our IDs back and says, "Go right through those doors." He points to the main entrance.

"Thank you," we both say, and run inside where we're promptly greeted by a large security guard.

"Lucy Bennett?"

"Hi, yes, I'm Lucy Bennett. This is Sebastian Ford. Miles Angelo was supposed to leave tickets for us?"

"You don't need tickets, just come with me." He hands us laminated lanyards. "Put these on."

We drape them around our necks and follow him to a set

of double doors. I feel the roar of the crowd rumbling against them before he even opens them.

"Oh, wait," I say, taking off Sebastian's jacket. I hand it to him and he slides it back on. "You look great," I say, smiling at him.

"So do you." He winks at me.

The security guard opens the door, and we're blasted by the music thumping through the arena speakers. Just like in New York, the lights dance around the arena and everyone is on their feet, cheering and clapping. But when I look up at the giant scoreboard monitors over the ring, I realize that they're cheering for Beau Ackerman.

And the bell marks the end of the seventh round, the announcer says over the steady roar of the crowd. *I have to tell you, I'm amazed that Cole has lasted this long... I have a feeling this next round may be his last.*

I glance up at the giant monitor again as we follow the security guard toward the ring, and I gasp when I see Sam. "Oh, my God." He's bleeding from his left eye and blood is dripping down his chest and stomach. I look away and grab Sebastian's hand, but when the security guard takes us to our seats, I can't look away. Sam's right in front of us. We're right next to the ring. And Miles. And a few other faces I recognize from the New York fight.

"Hey, honey," Miles says, wrapping his arm around me when I sit down. "I wasn't sure if you were going to make it," he says, hugging me. He reaches across me and shakes Sebastian's hand.

"I take it you got my message," Bas shouts over me.

"Yeah, but I think I should have told Sam you were coming. He's a fucking mess. Look at him." He rubs his jaw. "Ackerman's using him as a punching bag. Come on, Sam! Get off those ropes!" he screams, jumping to his feet.

Sebastian jumps up too. "Come on, Sam!"

I can't stand up. I feel sick. I can barely look up, but I do. I look up at Sam between my hands that are shielding everything else from my eyes. I see only him, beaten and bruised, hugging Beau Ackerman. His thick arms are wrapped around Beau's neck, but not for long. Beau throws a punch at his ribs and Sam lets go.

"Put your gloves up, Sam!" Joe yells at him.

Sam blocks a couple of punches and then throws a left hook that makes Beau stumble back.

"There you go, baby, there you go!" Joe shouts.

"All right, Sam, there it is. Come on now!" Miles yells.

But all Sam did was piss Beau off, because Beau comes right back with two body slaps and an uppercut to the jaw that knocks Sam backward onto the mat.

I gasp when I see the blood coming from his nose and bolt up between Miles and Sebastian. "Get up, Sam," I say, but it's so loud in here I can barely hear my own voice.

The referee counts, *One...two...*

"Get up," I say again, but it might as well be a thought.

Three...four...

"Get up, Sam!"

He just lies there.

Something's wrong. My skin pricks with fear and my blood pulses behind my ears.

Five...

"Sam!" I scream and he opens his unfocused eyes.

Wait a minute, the announcer says, and the crowd erupts. *Let's see if Cole can get back on his feet... He's done it before.*

"Come on, baby, get up, get up!" I beg.

Seven...

He pushes himself up and every muscle in his body strains as he pulls his feet beneath him and stands up.

I don't believe it. Sam Cole is back on his feet, ladies and gentlemen.

The referee grabs his gloves and pushes on them. "You okay?"

Sam looks at me and smiles over his bloody mouthpiece.

"You good? You ready?" the referee asks him again.

He nods and stretches his neck from side to side. He pulls his gloves up to his face and screams when Beau takes his stance across from him. "Ahhhhhhh!"

The crowd goes crazy, and I pull my hands to my mouth to cover my smile.

"Yeah, baby, yeah, baby. Show him who the fucking champ is!" Miles screams.

The referee drops his hands away and steps back.

Beau throws the first jab, but Sam dodges it and throws a right hook, a left hook, and another right hook that knocks Beau back against the ropes. Sam hovers over him, throwing jabs faster than I can count.

Sam Cole is back, ladies and gentlemen. I don't think he's ready to give up his title just yet.

Beau holds his gloves up to cover his face, but Sam connects with an uppercut that leaves him hanging on the ropes. He swings his arm around Sam's neck and hangs on him until the bell rings.

The tide has turned in this fight.

The referee pulls them apart and Sam falls into his corner.

"He's back," Miles says. "I can see it in his eyes."

"How can you see anything through all that blood?" I ask, looking away.

"He's okay. The doc will fix him up," he says, like it's nothing.

I look at Sam, slouched in the corner of the ring, spitting blood into a cup while Joe crouches in front of him.

"He's okay," Miles assures me.

Sam gets to his feet and waits for the bell to ring. When it does, he circles Beau like a shark, waiting to attack. As soon as Beau comes within two feet of him, Sam throws a left hook that knocks him to the mat, and the crowd erupts again.

One...two...three...four...

"He fucking did it!" Miles shouts.

I hold my breath and feel the blood racing through my veins.

Five...six...seven...

Beau pulls his glove under him, but he can't push himself up.

Eight...nine...ten...

And that is it. A comeback win for Sam Cole!

"Yeah, baby!" Miles shouts, jumping up and down. He rushes to the ring.

I let out the breath I was holding and feel Sebastian's arms around me. He lifts me up off my feet and shouts with excitement.

"I need you to come with me, please," the bodyguard says, but it feels like an order. I'm quickly consumed by a crowd of people, and I understand why he's here.

"Lucy, can you confirm your relationship with Sam?" a photographer asks, taking my picture.

"Don't answer," Sebastian says.

"I'm going to need you to back up," the bodyguard says, putting his hand up in front of me, and I gratefully follow him through the crowd, around the ring, and out of the arena to a quiet room in the back.

* * *

"Lucy," Miles says, walking into the room that Sebastian and I have been anxiously waiting in for the last ten minutes. "Sam's asking for you."

I bite my smiling lip and look at Sebastian with excited eyes.

"Go," he says. "I'll wait here."

I hurry toward Miles, but pause when I reach the door. "Hold on," I say, putting my finger up. I turn around and walk back to Sebastian.

"What are you doing?" he asks with smiling eyes.

I stand in front of him and reach for the lapel on his jacket. "I just wanted to say thank you."

He smiles softly and nods. "You're welcome."

"Not just for today, Bas. For everything. I know we have

this running joke that I couldn't live without you, but... I couldn't live without you. And not just because you know my dress size or how I like my coffee. But because you're my best friend. And I love you."

He wraps his long arms around me and hugs me tight. "I love you too," he chokes out. He releases me and clears his throat. "Now, go get him."

I smile wide.

"Lucy, you coming or what?"

"Yeah, I'm coming." I hurry over to Miles.

"Listen, before you go in there, you just need to know, he's pretty beat up."

My heart sinks and my smile fades. "Is he okay?"

"He will be. But he got hit a lot tonight. It slows him down a little. He'll be better by the morning, but he's gonna be hurting tonight."

"Okay."

He leads me to an adjacent room that's filled with a few familiar faces, including Joe's. I assume the other guys make up the rest of his team. But I don't see Tristan.

"Hey, champ, there's someone here to see you. She's a hell of a lot prettier than these guys." They grumble at Miles, but as soon as they move out of the way and I see Sam, the room might as well be empty.

He looks up at me from the table he's sitting on and my guarded heart pounds inside my chest. His handsome face is swollen and bruised, and his hair is soaked with sweat. He pulls the bloody towel away from his mouth and says slowly, "You came."

"Yeah," I say, smiling over the tears that fill my eyes.

He smiles weakly, but I see the question in his tired eyes through the dried blood.

I nod and walk toward him, ignoring everyone else in the room as I close the space between us. "I'm yours, Sam. Only yours. From now on. No more strings."

He wraps his heavy arms and gloves around my waist and drops his head to my chest, making me stumble back a little. "You sure?" he mumbles without looking up.

I laugh softly and push against him so that he doesn't knock me over. "Yeah, I'm sure."

He turns his head and looks at Joe. "Get these fucking gloves off me," he says with a little more gusto, though it's still slightly slurred.

I laugh and watch Joe tug and pull at the laces. "It's good to see you, sweetheart," he says, smiling up at me with his warm, familiar eyes, and it fills a hole in my heart I didn't even know was there.

I swallow down the sudden burst of emotion and put my hand on his shoulder. "It's good to see you too, Joe. It's been too long."

When he gets Sam's gloves off, Joe pulls me into a hug and says, "Don't let it happen again, okay?" He squeezes me tight.

"I won't."

Sam wraps his taped hand around mine and pulls me back over to him, knocking Joe out of the way.

Joe just smiles. "All right, let's give 'em a minute," he says, leading everyone out of the room.

Sam reaches for my face, but he barely has the strength

to hold his hand up. It falls to his lap. "You are the only reason... I won tonight."

I shake my head and hold his battered face in my hands. "You won because of the lion inside you. I saw it tonight."

He shakes his head slowly and says quietly, "You are the lion inside me." He drops his head and leans against me again. "Without you... without you, I..."

"Shhh... it's okay," I say, wrapping my arms around him to hold him, but he leans on me with all his weight. "Sam." I grab his shoulders and push against him, but it's like trying to hold up a stone statue. "Sam, sit up," I grit out, digging my fingers into his arms, but he's too heavy. He leans forward, knocking me back on my heels, and we both fall onto the floor with a loud thud. "Sam!" I frantically reach for his face, but his eyes roll back in his head. "Joe!"

Don't miss the riveting, powerful conclusion to the Love Story duet.

A Story Like Ours
will be available in June 2019!

Acknowledgments

Thank you to my agent, Joanna MacKenzie, for taking a chance on me, showing me the publishing ropes, and occasionally talking me off the ledge. Your guidance and advice is invaluable. I'm so thankful to have you in my corner.

Thank you to my editor, Lexi Smail, for your direction and vision. Your enthusiasm and drive is unparalleled! You shaped this story into something that I'm so proud of (and made me a better writer in the process). I have loved working with you on this book!

Thank you to the amazing women in my life who have been a part of this journey since the beginning. My mom, Kathie Brewer, for your endless support and encouragement. My sister, Karen Shalters, for always making me laugh (especially at my rough drafts). Shannon Baum, for being my biggest cheerleader (and unofficial publicist). Angie King, for always believing in me (and staying up all night to get to the good parts). And Anne Rae, for your unwavering pride in my ability to write a book—I'm still just as surprised each time that it happens.

Thank you to my beta readers, who loved Sam and Lucy

even before their story was complete. Your feedback and words of encouragement mean the world to me. To all of my family, friends, and coworkers who have encouraged me along the way, thank you!

Most of all, thank you to my husband, Kevin Huber. Not only are you my biggest fan; you're my favorite person (even though you leave your clothes on the floor). Thank you for teaching me to be brave and for giving me three incredible kids that I adore. I love and cherish our family more than words can express. It's because my heart is so full that I'm able to daydream and create love stories like this one to share with the world. Also, thank you for teaching me the difference between an uppercut and a right hook.

About the Author

Robin Huber is a lifelong daydreamer, a lover of music, and an avid cook with a knack for plotting emotionally charged love stories on her way to work. It keeps her from losing it in traffic. She's admittedly an introverted extrovert and a proud Aries with a somewhat unhealthy dependency on her horoscope. She's a director by day, a writer by night, a wife to her high school sweetheart, and most importantly a mom to her three crazy kids (she means beautiful children). When she's not writing, you can find this Florida native with her toes in the sand, holding her Kindle, and probably a Corona too.

Learn more at:
  robinhuberbooks.com
  Twitter @RobinHuber80
  Facebook.com/RobinHuberWrites

You Might Also Like...

Looking for more great digital reads?
We've got you covered!

Now Available from Forever Yours

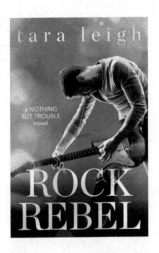

He's a rock star with a secret, she's a pop princess with a painful past—can their forbidden romance survive, or will their lies destroy them both?

I've earned my bad reputation.

A few years ago, I was New York City's hottest classical music prodigy. But I wanted something else, something *more*. So I chased my real dream, and now...I'm rock royalty. Dax Hughes, lead guitarist of Nothing but Trouble. But to my family and former Juilliard classmates, I'm an outcast. A misfit. A rebel.

They're not entirely wrong. I *don't* give a damn what other people think, and I'm all for breaking the rules...except when it comes to our new opening act, Verity Moore.

Rock gods don't tour with pop princesses.

It's not personal. Actually, under that fallen diva reputation, Verity's incredibly talented. And her fiery redheaded personality is...intriguing. But I'm convinced the skeletons in Verity's closet are as scandalous as my own, and when we're not sparring, she has a way of drawing out all those secrets I'm determined to keep hidden.

Yeah. Verity Moore is definitely off-limits...

But since when do I give a damn about the rules?

Get ready for all the feels in this sexy, "emotionally charged" (*Library Journal*) romance about a bad boy hockey player who wants a second chance to win the heart of his high school crush.

All Winnie Braddock wants is a quiet place to be alone and time to heal her battered heart. But the refuge she'd hoped for in her family's summer cottage is destroyed when she gets there to find Holden Hendricks literally camped out in the driveway. He made her life hell when they were kids, and despite what he says, it doesn't look like much has changed. She doesn't care if her brother hired Holden to renovate the house this winter; she wants him gone.

You miss 100 percent of the shots you never take. Holden knows that hockey saying all too well. After all, he could have gone pro if he hadn't messed up so much as a kid. But now he's desperate to prove he's changed for the better, especially to Winnie Braddock. As the two work together to fix up the cottage piece by piece, they realize that perhaps they can give each other the new beginning they've both been waiting for—if they're just willing to take the shot.

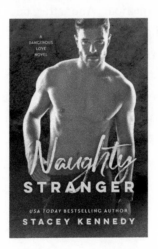

From *USA Today* bestselling author Stacey Kennedy comes a thrilling, sexy romance about a woman in danger and a small-town police detective who will do anything to keep her safe.

After a sudden tragedy blew her world apart, Peyton Kerr fled her big city career and started over in Stoney Creek, Maine. So far, she's loving small-town life—no one knows about her past, and her easy flirtation with Boone Knight gives her a reason to smile. But then someone is murdered in Peyton's store, and her quiet, anonymous existence is instantly destroyed. To make matters worse, Boone—a police detective—is assigned to the case, and Peyton knows she can't keep him at arm's length any longer. She's resisted the simmering heat between them—but now this gorgeous man is promising to keep her safe—and satisfied...

Boone Knight doesn't want the complications of a relationship. But when he volunteers to protect his town's newest—and sexiest—resident, he finally admits he'd like to explore their sizzling attraction. And after one incredible night, everything changes for Boone. Peyton is sweeter—and braver—than anyone he's ever met, and with her in his arms, everything makes sense. He just needs to convince her to trust him enough to reveal her secrets, or risk losing her to a merciless killer who seems to grow bolder with each passing day.